BRODIE DUKE

Brodie Duke

CORA DARRAH

First Printing, 2025

Cover Design and Illustrations by Hannah Darrah
Chapter Illustrations generated by Ellie Thomas using ChatGPT

www.coradarrah.com

Dedication

I would like to dedicate this book to Robert F. Durden, Jean B. Anderson, and the staff at Rubenstein Library.

Thank you for your tireless work and dedication in preserving Durham's rich history.

DUKE

Taylor and Dicey Jones Duke
marriage #1
Mary Caroline Clinton Duke
Washington Duke
marriage #2
Artelia Roney Duke
Sidney Taylor Duke
Mary Elizabeth Duke Lyon
marriage
Robert Lyon
Brodie Leonidas Duke
Mary Stagg
Benjamin Lyon
George Lyon
Edwin Lyon
marriage #1
Martha McMannen Duke
Mabel Goodall
Lawrence Duke
Pearl Buchman
marriage
Sarah Angier Duke
Benjamin Newton Duke
George Duke
Angier Duke
Mary Biddle
marriage #2
Minnie Woodward Duke
Woodward Duke
marriage #3
Alice Webb Duke
marriage #4
Wylanta Rochelle Duke
marriage #1
Lillian McCredy Duke

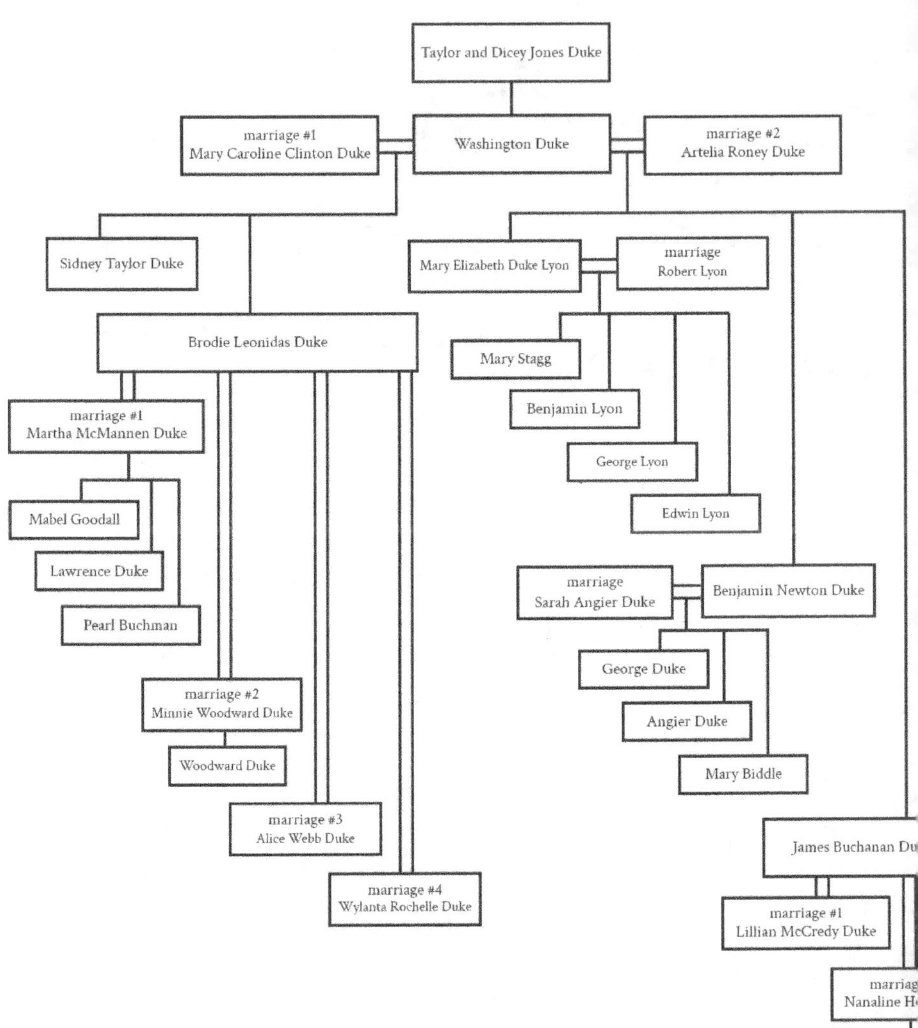

Author's Notes

For many years, I have had the honor and privilege of having access to the Duke University campus. As a small child, I took my wooden tennis racket and used balls, and walked the mile from my house to the Duke University tennis courts where I actually taught myself to play. On Saturdays, I could hear the football fans from the home I grew up in on Wrightwood Avenue. As a teenager, I enjoyed the freedom of walking to the campus and actually making my way up to the top of the chapel to peer down onto the Gothic style architecture of the buildings that were built in the early twentieth century.

Of all the places on the campus, the Sarah P. Duke Gardens was, and is still, my favorite destination. No matter the time of year, flowers and plants adorn the grounds, causing me to stop and reflect on the incredible beauty of the gardens. But, as many of us realize, when something is part of our daily lives, we tend to take it for granted. So, as an older adult with the ability to travel to many destinations, I have come to realize that this campus, with all of its intricate details, is a gift that should be treasured.

Over the past few years, I have spent a great deal of time in Rubenstein Library researching through the archives. To reach my destination, I usually pass the chapel and look in the direction of James Buchanan's larger-than-life monument. Often, I find myself pausing to gaze up at this man with a cigar in his hand, leaning on his cane. It was here that questions began to interrupt my thoughts, along with a burning desire to know more about this man and his family.

This book is the story of the Duke family, but particularly of Brodie Leonidas Duke, Washington Duke's second son and half-brother to James Buchanan. Brodie, unlike his brother James Buchanan, lived a scandalous life that, at times, marred his brother's image. Historians have primarily focused on Washington and James Buchanan, along with Benjamin Newton Duke. But as I studied this family, I believed it was time to hear Brodie's voice and the gifts he also left behind.

Prologue

Durham County is located in the Piedmont region of North Carolina, about an hour from the Virginia state line, two hours from the Atlantic coast, and three hours from the Smoky Mountains. Native Americans lived in this area long before Europeans arrived. Once the Europeans made their way to the Piedmont, Native Americans were hired as guides to lead them along the Indian Trading Path. This path begins in Augusta, Georgia, and passes through Hillsborough, N.C., where it is commonly referred to as the Occoneechi Trail. It then winds its way into the northern part of Durham County and ends near Petersburg, Virginia. Because of the excellent design and placement of the trail, engineers later constructed Interstate 85, which roughly follows the same route as this ancient path that dates back to the 1600s.

As early as the 1700s, settlers who sought to make the Piedmont of North Carolina their home faced an arduous task. Most of the land was densely forested, and trees had to be cleared before crops could be planted. Once the soil was broken up, farmers typically planted wheat or tobacco. Tobacco was a difficult and time-consuming crop, often grown by farmers who had several workers to tend the fields. Wheat crops needed to be harvested and then taken to a nearby mill to be ground into flour before it could be sold. Most farmers also owned swine that roamed freely around their property.

Many of the first settlers of North Carolina came down from Virginia and purchased property in the Piedmont region. One such settler was Washington Duke's grandfather. Originally from Europe, he made his way to Virginia and ultimately settled on a piece of land in Orange County. His son, Taylor Duke, Washington's father, spent his entire life farming the family's land while raising ten children. Washington was the eighth child, and like his brothers, he was taught from an early age how to farm. Once Washington was old enough to handle a plow, he could often be found plowing the soil, dreaming of a future beyond the farm.

In the mid-1850s, several miles east of where Washington lived, three men—Andrew Turner, William Pratt, and Bartlett Durham—owned property that would later become the city of Durham. The railroad approached William Pratt about selling a portion of his land for a station, but Pratt refused, concerned that the noise from the trains would spook his customers' horses. The railroad then approached Bartlett Durham, who sold a portion of his land to the railroad. In response, the railroad named the station after him.

The hamlet of Durham did not prosper as quickly as some had hoped. In 1855, John McMannen, an entrepreneur and minister, purchased land from Durham with hopes of subdividing it and selling the lots. In his advertisement, he stipulated that there would be no sale of ardent spirits and no people of questionable character. Two years later, with only a down payment made to Durham and no substantial sales, John McMannen had to return the land.

At this point, Durham consisted of only a tavern, a store, and a couple of churches. There were no industries, and most of the people living near Durham were farmers. Despite the efforts of men like John McMannen to draw people to this sleepy hamlet, it seemed that Durham would never prosper.

| 1 |

1851

Brodie picked up a rock and flung it over the creek bed, watching it land in the muddy water. He leaned down to take another rock when he heard his father calling his name. Normally, he would respond to his father's voice, but not now. It didn't matter that his father was mad at him for running down to the creek bed. It didn't matter that his older brother, Sidney, had tried to hold him back. Nothing mattered, except for the anger he felt toward the woman who now visited his home.

Brodie had never known his mother. She had died when he was only an infant. Sidney and his father, Washington, had always been enough. The three Dukes worked the fields during the day and cooked their food together in the evening. After the dishes were cleaned and put away, the three would sit near the fire and read the Bible or the few treasured books they owned. The days were predictable and set in a structure that provided comfort for the young boy.

Over the past couple of weeks, the predictable routine had changed. Instead of eating together on a nightly basis, his father had begun to send the boys over to the home of his brother, William, for dinner and they did not return until late in the evening. Brodie found this unusual at first, not understanding what his father could possibly be doing. But then one Sunday after church, a woman arrived on their doorstep asking for Washington.

Brodie had been the first to open the door and look up into the stranger's face, not knowing if he wanted to let the pretty woman in, or pretend she didn't exist. With the door ajar, the young boy continued to peer through the crack, trying to grasp the implications of letting her into the house. But, before he could make up his mind, the woman smiled down at him, "Hello, you must be Brodie."

Unsure if he liked the idea of this stranger knowing his name, Brodie responded, "How did you know my name?"

"Well, your father told me he had two sons, the eldest being Sidney and the youngest being Brodie. So, I assumed you must be Brodie."

By this time, Washington had come up to the door and opened it so he could see who his son was speaking to. "Hello, Artelia. I'm sorry my son has been so rude by not asking you to come in."

Brodie looked up at his father and this woman named Artelia, noticing the way they were staring at each other. The young boy was confused by his father's expression and how he beamed at the sight of the woman standing in the doorway. His first thought was to slam the door, but instinctively knew that it wouldn't go well if he did.

"Artelia, please come in."

"Well, thank you, Washington. I'd love to."

As Artelia slipped by, Brodie looked up and noticed the solemn expression on his father's face. He soaked in the reality that this woman was somehow important to his father and didn't like it one bit. He wanted to scream out loud as he took in the scene that was playing out in front of him. Sidney, who should've been an ally, stood from his place at the table, offering his hand to the woman. It was in this moment, that Brodie charged out of the door and ran down the hill that led to the creek. Sidney ran after him, but couldn't catch him.

Several minutes passed, before his brother found him with a rock in hand. Brodie was tempted to throw it at him, but thought better of it. The rock dropped into the water as his entire body slumped over. "I don't want a woman around."

Sidney came up beside his brother, placing his hand on his shoulder. "I know you were too young to remember Mother. She was so good to all of us. She loved me, but I believe she loved you best." Sidney paused in order to let Brodie process what he was saying. "When you were born, I didn't want to share her with you. I was mad at you, and one time I pushed you too hard. Mother saw this and came up beside me. Instead of yelling at me, she placed me beside her and held me close. At first, she didn't say anything, but after a few minutes, she spoke. "Sidney, I'm sorry you feel I love your brother more than you. I don't. I just love you differently."

Brodie didn't know how to respond. He wished he could remember the brief time when his mother was alive. But he just couldn't. Out of frustration, he exclaimed. "Sidney, I don't want to share Daddy or you with anyone else."

"I know. I feel the same way. But I also know that Daddy seems happier. I can't expect you to understand now, but one day you will. Just remember this, no matter if Daddy marries Artelia or not, I'll be here for you. I promise."

Brodie looked up at his older brother and sighed. "Okay, as long as we're together, I guess that's all that matters."

"Come on. Let's give Artelia a chance. You have to admit she is pretty."

"Okay."

The boys walked up the hill toward the house and saw their father and Artelia sitting on the porch. They seemed to be deep in conversation, but once they spotted the boys, they rose from their seats. When Brodie got close enough, he looked first at his father and then to Artelia. "I'm sorry I was so mean."

Washington smiled and patted Brodie on his head. "Brodie, you know I love you very much and don't want to hurt you."

"I know."

"But, you see, I've come to love Artelia and want her to become my wife."

Artelia leaned down to Brodie's eye level. "Brodie, I know I can never replace your mother, but if it's okay with you, I'd like to start by being your friend."

Brodie looked at her and could tell she was being sincere. "Okay, I guess we can be friends."

Washington smiled and placed his arm around Artelia's waist. "I also wanted to tell you that Artelia is a really good cook."

"Can you fry chicken?" Brodie asked.

"I surely can. And people are always telling me how good my apple pie is."

"Well, in that case, I guess you can stay."

Several weeks later, in the spring of 1851, Washington and Artelia were married. It was a church wedding followed by a supper on the grounds. Artelia made fried chicken and apple pie as a way to demonstrate her love for her new stepsons. Brodie and Artelia did become close and, for once, the young boy felt like he was having a taste of what it had been like when his mother was alive. As for Sidney, he kept his promise and the two boys grew closer than ever.

| 2 |

1851-1856

Once again, life was good and Brodie began to enjoy having Artelia around, particularly during meal time. Each day around noon, the boys would come in from farming the tobacco crops and a large meal would be ready and waiting for them. In the evening, after dinner, the family would once again sit around the fireplace where Artelia taught Brodie how to read and write. Her attentive nature and soft manner gave Brodie exactly what he needed in order to feel loved.

In 1853, Artelia gave birth to a baby girl and named her Mary Elizabeth. At first, Brodie ignored the baby and didn't want to have anything to do with her. But, after a few weeks of gently prompting Brodie to hold his sister, he began to feel an affection for her.

Two years later, Artelia gave birth to a boy and named him Benjamin. The next year, Artelia once again delivered a baby boy and named him James Buchanan.

By this time, Brodie and Sidney were spending most of their waking hours outside assisting their father with the family crops. It was difficult work, but Brodie never complained. As long as he could spend time with his brother and father, he was happy. When asked, he did help with his half-siblings, but always preferred the work in the fields, or the times he and Sidney would slip away into the woods which surrounded their property.

There was one particular spring day that would always be ingrained in Brodie's mind. After several hours of working in the fields, Washington encouraged the boys to go off and enjoy the beautiful afternoon. So, at a good stopping place, Brodie ran to the shed located in the backyard and grabbed their fishing poles. As he was headed toward the creek, he looked back to see Artelia hanging the sheets onto a line with her three little ones sitting on the ground nearby. She appeared so happy that he almost wanted to try and insert himself into the scene. At that moment, he felt a turmoil deep inside, a feeling he couldn't identify.

"Brodie, come on," Sidney called from a distance.

"I'm coming." Brodie turned toward the creek bed and followed his brother down the hill and into the woods that bordered their property. As he walked, he couldn't help but think how thankful he was for his brother and the close bond they shared.

Drawing closer to the creek, they noticed how swollen the water was and the debris that was swirling past them. Neither boy wanted to step into the water, given the force of the current. Brodie was standing on a rock overlooking the water, when he slipped and tumbled into the raging waters below. He hit his head as he fell, and everything went dark.

Brodie awoke to Artelia's eyes staring intently at him. She was smoothing his hair back and speaking in a calm voice. His head began to throb and everything appeared blurry. He closed his eyes and, when he opened them again, his father and brother were standing behind Artelia. They looked both concerned and happy to see him awake. His father pushed forward, "Son, are you alright?"

Brodie tried to speak, but his head hurt so much, he could only nod. Artelia rose to let Washington sit down. Sidney was standing over him and smiling. "I knew you were going to be okay. Us Dukes are not going to let a hit on the head put an end to us."

Brodie looked at his brother and the red splotches of blood on his arms and legs. He wanted to ask what had happened, but Artelia placed her finger on his lips and said, "Brodie, you fell in the creek and your brother saved you. As you can see, he had to fight off the blackberry bramble and several rocks in order to get to you. You have a brother who loves you very much, just as your father and I do."

Brodie looked into the eyes of his father and brother and smiled. He wondered where the younger children were, but was glad to have the attention of the three people he loved most in the world. He drifted back into a deep slumber and woke again several hours later as the day was turning to dusk. The room was quiet, except for the sound of Artelia fixing something in the kitchen. He tried to sit up, but the pain was too much.

He laid back down and gazed around the room. Sidney was sitting at the table carving something out of wood. His older brother loved to pick out branches from the walnut tree in the backyard, then take his knife and whittle the wood into shapes of animals. Once they were finished, the wooden animals could be found all over the house, becoming perfect toys for the three small children.

Brodie called out to Sidney in a raspy voice. "What are you making?"

"I'm making a fox."

"Why a fox?"

Sidney placed his knife down and brought the wooden fox over to his brother. "I don't know. Maybe it's because, when I pulled you out of the water, I spotted a fox on the other side of the creek, looking straight at us. It's strange, but it appeared like he was telling me that you were going to be okay."

"Can I have it when you're finished?"

"I can't think of anyone else I would rather give it to."

"Thanks, big brother."

It took a couple of days before Brodie felt strong enough to get out of bed. While recovering, Artelia did her best to keep the small children at a distance. Mary Elizabeth was the only one who came near him, offering him some water or a biscuit. James was still breastfeeding and Artelia would sit near Brodie while the baby sucked on her breast. Something about this bond between the baby and Artelia agitated Brodie. He didn't want to feel the irritation that rose up, but he just couldn't shake it.

One day, as Artelia was trying to help Brodie walk, Baby James began to scream and crawled over to Artelia, clinging on to her leg. "Now, honey, can't you see I'm trying to help your brother? I'll be with you in a minute."

But, to no avail, James began to scream louder and wouldn't let go of her leg. Brodie sat back down and, without thinking, pushed the baby with his foot. In that second, he knew he shouldn't have done it. "Brodie Duke, we will have none of that. James is just a baby."

"I know. I'm sorry. It's just, he always gets your attention, and the one time I need help, he's in the way."

Artelia sat down next to Brodie and lifted James onto her lap. "I know it must look that way to you. Brodie, I love you. I know I'm not your real mother, but I love you like you're my own flesh and blood. All I want is for us to be a family who loves and takes care of each other."

"I'm sorry. I'll try harder."

"Good. Now let's see if we can get you up and walking around."

Brodie improved every day and, over the course of a couple of weeks, he was back to his normal self. But life was no longer normal. The younger children were taking up more and more of Artelia's time and energy. Everyone tried to pitch in, but the amount of work that needed to be done seemed overwhelming for everyone in the Duke family.

One October morning, Brodie woke to the smell of bacon cooking and the sound of a voice he didn't recognize. He rose and walked toward the kitchen where he saw a young black woman standing in front of the stove. She was silent as she placed the fork into the greased pan flipping over the thick slabs of meat. Washington was sitting at the end of the table, sipping a cup of coffee.

Washington looked up and made eye contact with his son. "Brodie, come here. I want you to meet Caroline."

Brodie was hesitant at first and didn't want to move. "Brodie, it's okay. Caroline won't hurt you."

Brodie walked into the room and drew closer to where his father was sitting. "Caroline will be living here so she can help Artelia take care of the small children and other household tasks."

Caroline placed the fork down and turned toward Brodie. He couldn't help but notice the tattered dress she was wearing and remembered when Artelia had placed it in the rag bin. The young woman appeared frightened and didn't raise her eyes as she spoke. "Hello."

Brodie was unsure what to say and looked to his father for an explanation. Washington gestured for Brodie to sit at the table while Caroline continued to monitor the bacon. "Brodie, I know you've heard me talk about how I don't believe in slavery." Washington took a sip of his coffee and continued. "Artelia has been working so hard and she needed some help with all the cooking and washing. Last night, I went to Hillsborough with enough money to purchase some help. When I saw Caroline, I believed the Good Lord had sent me there to bring her home to us."

Washington looked in Caroline's direction. "Caroline, please don't be afraid. If you work hard, I promise you that we'll provide for you and treat you with respect."

Caroline placed the bacon on a plate and took eggs out of a basket, cracked them, and let them slide into the grease. As Artelia walked in with James situated on her hip, she approached Caroline and spoke, "I see Washington found one of my old dresses. We'll work on making you a dress as soon as I can get to town for cloth. If you can take James from me, I'll finish breakfast."

Brodie watched as James clung to Artelia, not wanting to go to this stranger. Artelia kissed James on the head and, with a calm voice, soothed her son. "James, it's okay. Caroline is going to take good care of you."

The baby seemed to understand and was willing for Caroline to take him from his mother's arms. About this time, Sidney, followed by Benjamin and Mary Elizabeth, came into the room. Brodie noticed how his siblings were just as perplexed as he was about this strange woman being in their home. Washington called all the children to the table and introduced Caroline. His words seemed to ease the tension in the room. After a few minutes, everyone, including Caroline, appeared content.

Brodie was drawn to Caroline as a brother is to an older sister. He found her mysterious, as well as inquisitive. When the family sat around the table at night to read the Bible, she would stop what she was doing to listen to the words that poured from the reader's lips. One day, when Brodie walked into the house, he found her gazing down at a page in a book. She didn't hear him come in and, when he approached her, she jumped up from the chair. "I'm sorry. I know I'm not to touch the books."

"Why do you say that?"

"Where I was before, I was whipped for holding a book."

Brodie fell silent and tried to imagine a life without books. "Caroline, do you want to learn to read?"

"Yes, very much."

Brodie took the book and opened it to the first page. He sat down next to Caroline and pointed to the first word. "This word is 'the'. Do you know the names of the letters in this word?"

Caroline took her finger and touched each letter, calling them out. Brodie smiled. "That's right. Now let us look at the next word."

For the next hour, Brodie and Caroline took each word, identified the sounds, and said them over and over, until Caroline was confident to read the sentence. Reading came naturally to the young woman and, with every word she read, the more confident she became. Time slipped by and, before they realized it, the sun was dropping down below the horizon.

When Caroline realized how late it was, she was visibly shaken. "I've got to get dinner started."

"It's okay. I know everyone will be happy to know you're learning to read."

"I don't know about that."

"It really is alright. Our family is different from where you came from. I spoke to my father about teaching you to read and he assured me, he was happy I could help."

Caroline stood up, walked over to the kitchen and started preparing for dinner. Soon afterward, the family came into the house and gathered around the table. When the food was ready to eat, everyone bowed their heads as Washington said the blessing. "Lord, thank you for all our many blessings. Thank you for this home and the members of this family. And Lord, thank you for Brodie's willingness to teach Caroline to read. In your Son's name, Amen."

Brodie looked up at his father and smiled. Artelia reached over and squeezed Caroline's hand. Sidney exclaimed, "That's wonderful Caroline. I believed you'd be a fast learner."

Brodie noticed how Caroline smiled as she looked around the table. It was hard to believe how things had changed in the last few years since the time of it being only him, his brother, and father. For the first time in a long while, Brodie felt like everything was going to work out well.

| 3 |

1858

The tobacco crop was doing well and it looked like the fall of 1858 would be a good one for the Dukes. When the tobacco was ready for picking, Sidney, Brodie, and their father rose early and headed out into the fields. Once the sun made its way to the top of the sky, the three would return back to the house, where a piping hot meal was waiting for them.

One day, while picking the sticky leaves from the plant, Washington pulled the boys aside. He took a leaf and rubbed his fingers over the gummy surface. "Boys, I want you to dream of bigger things than just working here in the fields. We know that tobacco manufacturers are making a lot more money by selling the tobacco than us farmers who grow it. One day, I want us to try our hand at manufacturing tobacco, where we can make some real money."

Brodie looked down at his calloused hands and thought of how wonderful it would be to actually do something that didn't cause him so much pain. He thought of the prospects of making money; doing anything other than working among the tobacco plants. But, little did Brodie know, there would come a day that he would dream of being back in the fields with his father and brother.

One day, in the midst of the summer heat, he and Sidney were trailing behind their father as they checked for hornworms, the one pest that could wipe out a tobacco crop. Sidney had fallen behind as the two inspected the plants. Not thinking anything of it, Brodie continued to turn over each leaf, feeling for the pest. After a couple of minutes, Brodie turned around to look for his brother and didn't see him. "Sidney, where are you?"

Brodie waited a moment and then called out again in a louder voice, "Sidney, you know we both need to finish this row before we can go inside. Come on now, you need to do your share."

The young boy fell silent, waiting to hear a response from his brother. But there was only the sound of birds flying over the field. At that moment, all Brodie could think about was how eerie the silence was. Sidney had never fallen back on his work. He was the one that was always encouraging Brodie to work a little harder and faster. Brodie walked back through the rows of tobacco plants, trying to locate where Sidney could be. Just as he was getting ready to head toward the house, he spotted Sidney lying on the ground, groaning in pain. "Sidney, what's wrong?"

Sidney held on to his side, barely able to speak. "I don't feel well."

Brodie called out in a loud voice, "Daddy, come quick. Sidney is sick."

Brodie stayed near his brother, trying to console him the best he could. "Daddy will be here in a minute. Please be okay. You've got to be okay."

Brodie spotted his father and called out, "Daddy, Sidney is here. He's burning up with fever."

Washington looked down at his son and, without hesitating, picked him up, placed his body over his shoulder, and headed in the direction of the house. Brodie kept close by, trying to encourage his brother, as they trampled through the tobacco field that led to front of the house. Brodie ran ahead and called out, "Artelia, Sidney's sick."

Artelia opened the door, jarring it enough for Washington to slip by. Washington almost tripped as he stumbled on a toy, but was able to regain his balance long enough to carry Sidney down the hallway and into the back bedroom. Brodie followed them into the room and gazed down at his brother. Tears formed in his eyes as he saw the pain his brother was enduring.

"Brodie, go get the doctor. Tell him to hurry."

Brodie ran through the house, out the door, and into the barn. After quickly harnessing and mounting the horse, he rode as fast as he could toward town. A mixture of sweat and tears blocked his vision as he drew closer to his destination. Once outside the doctor's house, he slid off the horse, wrapped the reins on a post, and ran up the steps. He knocked on the door several times before a man appeared. "Dr. McGee, please come quickly. My brother is really sick."

"I'll be there as quickly as I can." The older man looked at the twelve-year-old boy with a grim expression. "Brodie, you need to stay away from him. Typhoid fever is running rampant."

Brodie was consumed with fear as he made his way back home. He didn't want to think that there could be any possibility that his brother would die. No, he wouldn't allow his thoughts to go there. His brother would be fine. He just had to be.

But, once Dr. McGee arrived and went back to the bedroom to examine Sidney, all hope that his brother would be all right, diminished. Even though Artelia, Washington, and the doctor, tried to speak as quietly as possible, Brodie heard Artelia gasp and begin to cry. A few minutes later, Dr. McGee left the house and Washington came into the room, where Caroline and the children were waiting. His shoulders were slumped over and it was clear he'd been crying. "Children, no one is to go back to see Sidney. Artelia will be with him to take care of his needs."

Brodie sat numb in his chair. He felt like he was in a nightmare and prayed that he would wake up. But, as the hours passed and darkness filled the room, all Brodie could do was sit and wait. Caroline fixed supper and fed the little children. Washington paced around the room, sucking on his pipe and mumbling under his breath. Everyone was on edge, and James and Benjamin sensed the tension in the air. Even though they were very young, they knew something was wrong. They cried out for their mother, but to no avail. The door in the back room never opened.

Brodie fell asleep with his head on the table. He didn't realize it was a dream when Sidney walked into the room, encouraging him to go get the fishing poles and meet him down at the creek. The dream seemed so real and right. As he walked down to the creek with his brother in front, Sidney turned to him. "Brodie, you can't come with me."

Puzzled by the words, Brodie called out, "I want to be with you. Please. Let's go to the creek and catch some fish."

Brodie tried to catch up with his brother. Just as he was about to touch him, Sidney disappeared. At that moment, Brodie heard his father cry out, waking him. He looked around the room and saw Artelia and Washington hugging each other. Both were crying and Brodie realized the worst had happened. Or would it be the worst?

Washington left the room and walked out the door. Artelia came over to Brodie and tried to comfort him, but her touch stung of death and he refused to believe his brother was gone. He ran back to the back bedroom and gazed over at the bed. A sheet had been pulled over Sidney's still body and Brodie dropped to the floor. "You can't leave me. You promised me that you would be here for me. Damn it. You can't be dead!"

Artelia came over and tried to comfort Brodie, but he was inconsolable. He pushed past her, ran down the hall, opened the door, and sprinted into the darkness. As he made his way toward the creek, he heard the sound of a shovel hit the ground. With tears streaming down his cheeks, he looked in the distance, where he saw the silhouette of his father digging a hole. It was in that moment that reality set in and all Brodie could do was run.

When Brodie arrived at the creek bed, he took a handful of rocks and flung them into the water. He began to scream and curse God. "How could you do this? Sidney was my brother and my friend. How could you take him away from me?"

After only a few minutes, Brodie collapsed onto the sandy ground. As he lay with his head on the sand, he watched the water cascade over the rocks and into the pool below. He could hear the birds singing in the trees and watched tadpoles slip around in the water. Flies swarmed in and began to sting him, causing him to sit up and swat at them. He brushed the sand from his face and made his way back to the house, unable to fathom what would happen next.

| 4 |

1858-1859

The following day, a small gathering of family circled around Sidney's grave, singing hymns and listening to Washington read from the Bible. At the conclusion of the service, each person took a handful of dirt and dropped it onto the top of the pine casket. When it was Brodie's turn, he approached the open grave, scooped up a handful of soil and allowed the red clay to slip through his fingers. As the dirt hit the casket, tears cascaded down his face. Not wanting to appear weak, he used his sleeve to wipe away the tears, turned from the onlookers, and walked back toward the house.

Moments later, the family entered and gathered around the table. Brodie sat with his head down, dazed by his grief. Silence prevailed for a while, until the sound of the little children playing in the corner broke through the stillness. As Brodie looked over at his siblings, he noticed James placing the carved fox into his mouth. He stood up and, without warning, went over and pulled it away from the small child. Immediately, James began to scream, causing the women in the room to run over and soothe him.

Washington yelled at Brodie, causing the boy to feel alienated and hurt. He stared back at his father, then turned and walked outside into the warm summer evening. He sat down in a rocking chair on the front porch and waited to see who might come out to reprimand him. After a few minutes, the door opened and Artelia walked out and sat in a chair beside him. She didn't say anything, and when Brodie looked at her, he noticed the pained expression on her face.

Brodie took the fox and rubbed it, thinking about the hours Sidney spent carving the wood into an intricately designed fox. Artelia remained silent, which concerned Brodie. He was expecting her to give him one of her speeches about how to treat James, but to his surprise, she said nothing.

Brodie looked over at the woman who he now thought of as his mother. "Are you alright?"

For a moment, Artelia didn't move. Then, in a tired voice she spoke. "Brodie, I can't imagine how you're feeling right now. I've lost family and friends, but never someone as close as you and Sidney were."

Brodie continued to rub the smooth texture of the fox, unable to find words worthy of speaking.

Artelia raised her head and, for the first time, Brodie noticed her bloodshot eyes and grayish skin color. He had been so obsessed with his own feelings, he didn't even consider that this woman, who had become such an important part of his life, could be sick. "Artelia, are you okay?"

"I didn't want to believe that I might have caught typhoid fever, but I don't feel well. That's why it's important for me to talk with you. I know you're grieving for your brother. I am, too. But, if I'm sick and don't make it, I need to know that you'll help your father and Caroline with the small children."

"Don't speak like that. You're going to be fine."

"Brodie, promise me, you'll help your father. He's a good man and he loves you very much."

"I refuse to believe you could be taken away from us!" Brodie looked over at Artelia. He wanted to run, like he had done so many times, but knew it wouldn't help.

"Now, I'm going to go lie down and I'd like it very much if you'd go inside and apologize to your father. Knowing that you're standing beside him during this very tough time would mean the world to me."

As Brodie looked into Artelia's eyes, he could see tears well up. He reached over and squeezed her hand. "You know, you do make really good fried chicken and apple pie."

Artelia smiled and brushed the tears from her eyes. Both of them walked inside. Artelia turned toward Brodie and smiled before making her way toward the back bedroom. Brodie stepped up to where his father was sitting. "I want to apologize for my outburst. I'm sorry."

Washington reached over and placed his arms around his son, squeezing him hard. Brodie couldn't remember a time when his father had held him so tightly and wondered if he was aware of Artelia's condition. "Dad, I love you, and want to be here for you. Go back and check on Artelia and I'll help Caroline with the children."

Washington didn't say anything, but turned and followed his wife back to the bedroom. For days, the door remained closed. Brodie and Caroline took on the major chores around the house, usually in silence. Every time Washington came out of the room, he would shake his head, clearly distressed over his wife's condition. Brodie continued to hope that Artelia would survive, but after a week of waiting, Washington entered the main room, found a chair, and sat down.

Everyone looked in Washington's direction to try to discern what had happened. Washington took a deep breath and announced, "She's gone."

Brodie couldn't comprehend how two people he loved so much could be taken from him. His brother, Sidney, was his rock and Artelia was the mother he had grown to love. Both of them had helped define who he was, and now, with their deaths, he felt lost.

The next couple of days were a blur. Brodie helped his father dig a grave out in the back near a maple tree that Artelia had enjoyed. The day after her death, a small graveside service was held with only a few close family members in attendance. A few of Artelia's favorite hymns were sung, but no one could sing the words without crying. With so many people in town dying of typhoid fever, a minister was not available, so Washington read a few scriptures and ended the service with a prayer that sounded more like a plea of protection over his family.

For several weeks, Artelia's sisters came to help Caroline with the household chores. They took charge of the young children, which gave Washington and Brodie the opportunity to return to their daily routine. It was out in the tobacco fields, working side by side, that the two began to come to terms with their own personal grief.

Everyone felt the loss of both Artelia and Sidney. The little children couldn't understand where their mother had gone, and leaned heavily on Caroline. Washington spent more time away, trying to deal with the loss of his second wife and eldest son. It was during these days that Brodie developed a strong attachment to the black woman who occupied their house.

One day, while the three small children were playing, Brodie looked over at Caroline and asked, "Do you know where your family is?"

Caroline gasped at the mention of her own family. "No. My father was sold when I was just a baby. Then my momma and I were brought to Hillsborough where your father bought me."

Brodie remained silent, pondering how this young woman must be feeling. Ever since Sidney's death, Brodie had begun to feel like he didn't belong. The three younger siblings had each other and his father was trying to get through his own grief. "Caroline, you're the only one who I can talk to."

Caroline sat motionless for a moment. "Your father is a good man. Just give him some time."

"But, how do you get over being apart from your family?"

"You pray to the Good Lord."

"I'm having a hard time believing in a good God. How could he take my mother, my brother, and Artelia away?"

"For me, it's believing there's more to this life than what we can see."

"Caroline, I hope you can find your family one day."

Caroline lowered her head and murmured, "I do, too."

The days crept into months as the summer changed into fall, and then into winter. One morning, Brodie woke to Benjamin crying in the distance. It was a pitiful sound that brought back memories of the last few hours of Sidney's life. He slid under the blanket and began to hum, hoping to push the sound away and, along with it, the grief he continued to experience.

In the next few minutes that followed, Brodie began to wonder why Caroline hadn't gone to his younger brother, and he decided to get up. She'd been like a mother to the young children and wouldn't neglect their cries, particularly, Benjamin who'd been so sickly. Brodie pulled a blanket around his thin body and entered the main living area. Looking around, he became exceedingly concerned. With no adult present, Brodie made his way into the room where the small children slept.

James was still fast asleep, oblivious to the cries of his older brother. Mary Elizabeth had positioned herself next to Benjamin, not sure of how to console the toddler.

Brodie looked at Benjamin and could see perspiration running off his forehead. Mary Elizabeth was wiping his brow and speaking to him in a calm voice. "Where's Caroline?" asked Brodie.

Mary Elizabeth shrugged her shoulders. "I don't know."

Brodie walked out of the room and went in search of Caroline and his father. He yanked his jacket off a hook, slipped into his boots, and opened the door. He could see smoke coming from the barn where the tobacco was being cured. Brodie walked over to the dilapidated structure and pulled the door open. The smell of cured tobacco filled his nostrils. He scanned the interior of the darkened room and noticed his father sitting on a chair near the open fire, smoking a pipe.

Brodie hesitated a moment before approaching his father, but knew he had to find help for his younger brother. He walked across the room and glanced down at the man, who appeared older and more fragile. "Papa, Benjamin is sick and Caroline is nowhere to be found."

Washington didn't move. He appeared deaf to the words that Brodie spoke. "Papa, where's Caroline?"

Washington looked into his son's eyes and said, "She's gone."

"What do you mean she's gone?"

"I had to let her go."

"But why?"

"I couldn't bear to keep her any longer. After Artelia died, it weighed so heavy on me. I had to let her have a chance at finding her mother. So last night, when all of you had gone to bed, she packed her belongings and left."

Brodie had never felt such an intense wave of anger. How could his father let Caroline leave? She was the only one who understood him; the only one who had any idea of how he was feeling. "So, who's going to take care of your children?"

Washington looked up into Brodie's eyes. "Artelia's family has agreed to come and help out. I know you don't understand. I don't expect you to. But it's not right to own someone. I told her if the day comes when slavery is abolished, she will be welcome to come work for me. But, until then, she needs to be free."

Brodie turned, slammed the barn door, and ran out to the frost covered field. He ran down the road that led to town, hoping he might find Caroline and convince her to come back. After an hour of running, he stopped in the middle of the road, leaned over, and screamed as loudly as he could. Tears streaked down his face and he wiped them away, refusing to allow his grief to transition into weakness. He took several deep breaths and, in that moment, he made a decision. A decision that would forever change the course of his life. Never again would he allow anyone to cause him pain.

| 5 |

1861-1864

On April 12, 1861, Confederate troops fired on Charleston Harbor to start the bloodiest war ever to take place on American soil. Brodie didn't understand the implications of the war and how it would alter his life. At first, it seemed like the war was far off, but as the months went by, more and more men in and around Durham were sent to the battlefields, many never returning.

In 1863, with the need for more soldiers, the Confederacy lowered the draft age from eighteen to seventeen and raised it from forty to forty-five. Given that Brodie had just turned seventeen, he knew he'd have to go to war. Upon reporting to Camp Holmes in Raleigh, he discovered that his thin stature would prevent him from participating in direct combat. Instead of going to the front lines, he was assigned to Salisbury, North Carolina, where he would serve as a prison guard. On the other hand, Washington was given orders to report to Charleston, South Carolina.

As Brodie was getting ready to leave, his father was also preparing for the worst. On October 20th, Washington sold all of his farming tools, wagon, livestock, and the remains of his recent harvest. He took most of the money and gave it to Artelia's family to assist with the raising of his three small children. Washington took the last of his money and purchased cured tobacco leaves from local farmers to process and sell once he returned. At that point in time, Washington Duke had no idea how this decision would change his destiny.

Days later, with the house empty and the small children gone to Alamance County, Brodie and Washington packed their few belongings and walked to the main road where they would each go their separate ways. Washington was headed south to Charleston, and Brodie west to Salisbury. When the moment came to say goodbye, Washington reached over and, with tears in his eyes, grabbed his son. "Son, I have no idea what our future holds. I just want you to know I love you very much."

Brodie didn't want to leave his father's embrace, but knew he had to go. "Pa, I love you."

The two men parted and Washington looked intently at Brodie. "Now, I hope this war will be over soon. But, if it isn't, please remember that the good Lord will be looking over you."

Brodie pulled out the wooden fox that his brother had made and rubbed his fingers over the curves. "I'm going to hold on to this and when I'm scared, I'll rub it and remember the days when you, Sidney, and I, were together."

Washington wiped his face of the tears that had trickled down his cheek. "They were really good days and I hope there will be more to come. Now take care of yourself and I'll meet you back here one day."

Brodie picked up his bag and began to walk down the dusty road, looking back on occasion to see if his father was still in sight. After a few minutes, his father was no longer visible. Anxiety swept over him and he was filled with a strong desire to run back home. Just as he was getting ready to turn back, he spotted a stagecoach heading in his direction.

A man riding in the front called out, "Young man, are you off to war?"

"Yes, sir."

"I'll be glad to give you a ride."

Brodie threw his bag onto the wooden bench and climbed up. The man turned to him, "You look mighty scrawny to go to war."

"That's what they told me when I went to Raleigh. I was hoping I wouldn't have to fight, but they told me I'd be fine in Salisbury."

"I've heard from some that, as long as the numbers of prisoners are down, that's the place to be."

Brodie sat in silence as the stagecoach made its way west toward his destination. He felt numb as he watched everything familiar slip behind him. Once they reached the train station in Greensboro, the man stopped the stagecoach. "You're going to need to catch the train from here."

Brodie hesitated a moment before stepping down. The man could sense how scared Brodie was and placed a hand on his shoulder. "Now, go on. The train will take you right up to the prison gates. I'll be praying for you."

Brodie stepped down and stood frozen on the train depot platform. He watched as other young men, dressed in gray or brown, drew closer to the track. When the sound of the whistle began to blow, Brodie picked up his few items and climbed up into the train. He found a seat beside a window and hoped no one would sit next to him. But, just as the train began to move, an older man sat down beside him. "Where are you headed?"

Brodie knew from the way the man asked, that he expected a response. "Salisbury, I've been given orders to serve at the prison."

"I'm sorry to hear that."

"What do you mean? I've heard that the number of prisoners has been manageable."

"Word has it that they are moving prisoners from Richmond as we speak. Thousands of men. The conditions at Camp Libby were intolerable and now they are creating the same nightmare in Salisbury. Typically, I would say it would be better to be a guard than a prisoner, but the way I see it, you're going to be just as much in prison as any of those Yanks."

Brodie didn't know what to say and sat in silence, as the train pulled into Salisbury and stopped outside the prison walls. When the train came to a halt, Brodie took out the wooden fox and rubbed it against his fingers. He thought of Sidney and asked him to be with him in spirit as he walked down the train steps onto the hard, red clay. Once the train had left, Brodie looked around to see only a few young men, not much older than him, standing outside the prison gate.

The walls surrounding the prison were ten feet tall with a ledge for sentries to look down upon the courtyard. One guard spotted the young men and called for the gate to be opened. Once inside, Brodie was overtaken by the stench. He had never smelled such a horrendous odor in all of his life and started to gag.

The prison guard looked at him with a sympathetic expression. "You'll get used to the smell. You'll have to."

Brodie turned toward the voice and gasped at the condition of the guard's uniform. In contrast to the clean one he was wearing, the uniform of the man standing in front of him was filthy. The gray was a muddied brown with several missing buttons. The man's cheek bones were sunken with a scruffy beard hiding any skin on his neck. He looked right at Brodie and then turned his attention to the other young men standing in front of him. "Major Gee would like to speak with you. Stand here until I can get him."

It was a chilly day to remain standing still, and the sudden flashes of cold air made Brodie flinch. He looked over at the others and could tell they were just as cold and nervous as he was. After a few minutes, a man about the age of his father walked out into the night air, and faced the young men. "Let me get to the facts. Prisoners from several different camps have been sent here due to overcrowding. Many of them are sick and all of them are hungry. We haven't been given the provisions that we need and chaos is sure to happen. You'll need to do your best to contain them until we hear of a prisoner exchange."

Brodie looked at the others standing in the cold and was immediately disheartened by his circumstances. This was the last place he wanted to be, but knew he had no choice but to do as he was told and, hopefully, this dreadful war would be over soon. Another guard led the young men into a building where there were several mats made of hay. He offered them a little water, bacon, and bread. The portions were meager, barely filling a small tin bowl.

"You'll sleep here tonight. First thing in the morning, you'll be given your assignments."

Brodie found a mat near the wall and placed his few belongings next to him. He lay down, pulled the wooden fox out of his pocket, and held it firmly. In the middle of the night, he heard a high-pitched scream that woke him. He was afraid to move, wishing he could be anywhere but here.

In the pitch darkness he heard a voice yell out, "Time to get up! I need everyone to line up and follow me."

Brodie rose and followed the man out of the building into the cold air. As the young men huddled together, trying to stay warm, the man looked over at them and spoke in a commanding voice. "Your first duty will be to serve as sentry on the upper ledge of the wall. Each of you will receive a musket. Don't shoot unless you have to. There's enough chaos going on here without any of you feeling your oats and shooting someone without cause."

After the muskets were handed out, the newly assigned guards were led up a ladder onto a ledge that circled the entire prison. The sun was just beginning to rise and, for the first time, Brodie could see the layout of the enclosure he would call home. There was a large brick building, four stories high that had been used for a cotton factory built in 1839. Several smaller buildings were scattered near the front, where the only entrance to the prison was located. Tents, barely large enough for two men were scattered throughout the premises of the prison. But, what caught his attention the most, were the mounds that were raised up above the ground.

As if the guard knew what he and the others were thinking, he called out, "The mounds you see have been dug by the men who have no other place to sleep. When the train arrived on October 5th, ten thousand men were brought in. Before then, there were enough places for the men to find shelter. But now, there's only room inside for the officers and a jail for the muggers."

One of the new guards blurted out, "Why did they send all these men here?"

"All the prisons are full. Major Gee has been trying to get more supplies, but there aren't any. The men on the battlefields are going without and the Confederate government doesn't want to give to the Union soldiers, when our own men are dying in the fields."

Brodie scanned the sixteen acres and noticed how little clothing the men had. Everyone looked like they were wearing rags and weren't dressed properly for the cold weather that naturally came to North Carolina in late October. He noticed a wagon, being pulled by two scrawny mules, proceeding through the prison grounds. At first, he didn't realize what was happening, but then it dawned on him that the wagon was being filled with dead bodies. He could hear a voice in the distance calling out, "Bring out your dead."

When the wagon stopped along the way, men pulled off clothes from the corpses and slung the bodies onto the wagon. A guard who was situated on top used a metal hook to pull the bodies to the front of the wagon, making room for more. Once the wagon was full, it continued to a building that had become known as the dead house.

Brodie was in a state of shock as he looked down upon the mass of suffering men. He could barely move and, when the guard called out, he didn't hear him. It was then, when the older man stood in front of him, that reality set in. "Young man, you need to get ahold of yourself. I need you to understand that those men down there are the enemy and should be treated as such!"

"Yes, sir."

"Now, once you receive your post, a guard will take you out onto the ledge where you will patrol until nightfall."

A young man, small for his age and clearly frightened asked, "When will we eat?"

"You'll eat twice a day, which is more than they have. Someone will bring you a slice of pork and cornbread. When you finish your shift, you'll have soup."

The muskets were made for men much larger than Brodie, which made them difficult to handle. He was thankful for the years of toiling in the fields with his father but, even with the muscles he had developed, the heaviness of the gun made it hard to manipulate.

Brodie followed the others to the ledge and was directed to go to the far corner of the prison. The sentry he was assigned to didn't appear interested in small talk. For the first couple of hours, the horror of what he was experiencing began to sink deeply into his soul. He had never seen such despair in all of his life and only wanted to be back home in Durham.

Afternoon came and, with it, a rainstorm. The rain started as a drizzle and then large drops began to pour down onto the prison. The prisoners who could find shelter did so, but many had no place to go, except down into manmade mounds of dirt. The hard clay surface made it next to impossible for the water to absorb into the earth. Within minutes, an inch of water was standing on the surface, creating streams for human waste to be transported in every direction.

From the corner of his eye, Brodie noticed a young man crouched against a corner of the stockade. His hair color and eyes looked just like Sidney's. Brodie stared at the young man and noticed how defenseless he was against the cold rain. A stern voice shouted at him from across the ledge. "What are you doing?"

Brodie turned toward the man on the ledge. "That man over there looks just like my brother."

"He's not your brother and, if others hear you talk like that, you'll end up down there alongside him."

Brodie turned around and began walking in the opposite direction, pretending to take his attention off of the prisoner. The torrential rain had soaked through all of his clothes and he began to shake. Maybe he was delusional, due to the lack of food and the chill that penetrated through to his core. But, every time he looked in the direction of the prisoner, he couldn't help but hope that maybe Sidney had somehow returned to life.

The routine of each day was the same. Brodie would stand on the ledge and look down onto this pit of hell. Sounds of moaning and cries filled the air, along with the occasional sound of a bored guard shooting his musket, wanting to demonstrate his power over defenseless prisoners. The smell of death and human waste filled his nostrils, causing him to gag. He had no idea how he would survive in this hell hole, but knew he had to somehow push through every minute, hour and day.

One cold day in early December, Brodie was given orders to walk among the prisoners. As he opened the door and began to circulate among the crowds of men, he noticed how apathetic they were. Most were so weak, and their bodies so depleted from lack of nourishment, that all they could do was huddle together around makeshift fires. Occasionally, a few prisoners could be seen shuffling around in hope of finding a piece of wood to burn or a morsel of food.

On one side of the camp a trench had been dug for the men to empty their bowels. As Brodie walked around the prison yard, it became clear that many of the men couldn't reach the trench, leaving piles of human waste everywhere. Brodie tried to avoid the piles, but realized it was useless. He wondered how much more of this hell he could take, unsure if he would ever be able to wipe these moments from his memory.

When he had made it to the far end of the prison, he saw the man who reminded him of Sidney crouched down near a mound of dirt. His hair and beard were matted and he was scratching his body, apparently from the lice that had infected everyone. Even as horrible as he looked, the man reminded him of his brother, whom he had loved so much.

Brodie scooted down so that he could talk with the stranger. "Hello."

Apparently startled, the man looked up and flinched backwards.

"I'm not here to hurt you. I just want to talk."

"Why do you want to talk with me?"

"I had a brother who died several years ago. When I saw you, I couldn't help but be reminded of him."

The man looked down, grabbed a stick, and tried to move some of the red clay away from his mound. Brodie thought it best to leave the man, but his desire to, in some way, draw close to his brother, even in death, provoked him to continue. "What's your name?"

The man looked up into Brodie's eyes. "William Raulston."

"Where are you from?"

"New York."

"My name is Brodie Duke. I'm from Durham, North Carolina."

"Brodie, what are you doing?"

Brodie looked behind him and saw one of the sentries he had worked with on the wall. "I was just asking this prisoner where he was from."

"You know we aren't allowed to get friendly with the prisoners. If one of the officers sees you talking with a prisoner, you might be charged. Now, move away before I have to report you."

Brodie looked once more in William's direction, then continued to walk. Everywhere he looked, he saw men who were close to death. There was no food or supplies. He had heard the guards talk of how Major Gee had tried to seek help from the Confederate government, but there was just no money.

Word had reached the prison that there might be a prisoner exchange, but it couldn't come quickly enough. Men were starving and others dying from diseases due to the filthy conditions. The guards were getting antsy and it was harder every day to keep them from causing a riot among the prisoners.

Brodie was brought back to reality when he heard the sound of an artillery shell exploding near the front gate. Prisoners had moved to the open gate, hoping for freedom, but instead were halted by the explosion. Sentries began to shoot at the prisoners, killing at least a dozen men. Other prisoners, trying to get back, trampled on the wounded, leaving them for the safety of the brick buildings.

Up to this point, Brodie hadn't fired his musket and hoped he wouldn't have a reason to do so. Men were screaming as they crawled back away from the gate. Brodie, unsure of what to do, raised his gun and pointed it in the direction of the men who were moving back. One of the guards shot in the direction of the fleeing men. One man jerked back and fell to the ground.

Without hesitating, Brodie screamed at the guard, "Why did you do that? They were retreating!"

The guard glared back at Brodie and yelled, "If you care so much, then you pick up the bodies and have them moved to the trenches."

Several other guards had joined them. One of them pressed his musket up to Brodie's chest. "Go on. You heard him. When the wagon comes for the dead, you take them to the trenches."

Brodie had heard of the trenches that were being dug to bury the dead, but hadn't seen them. When the wagon came up, Brodie supervised the prisoners as they tossed the bodies onto the wagon. Once the wagon was full of entangled bodies, the gate was opened and several black prisoners, along with two other guards, walked through the gate toward a cornfield on the southeast edge of the property. Several guards were monitoring the digging of a trench, while the black prisoners tossed the bodies into the shallow grave. Another prisoner stood on top of the bodies trying to press them down into the earth to make room for more.

It felt like a bad dream that Brodie was sure he would wake up from. He was in a state of shock as he observed the bodies being tossed into the hole, hearing the crunching of broken bones and smelling the gagging odor of death. When the last body was tossed into the trench, the man's face gazed upward, eyes still open.

Brodie gasped as he recognized the man's face. It was William Raulston.

Tears pooled in his eyes as he watched the men toss dirt over the bodies. William's face was the last to be covered. Brodie turned and wiped his eyes, without allowing the other guards to see his grief. After several hours of shoveling dirt, pressing it down to make the ground level, Brodie turned and made his way back to the ominous structure that he had come to hate.

| 6 |

1865

The winter of 1865 was brutal. Never had Brodie remembered such a cold dismal winter. He and the other guards suffered from the lack of food. He did have a shelter over his head at night, along with a straw-filled mattress, but he rarely was able to stay warm. As bad as it was for him and the Rebel guards, life for the Union prisoners was a living nightmare.

Every day, the wagon was pulled through the prison grounds, picking up the dead and taking them to the awaiting trenches. The stench grew stronger and the snow-covered ground glowed blood-red and a dark brown. And every day, Brodie's heart hardened to the reality of the senseless deaths of so many.

In late February, Major Gee called the guards together to tell them of the orders he had received. They met in the barracks, awaiting the words that would finally change everything. Brodie stood in a corner, away from the majority of the soldiers, and listened to them exchange thoughts of what Major Gee might say. When the major finally opened up the door, everyone stood at attention.

The older man, who had tried so hard to advocate for better conditions in the prison, appeared sober by the news he was about to share. "Men, the day has finally come. The terms for an exchange of prisoners have finally been agreed upon. Tomorrow, we will open the gates, and everyone who can walk will be able to leave."

One man in the crowd called out, "Won't that cause bedlam?"

Major Gee responded, "Not unless we provoke them." He then looked at one particular guard and gave him instructions. "Tell the prisoners that they have something good to sleep over tonight."

"Yes, sir."

Brodie looked over at the major and asked, "What will happen to the others? The ones that can't walk."

"Once the prisoners that can walk leave, we will transport the sick to the trains, where they will be taken north."

For the first time since arriving in Salisbury, Brodie felt a sense of hope. A hope that maybe the war was coming to an end and he, along with the other guards, would be able to go home. But, before he could set his sights on home, he knew he needed to assist as many of the prisoners as possible.

The next morning, as the sun was rising in the sky, the heavy gate that had served as an obstacle between life and death, slowly began to open. The guards were in position with their muskets raised, wondering if the prisoners would try to retaliate. But, once the door was open wide and the first couple of prisoners walked through, the guards began lowering their muskets. Some left their positions and went down among the prisoners, trying to encourage the hesitant ones to leave.

Brodie observed from above as the men quietly left the compound. There were no shouts of retaliation or threats. Instead, tears of joy could be heard from some, while most walked in a somber manner, reserved for people close to death. As the last of the able-bodied walked out of the gate and toward the road that led to Greensboro, Brodie left his post and walked down among the dying. He picked up the planks that provided a minimal amount of cover for the mounds and found several bodies frozen in the snow.

For the next two months, the guards buried the dead and waited for the war to end. News had traveled quickly that General Robert E. Lee had surrendered in Virginia and the remaining troops were gathered around Durham waiting for a treaty to be signed, to officially end the war. But before a treaty could be signed, Major General George Stoneman led his Union troops through Western North Carolina, destroying everything in their path.

Days before the assault on the prison, Brodie, along with many of the other guards, left and headed home. They had heard of the destruction caused by Stoneman and knew they would probably lose their lives if they stayed.

On April 12th, the prison was set on fire and burned to the ground. Though the true accounting of deaths will never be known, it was recorded that over 3,700 Union soldiers died in Salisbury between October 1864 and February 1865.

| 7 |

1865

Brodie didn't know what to think. He had lived through hell and witnessed so many men die, all because the Secretary of War, Edwin M. Stanton, refused to allow an exchange of prisoners. Although Stanton was aware of the poor conditions in Confederate prisons, he stated that it was not policy for the North to exchange prisoners with the South. He reinforced that position by stating that the North couldn't afford to exchange well-fed, rugged, Confederate prisoners for Union soldiers who were now practically skeletons.

As Brodie made his way home, he was filled with anger, frustration, and anxiety over what he had experienced. He was numb and unresponsive when people tried to speak to him. He couldn't begin to return to the normalcy of life on the farm. The one question that was the hardest for him to move past was, why not me? Why didn't I die? Feelings of guilt invaded his thoughts, making it difficult to think clearly.

Brodie took the wooden fox out of his pocket and rubbed it. It had served him well during the months in Salisbury. Each night, while going to sleep, he had held it, and thought of what it would be like to return to Durham. But now that he was free, it served as his only source of normalcy. His faith in a good God had dissipated while observing the constant ongoing suffering. No more could he trust the words of any man, particularly a man of God, with their words of hope and salvation.

As he crossed into Orange County, Brodie slowed his pace. He just didn't know how he would be able to return to his family's farm and face his father and half-siblings. He needed time to himself, away from all who might expect him to be the same boy he was when he left home. So, instead of walking to his father's house, he made his way to the home of his Uncle William.

After days of walking, Brodie was exhausted and hungry, and he only wanted to lie down. Every muscle ached and his stomach churned from lack of food. He had lost weight since leaving home and his clothes hung loosely off of his tall frame. He stopped every couple of minutes to catch his breath, but was determined to make it to his uncle's house before the sun set.

When Brodie spotted the path that led to his uncle's property, he increased his pace. All he could envision was a hot meal and a bath to remove the dirt that had caked onto his skin. He knew he must look atrocious, but it didn't matter; he was back on familiar ground with someone he could trust.

Uncle William was working in the field when Brodie spotted him from a distance. When he was about hundred yards away, Brodie called out, "Uncle William, its Brodie."

Uncle William looked up from where he was tending the small seedlings and dropped the hoe he held in his hand. "Brodie, is that really you?"

"Yes, sir."

Brodie stopped, leaned over to take a breath, and finally fell to the ground. He felt lightheaded and, when he opened his eyes, he saw his uncle looking down at him. "Brodie, are you alright?"

"I'm really tired."

"Can you stand?"

Brodie put his arm on his uncle's shoulder and pulled himself up. He leaned into his uncle as the two walked back to the house. "Mary, Brodie's here. Make some of your biscuits and cut off a slab of the ham."

The two men barely made it up the steps without tripping. Brodie collapsed in a rocking chair on the front porch. His Aunt Mary came out of the house carrying a tin cup filled to the top with ice cold milk. Brodie pressed the cup to his lips and drank it down in one long swig. He wiped his mouth with the back of his dirt-caked hand, and leaned his head back.

No one spoke, letting Brodie take a moment to get his bearings. Aunt Mary poured more milk from a pitcher into the cup, handing it back to Brodie. This time, he drank a few sips, then held the cup to the side. "I don't believe I've ever tasted anything as good as this milk."

Uncle William sat down in the chair next to Brodie, while Aunt Mary went inside to fix him a plate of food. The two men sat quietly for a few minutes before Brodie spoke. "I truly didn't believe I'd ever see this place again."

"We're very glad to see you. We got word that General Stoneman came through Salisbury on the 12th, burning the prison to the ground. We didn't know if you got out."

Brodie leaned back and shut his eyes, experiencing visions of dead bodies pressed into the trenches. He flinched as he remembered William Raulston's piercing eyes staring up at him. "Uncle, can I stay here awhile?"

"Of course." Uncle William paused a moment and then asked, "Don't you want to go home?"

"I can't."

"You're welcome here as long as you feel the need."

"Have you had any word about my father?"

"I heard he was captured in Richmond and then released when the treaty was signed in Virginia. Word is he was taken to New Bern and is making his way back here."

Brodie stared out into the air. "I'm sure he'll be glad to get his children back from Artelia's family."

Once Aunt Mary returned with the biscuit and ham, Brodie bit into it and savored the flavor of each bite. Instead of consuming it quickly, he bit off a little at a time, trying to enjoy each chew. Tears welled up in his eyes and he quickly brushed them away. He didn't want his uncle to see his weakness. No, he had to be strong and hold back the emotions that were fighting to be released. No one needed to know what he had been through. It was just too painful to state out loud.

After a few minutes, Aunt Mary called out, "Brodie, your bath is ready. I have some fresh clothes for you as well. I'm not sure if they'll fit, but they'll do."

Brodie raised himself up out of the chair and, for the first time since he could remember, his stomach felt full. He carefully walked down the steps, going around to the back of the house, where the tub waited for him. He hesitated a moment before ripping the filthy clothes from his body, but as the thoughts of what he had been through crept into his memory, he used all of his strength to tear them up into tiny shreds. Anger swept over him and, before he knew it, he was stomping them into the ground.

The water was warm and felt like a soft blanket enveloping his body. Aunt Mary had left soap and a cloth for him to use to scrub away the filth. But, before he could actually get himself clean, the water had already turned dark brown. As if his aunt knew of his plight, she brought out another warm bucket of clean water. She poured the water into the tub and left him to finish his bath.

Once Brodie had shaved his face and allowed his aunt to cut and shave his head, he dressed and then entered the house. The sun had set and the stars were beginning to make their appearance in the spring night sky. He couldn't help but think about how quiet it was, almost eerily so. When he came into the large room, Brodie noticed his aunt and uncle sitting in front of a large fireplace, she knitting and he reading.

Aunt Mary rose from her seat. "Brodie, I know you must be exhausted. I've made a bed for you. Come lie down."

Brodie followed his aunt into the small room that contained only a bed and a nightstand. He lay on the bed and covered his body with a clean blanket. Drawing the blanket close to his neck, he enjoyed the feeling of warmth for the first time since leaving for Salisbury. When he opened his eyes, the sun was shining brightly in the sky. At first, he didn't know where he was and thought he must be dreaming. But, then, when he looked over into the large room and saw his aunt stirring a pot, he realized that he was finally safe.

| 8 |

1865

For the next few days, Brodie spent his time working beside his uncle in the fields. They worked in silence, tilling up the earth and planting each tobacco seedling by hand. In the evening, the three sat at the table, Brodie remaining quiet, except to tell his aunt how good the food was or to thank his uncle for his hospitality.

One day, as they were getting ready to retire from the fields, a young black boy walked up the path toward them. William and Brodie waited as the boy approached them. William wasn't sure if they should be concerned and stood in a defensive manner. The boy stopped a few yards away before speaking. "Mister, my name is Elijah and I come from the Stagville Plantation."

William responded, "What do you want?"

"I'm now free and I need a place to work."

"Why didn't you stay there?"

"Mr. Cameron isn't treating us well. He's gotten a federal officer to come and tell us to stay there and work like we always have, getting nothing for our work."

"Well, as you can see, I don't have much need for someone to work for me."

"I can work hard for you. I won't be any trouble. I just need a shelter to sleep in and some decent food."

Brodie looked at his uncle, waiting to see his response to the boy. They had known about the thirty-thousand acre plantation that housed nine hundred slaves. Many farmers in the area had wondered if the freed slaves would travel to nearby farms for work. "Uncle William, if we're to grow enough tobacco for manufacturing, we might could use an extra pair of hands."

Uncle William looked directly at the boy, paused a moment, and then stated in a firm voice, "We can give it a try. Now, I don't want any trouble out of you. If you work hard and make it worth my while, I'll pay you a little money and give you a place to sleep."

"Mister, thank you."

"You can call me Mr. Duke."

"Yes, sir, Mr. Duke."

"It's late and we have a lot of work to do tomorrow. Let's get you washed up and find a place for you to sleep."

Elijah was up and ready the next morning. He followed directions and was very helpful. He stayed in a shelter at the back of the property, and only came into the house when given permission. One day, over lunch, Brodie asked, "Elijah, what was life like at Stagville?"

Elijah stopped eating and paused a moment. "If you did your work and didn't talk back to the overseers, it was okay. But, the worst part was how my mother was sold. I don't know where she is. We were living in the Fish Dam Quarters. One night, the overseers came and grabbed my mother up out of bed, took her out the door, and I haven't seen her since."

Brodie responded, "My mother died when I was a baby. I never knew her."

Elijah looked at Brodie. "I'm sorry about that."

Brodie felt a connection to the boy. He knew Elijah had experienced some horrible injustices in his short life and must be feeling the same kind of anger he couldn't shake. "We heard about the raids by the Confederate and Federal troops."

"The Federal troops were bad, threatening to kill us if we didn't show them where Mr. Cameron's gold was hidden. They finally left us alone after taking everything they could carry away. But it was the Confederate troops that treated us the worst. They came into our quarters, demanding for the men to tell them if they wanted to be free."

Elijah closed his eyes and shook his head. Tears started to stream down his cheeks. "My uncle stood up and told them he wanted to be free. And then, before we could move, one soldier shot him right in the head. He then waved his gun at all of us, laughing at how scared we were. Then another soldier took one of the girls outside. In the next few minutes, all I could hear were her screams and the soldier hitting her and yelling at her."

Brodie didn't know what to say, so he remained silent.

Elijah placed his head down on the table and sobbed. Through his tears, he cried out, "I could've done something to protect them, but I didn't. Why didn't I?"

Brodie understood how haunted the young boy was feeling. As much as he wanted to change his own feelings, he couldn't shake off the vision of so many men dying and doing nothing to stop it. As hard as he tried, the guilt was like a shadow, following him everywhere he went.

Working the fields was the only pastime that kept the demons away. Brodie worked so hard every day that he could hardly crawl back to the house. After washing up and eating a meal, he would fall into a deep sleep. But as hard as he tried to keep the memories at bay, they always crept in through his dreams. Night after night, he would dream of William Raulston and the sight of his body entangled among the others. His piercing eyes staring right at him, pleading for Brodie to do something, anything, to save him.

9

1865

April turned into May, and as much as Brodie wanted to avoid going back to his father's house, he knew he needed to go. Word had reached him that Washington had arrived home after walking over a hundred and thirty miles from New Bern. He had also heard that his younger siblings had returned and were asking for him. So, one warm day with the dogwood blossoms out in full bloom and the hummingbirds zipping across the yard, Brodie walked the three-mile trek through the woods and down the dirt road leading toward Durham.

He took his time, trying to put off the inevitable, but as slow as he walked, he finally arrived. The first person he spotted was Mary Elizabeth, walking through the grass picking dandelions and creating a bouquet. She had grown so much since he last saw her. Instead of a little girl, she had taken on the shape of a young woman. Her hair had grown and was braided down her back. When she looked in his direction, she dropped the dandelions and ran toward him.

Brodie was surprised at the emotion that welled up inside him. He had always cared for his younger sister and how different she was from him. She always found the good in everyone and loved to laugh at the smallest of things. Approaching him, she reached her arms up to give him a hug. At first, Brodie hesitated. He hadn't touched anyone since leaving for Salisbury. But when he leaned down to hug her, he found himself picking her up and swinging her around.

When he placed her down, Mary Elizabeth called out in the direction of the house. "Daddy, James, Benjamin, come quickly! Brodie's home."

Washington walked out of the door with a pipe in his hand. He smiled as he approached his son. "Brodie, it's so good to see you!"

Brodie extended his hand toward his father, but didn't receive the response he expected. "Son, we aren't going to have none of that. I want a proper hug. Now, pull in."

Washington placed his arms around his son and hugged him hard. He then pulled back and the two men made eye contact. It was then that Brodie looked past his father and saw Benjamin, followed by James. Benjamin appeared happy to see his older brother, but James looked annoyed and stood back.

Benjamin called out, "Brodie, I missed you. I'm so glad you're home."

James stood outside of the circle, observing his older brother. He could feel James' eyes on him, not moving forward or speaking. "Hello, James."

"Hello."

"Now, that's no way to greet your brother. He's been away for a long time and I'm glad we're all together again." Washington placed his pipe into his mouth and sucked in. "Now, give him a hug."

The two hardly touched as they hugged and quickly pulled back. Apparently satisfied with the embrace, Washington said, "Let's go inside and talk."

Once they opened the door, Elizabeth Roney, his stepmother's sister, met him with a hug. "Brodie, it's so good to see you! Now you look like you could use a good home-cooked meal. Come in and sit down."

Brodie glanced around the cabin and noticed the changes that had been made. Changes that made him feel like a stranger in the house that he'd grown up in. A house where Artelia had brought him so much joy from cooking her apple pie and fried chicken. A place where he had sat near the fireplace learning to read and write. But, mostly, a place where he had observed Sidney whittling an animal while talking about their next adventure.

The memories from the past, coupled with the reality of the present, caused him to feel suffocated. He took a deep breath and sat down next to his father. "So, Brodie, how are you?"

Immediately, Brodie's expression changed. His body became limp and he almost wanted to laugh. How do you answer such a question? This was why he had avoided coming. He loved his father so much and didn't want to burden him with the truth. "I'm making it."

Washington took his hand and placed it on top of Brodie's. "I heard word of Salisbury. I didn't want to believe the stories. I hoped that, when you came home, you would tell me that the stories weren't true." He took his hand and wiped the tears away. "I'm so sorry, son. I would've done anything to have taken your place."

Everyone sat in stillness as the two men muffled their tears. No one had words. Elizabeth poured cups of coffee for Brodie and Washington, placed a tray of biscuits on the table, and encouraged

Mary Elizabeth, Benjamin, and James to follow her outside. Once the door had closed behind them, Brodie looked up at his father. "Dad, I'm going to live with your brother for a while. We're growing a crop of tobacco."

Washington took a draw from his pipe and exhaled, allowing the smoke to lift into the air. "Brodie, I was hoping you would live here."

Not knowing how to respond, Brodie remained silent.

Washington took another draw from his pipe. "Before I left for the war, I bought some leaf tobacco and hid it. Now that the war is over, I'm planning on selling it. I could surely use your help."

Brodie looked down and shook his head. "I can't. Too much has changed. I love you, but I can't be here."

Washington didn't say anything. He took a sip of his coffee and remained silent. Brodie knew his decision wasn't what Washington wanted, but he appreciated his father's acceptance.

"So, Dad, tell me how you plan on selling this tobacco you purchased."

Washington leaned in and, with excitement in his voice, stated, "We've been beating the tobacco with wooden flails, sifting it and placing it in cloth bags. We're calling our product *Pro Bono Publico,* which means 'for the public good'. I thought through it as I walked the one hundred thirty-seven miles back from New Bern. I'm planning on leaving this autumn and returning to the eastern part of the state. I was sure hoping you would come with me."

Brodie looked downward for a moment. "I don't think I'd be any good for you right now. It's best for everyone if I stay away for a while."

Washington took his pipe and knocked it against a bowl, allowing the ashes to fall inside. He then took a pinch of tobacco from a bag and placed it into his pipe. He lit the pipe and watched as the smoke lifted toward the ceiling. In a very subdued voice, he said, "I understand."

Brodie stood up. "I need to go now."

"Son, if you need anything, please let me know."

"I will."

Washington rose and the two men hugged. They walked out onto the porch where the children were sitting. Brodie looked over and watched, as they played with several of the wooden animals Sidney had whittled so many years ago. His pulse quickened as the memories of days gone by flowed through his mind. Instinctively, Brodie took the wooden fox from his pocket, rubbing it with such force he thought it might break, and walked down the path leading in the direction of his new life.

10

1865-1874

For four years, Brodie tended his uncle's tobacco fields, striving to grow some of the best tobacco in the area. Over time, he learned how to process the tobacco that had become so sought after by the Northern soldiers. As the years went by, he developed relationships with other tobacco farmers around Durham and Orange County. The farmers wanted to get the best price for their tobacco, so when Brodie talked of starting his own manufacturing company, they were eager to assist him in his pursuit.

While Brodie stayed on the farm, his father, Washington, with the help of his three youngest children, headed to the eastern part of the state, selling tobacco and flour, bartering as they went. Mary Elizabeth spent hours sewing the small bags that were used for the tobacco. Benjamin and James helped their father manufacture the tobacco and prepare it for selling. But, their success came primarily because of Washington's sales skills.

In 1866, Washington peddled over 15,000 pounds of tobacco for fifty to sixty cents a pound. It was hard work, but Washington never gave up. And neither did his children. They were all determined to make a success of the business. As time passed, the business continued to grow and, along with the growth, the number of buildings for manufacturing increased.

Even though Brodie didn't work with his father, he was inspired by him to build his own business. In 1869, Brodie made the decision to move to Durham to be closer to the railroad, as well as to the other tobacco factories that were making a name for themselves.

One of these tobacco companies was begun by a farmer by the name of John Ruffin Green. John used a different curing process than the other farmers. Instead of wood, he used charcoal as a means of curing the tobacco, giving it a bright gold color and a distinctive flavor. When the soldiers came through North Carolina waiting for the treaty to be signed at the Bennett home, they plundered all of John's tobacco, causing him to feel like his days as a businessman were over. But after the war was over, and the soldiers were back up north, letters starting pouring into the Durham post office, asking for this particular brand of tobacco. It was then that John knew he had a product that would sell.

John called in two men, William T. Blackwell and James Day, to help build his business. But tragedy struck, and six months into the start of the company, John fell sick from tuberculosis and died. William knew that, in order for the company to be successful, he would have to bring on someone who had a strong business mind. So, after placing ads in local newspapers, a young man by the name of Julian Shakespeare Carr was hired.

The combination of Julian's knack for advertising, using a bull for the brand, and William's and James' knowledge of the tobacco business, pushed the company to the top of the industry. In 1869, they produced sixty thousand pounds of tobacco with a workforce of twelve. In 1883, the company employed over nine hundred hands and produced over five million pounds of tobacco.

The William T. Blackwell Company wanted to make sure that everyone knew who was the king of tobacco in Durham. To do that, they changed the steam whistle of the train that traveled alongside Main Street to sound like the snorting of a bull. In these early years, it was clear that the William T. Blackwell Company would dominate the industry for years to come.

The move to Durham was a perfect fit for Brodie. He purchased a building on Main Street, using the space on the ground floor to manufacture tobacco and the top floor as his living quarters. He produced tobacco under the brands of *Duke of Durham* and *Semper Idem.* Initially, the business started slow but, with the support from his father and local farmers, it soon began to thrive.

On occasion, when sleep wouldn't come, Brodie would go to a local tavern to sip on rye whiskey and listen to men speak of their own dreams being realized here in Durham. On one such night, in late June 1872, he opened the door to the tavern, only to be bombarded with the emotional debate about who would be their new state representative. Brodie never cared about politics, but knew his father, Washington, was running on the Republican ticket against Democrat W.N. Patterson. The discussion was heated, but even so, Brodie kept quiet and listened intently as the men spoke in favor of the Freedman's bureau, and others, in total opposition to blacks having more rights.

One young man, who was clearly from the North, but sided with the conservatives, spoke up. "We cannot have Washington

Duke elected. Negroes should be kept in their place and, if Washington is elected, they will think they can run the city."

Someone in the crowd called out. "Louis Austin, I don't care for you coming here and telling us how to run our town or our state."

Louis, appearing arrogant and full of himself, exclaimed, "I have every right to speak my piece! I work hard as a roofer and pay my taxes."

A man sitting in the corner called out, "Mayor Durham told me about you coming into his office, demanding that the land that has been allotted as a cemetery should be used as a baseball field."

A confident Louis answered, "That's true. A cemetery is a waste of money. People can be buried in their churchyards. Anyway, I've been hearing about the baseball fields in Raleigh and Greensboro bringing in people from all around."

Brodie called out, "That's great for those two cities, but Durham is growing and we need a place to bury our citizens."

"Hogwash! Brodie Duke."

"I can tell you that when I was in Salisbury, a cemetery was needed far more than any baseball field."

Louis stood up and looked right at Brodie. "And what do you think of your father running for state representative?"

Brodie looked around the room, wondering which side of the political fence most of the men were on. But, as he thought about it, he didn't care. "I believe my father is a fair man and cares about the rights of all people."

Louis drew close to Brodie and then turned so that everyone could hear him. "That's more of a reason not to vote for him. And I can tell you this, I'm going to tell everyone I know that Washington Duke will take the jobs away from the white man in order to ensure the Negroes have paid jobs."

Brodie appeared annoyed as he proclaimed, "Louis, I don't believe that for one minute. Anyway, William Patterson is a little too small-minded for my taste."

Louis started walking toward the door, turned, and stated, loud enough for everyone to hear, "We'll see in a couple of weeks who wins. Either way, my vote will be for a baseball field over a cemetery."

Little did Louis Austin know what would happen the night that William Patterson won the state House of Representative's seat for Durham's district. After having a little bit too much to drink, Louis and several of his friends decided to demonstrate how excited they were over Patterson's victory. The young men carried an antique cannon up to the roof of the William T. Blackwell factory and began firing cannonballs out over the city. Thinking it was great fun, they continued to fire the cannon until it exploded, blowing off his arm, and ultimately killing Louis. Days later, with no other place to bury Louis, ironically his grave was the first to be dug on the property that is now Maplewood Cemetery.

In 1874, after leaving political life behind him, Washington decided to move his manufacturing business from the farm into town. He purchased a building large enough to accommodate both Brodie's business and his own. Even though Brodie wasn't keen to be in business with his two half-brothers, he knew that his father had had far more success in selling tobacco and had a lot of expertise to share with him.

One day, not long after Brodie moved into the building adjoining Washington's business, he overheard a conversation his younger brother, James, was having with his father. James, now being referred to by all as 'Buck', was speaking to Washington. "Dad, I don't know if I want us to work with Brodie. We've done so much work to promote our brand, and I don't think it's fair to give him an equal share of the profits."

"Now, Buck, I know you and Brodie don't see eye to eye on many of the issues pertaining to the tobacco business, but he's my son, and I want him involved in the business. He has made some great connections with many local farmers and his Duke of Durham brand has been very successful."

"I just don't understand why he didn't stay home and help us with the startup of the business."

"Buck, you didn't go off to war. Your life was difficult, but you didn't experience the hell he went through. I personally believe it was best for him to work for my brother, William. It gave him some time to work through things. I'm not sure if he'll ever be able to come to terms with what he experienced, but I'm going to be here for him. Now, we aren't going to discuss this further."

After hearing the conversation and observing Buck, Brodie began to realize that life was going to be a challenge. Instead of asking for his input, Buck made decisions regarding the tobacco business without consulting him. As time went on, Brodie was pushed out of the discussions that took place between Buck, Benjamin, and Washington.

Brodie spent more and more time away from the factory, walking the streets, and getting to know the people who were moving to Durham on a daily basis. One day, as he was strolling down the dirt street in front of the factory, he spotted a young woman walking in his direction. She appeared determined in her walk as she came toward him. Once she approached, Brodie looked down and couldn't help but smile at the woman with the white cotton dress and large brimmed hat. "Are you Brodie Duke?"

Brodie liked the woman's voice and couldn't wait to hear why she wanted to speak to him. "Yes, I am. How can I help you?"

"My father is starting up a church and he told me to come over and invite you and your family."

"I usually don't attend church."

"We know. That's why I'm inviting you to come this Sunday. We'll be having a meal on the grounds after the service. Please ask your family to join you."

"So, if I do come, who can I tell people invited me?"

"My name is Martha. Martha McMannen." She raised her hand to shake his. As Brodie touched the small delicate fingers, he squeezed them, not wanting to let go. After a moment, Martha looked up at Brodie. "I'll take my hand back. And, by the way, I'll be praying for you and your family."

"So why are you going to be praying for my family?"

"Tobacco is from the devil. No good can come from it."

"Now, Martha, I have to disagree. Durham is growing because of tobacco. That means more people are coming here. People who can attend your father's church and be saved."

Martha fell silent for a moment. "I never thought about it in that way."

"Well, Martha McMannen, I look forward to seeing you on Sunday."

Martha tipped her hat, turned, and scurried away.

As much as Brodie didn't want to extend the invitation to his father and family, he knew it would be best. But, to his delight, his father had already committed to attend the Trinity Church Missions, given that they were using his factory to hold a service. This pleased Brodie, and he was surprised at how much he looked forward to the opportunity to spend time with Martha without the distraction of his younger siblings.

Sunday was a beautiful day, with cool temperatures and a slight breeze. Brodie felt a sense of joy he hadn't felt since the days when he and Sidney were playing on the farm. Just the thought of seeing Martha made him smile. When he entered the small building, with rows of pews set on both sides and a picture of Jesus on a cross above the pulpit, he wondered if he wanted to stay.

Brodie hadn't been to church since leaving for war and, though he felt uncomfortable, the thought of seeing Martha outweighed his desire to leave. He sat on the back pew and watched as people walked in, filling in the seats. When the service was beginning, and there was no sign of Martha, he started to rise. But, just as he was headed toward the door, he heard the sweetest voice singing the song, *Amazing Grace.*

Brodie turned toward the front and looked right into Martha's eyes. He was mesmerized by how beautiful she was. It wasn't just a physical beauty, but something much deeper. In that moment, as she sang each word, a current of emotion struck him. He sat down, feeling light-headed and perplexed by these feelings. Feelings he had never had before. Not knowing how to react to such a vulnerable emotion, Brodie rose and walked out of the church. He sat down on a bench and placed his head in his hands. Tears welled up inside him and he began to sob.

Oblivious to his surroundings, he flinched when he felt the presence of a person sitting down beside him. When he looked up, Martha was staring out into the field of trees that lined the property. She didn't say a word. And, in the calmness of the moment, for the first time in his life, he understood how it felt to be loved by a woman.

11

1873-1874

In the months that followed, Brodie was either working in the tobacco factory or spending time with Martha. Brodie enjoyed her company and was surprised at how comfortable he was with her family. Martha's father, John, was first a preacher, but second an entrepreneur, who made contraptions for different purposes. This gave Brodie and John a topic to discuss when they weren't conversing about Martha. John was also an excellent fiddle player and loved to entertain his guests with his talents.

One particular night, in late fall, Brodie arrived to hear the sounds of music filtering out into the yard. He was momentarily taken aback at hearing Martha playing the piano and singing. He could never get enough of her voice, which increased his desire for her more and more. It was then that he knew he wanted to ask her to marry him. And that meant he would have to talk with John.

Brodie walked into the house as the last notes were being played. Once he was able to get John's attention, he waved at him to join him outside. As Martha approached the two men, Brodie made a motion in her direction, letting her know he wanted to be alone with her father. She appeared puzzled by his refusal to let her come, but complied.

It was an unusually warm fall night with the wind blowing from the south. Leaves had fallen from the trees, making a yellow, orange, and brown carpet. The two men sat in the rocking chairs that lined the front porch and lit up their pipes. Brodie turned to this man, who he had come to admire, and stated, "John, I've grown very fond of your daughter."

At first, John didn't speak, which made Brodie nervous. Then, after taking a swig of coffee, John looked out into the distance. "I've noticed that."

"I'd like to marry her."

John sat back, causing the rocker to hit the floor in a rhythmic motion. The silence was almost unbearable for Brodie, but he knew he needed to give John some time to process what he was asking. "Brodie, I know you'll be able to provide for my daughter. You're a hard worker and I can tell that your tobacco business is beginning to expand."

"Yes, sir. When I was growing up on the farm, one thing that my father instilled in me was to work hard and never give up."

John took another sip of coffee and placed the cup down on a small table. "When I was a little boy, my sister, Margaret, and I used to ride horses out into the fields that surrounded our homestead. I was twelve and she was nine. Margaret was one of the sweetest human beings to ever set forth on this earth. Anyway, we were riding beside each other when her horse got spooked and pulled upward. Margaret tried to hold on, but the force was too great. She fell off, hitting her head on a rock."

Brodie wasn't sure why John felt the need to tell him this story, but remained quiet as he continued. John was looking off into the distance as if he could actually see the scene play out in front of him. "Margaret didn't die right away. And the whole time I was riding back to the house with her still body in front of me, I kept praying to God to take me, believing that I was at fault, not her." He paused a moment. "You see, I've carried with me a sense of guilt since that day. And I can recognize when someone else carries a heavy burden. I heard what happened in Salisbury and have spoken to men who were there. And everyone who I've spoken to that served in that God-forsaken hellhole, can't let go of the burden of survival."

Brodie could feel the wooden fox in his pocket. It was a reminder of his brother, but also a testimony to his own survival of such a gruesome experience. He preferred to leave Salisbury in his past, but he knew John understood how impossible that was. John was right. The guilt of surviving, while men like William Raulston died, still haunted him.

Brodie lowered his head, falling silent. He had no defense. All he knew was that he loved Martha and would do everything in his power to take care of her. "John, I can't deny what you're saying. I'm still troubled by the demons. Every night, when I lay my head down, I pray to God to keep them away. Most of the time I can sleep, but I have to be honest, there are nights when I wake in a sweat, suffering by reliving those months all over again in my dreams."

John reached over and placed his hand on Brodie's shoulder. "Brodie, you've got to promise me that you'll get help when you struggle. I'll be glad to talk with you anytime. But you need to understand that, if you ever hurt my daughter, you'll have me to deal with."

"Yes, sir. I understand."

The next day, Brodie rode up to his father's house to share the good news. Washington was ecstatic and offered Brodie his mother's wedding ring. He wasn't sure how he felt about taking such a treasured item from his father. But, when Washington took it from a drawer and showed it to him, he knew it was perfect. It was a simple gold band that he believed Martha would love.

Brodie decided he would ask Martha to ride out to the country and have a picnic lunch. Thankfully, the day wasn't too cold and the ride was relaxing. The ring was snug in his pocket, but, even so, he checked for it every couple of minutes. When they arrived at the same river bank where he and Sidney played, he took out a blanket and spread it across a soft bed of moss. He opened the basket, which held sandwiches and potato salad, and placed the food in front of them.

"Brodie, this is a beautiful spot. I know you must've enjoyed growing up here."

The question caught Brodie off guard. It was hard for him to define his feelings about this place. He had loved the years when it was just him, his father, and Sidney. He had even enjoyed it when Artelia first became part of their family. But, after the births of his younger siblings, life had gotten more complicated. "I do have some special memories. I just wish you could've met Sidney. He was the best brother I could've asked for."

"I'm so sorry about the loss of your brother. Are you close to Benjamin and Buck?"

"No, not really. They are extremely close, which sometimes makes me angry. I know I shouldn't dwell on things I can't change. They were so much younger than me. When I left for the war, they stayed with my stepmother's family in Alamance County. Other than not having a lot of food, they were practically unscathed by the war. When I returned from Salisbury, I knew I couldn't be around them. It was just too painful to see them enjoy life, while I was suffering."

"Brodie, I can't imagine what you went through, but I'm going to pray every day for you to enjoy the peace that comes from forgiving yourself."

Brodie reached over and traced Martha's face with his finger. "You sure are beautiful."

"I'm glad you think so."

"I have something to ask you."

Martha looked puzzled, but remained quiet. She reached into the basket and pulled out a sandwich. She had just taken a bite when Brodie changed his position. He was leaning on one knee as he pulled the ring out of his pocket.

"Martha McMannen, will you marry me?"

Martha was chewing the sandwich and couldn't speak. She placed her hand over her mouth, waiting for the remainder of the sandwich to go down. She was shaking her head in an unusual way, which confused Brodie. His first instinct was to become angry, thinking that he had embarrassed himself by asking her. He got up and started walking away. Martha finally swallowed the remainder of her sandwich and blurted out, "Brodie Duke, where are you going? I'm sorry, I couldn't speak. Of course, I'll marry you!"

He turned around and she was standing in front of him. "Brodie, I love you and want to be your wife."

Brodie took her hand and gently kissed it. He then cupped her neck with his hand, leaned in, and kissed her lips. "I have to admit, I'm looking forward to being your husband with all its benefits."

Martha slipped out of his embrace and playfully slapped him on the rear. "Mr. Duke, you should be ashamed of yourself."

"I'm not a bit, my future Mrs. Duke."

The couple was married on March 26th in the Methodist Church in Durham. J.J. Renn officiated the ceremony. John walked his daughter down the aisle and, once they reached Brodie, he reached over and hugged him. "Take care of my daughter," he whispered. Brodie nodded his head and then took Martha's hands in his.

After the service was over, Brodie and Martha moved among their guests, thanking them and engaging in small talk. As they made their way toward his family, feelings of insecurity swept over him. He hated feeling like this, but didn't know how to change it. Once they reached Washington, he leaned in, allowing his father to give him a hug. Brodie wanted to pull away, but knew how much his father cared for him. "Brodie, take care of Martha, but most importantly, take care of yourself."

"I will."

"Please, if there is ever anything I can do to help you, don't hesitate to ask."

"Thank you."

Brodie looked over at Buck, who took out a bag of tobacco, pinched some flakes into his pipe, and lit it with a match. "I sure hope you will be able to take proper care of your new wife?"

"What are you talking about?"

"Martha seems like a sweet girl from a good family. I just wonder if you'll have it in you to do the right thing and put her needs before your own?"

Brodie sensed an anger rise up in him that he hadn't felt since Salisbury. How dare his brother question his ability to be a good husband! "Buck, you and I have never seen eye to eye and I'd appreciate it if you'd keep your opinions to yourself. I don't have to answer to you or anyone. I love Martha and I plan on being a faithful husband and a good provider!"

Buck shrugged his shoulders and turned away. Brodie had never felt the urge to hit someone as much as he did his younger brother. But instead, he turned toward Martha, took her by the arm, and walked back toward the wedding party.

Martha pulled her arm away and looked right into his eyes. "Brodie, are you okay?"

"I'm fine."

"Please, if you need to talk about how you're feeling, I'm here for you."

"Martha, I told you I was fine."

The next morning, when Brodie woke up, he looked over at Martha lying beside him, and was consumed with anger at his brother, but more so at himself. He had messed up their first night together and, what should've been a night to remember, was one they both wanted to forget.

As the light of the sun creeped into the room, he noticed, for the first time, how beautiful she was without the usual clothing that hid her fair skin and round breasts. Martha was wearing a thin cotton gown that slipped off of her shoulder, revealing the curvature of her neck. Without thinking, Brodie reached over and touched her exposed skin, smiling at the thought of this woman being his wife.

Brodie knew he had messed up last night, but today was a new day. A new beginning. One in which he would beg for forgiveness and create an atmosphere that would bring them together, emotionally as well as physically.

| 12 |

1874-1879

Brodie looked over at his wife as drips of perspiration trickled down her forehead. Martha's hair was matted and she was drenched. Her sister was at her side, wiping her face, as Martha let out a bloodcurdling scream. It had been hours since the first labor pains began and, even though the two sisters tried to get Brodie to leave, he refused. This was his first child and he wanted to be present for the birth.

As the hours passed, Brodie knew better than to speak and stood in the shadows, waiting. He hated waiting, and questioned the higher powers as to the reason for the wasted time. He grew tired and began to ask why it was taking so long. But, just as he was getting ready to leave the room, Martha's sister yelled out, "Push! You can do this, Martha. The baby's coming!"

"It hurts!"

"I know. Use the pain to push."

Moments later, the baby slipped into Martha's sister's arms. Brodie walked over to see the baby and was immediately overtaken by the miracle that was occurring before his very eyes. "Can I do anything?"

Martha's sister yelled out, "Yes, bring me some water and fresh sheets."

Brodie walked outside, brought up water from the well, and then rushed back into the room. The baby was lying on Martha's chest. It was in that moment that the responsibility of taking care of, not only his wife, but this small vulnerable human being, began to weigh heavily on him. How could he ever be good enough to raise this child?

The voices inside his head were too much for him. He left the room and walked out into the darkness. The cold, brisk January wind hit Brodie without warning. He closed his arms against his chest as he paced under the light of the bedroom window. His thoughts of being a father, and how he would be the man that everyone expected him to be, tore at his soul. After only a few paces, he went to the steps, reached under the wood plank, and pulled out a flask of rye whiskey.

Without hesitating, he pulled off the cork and took a long swig of the burning liquid. Instantly, his body warmed and his thoughts became fuzzy. The seriousness of his situation dulled and he regained his composure. When he walked back inside, the baby was wrapped and snuggled next to Martha. As he drew closer, Martha's sister winced from the smell of the liquor on his breath, but didn't say a word as she left the room.

Once he was sitting next to the bed, Martha looked in his direction. "Brodie, do you want to hold our baby girl?"

"I'm afraid I might drop her."

"Don't be silly. She needs to know you."

Brodie reached over, took the baby, and placed her against his chest. He felt the warmth of the little body against his and smiled. "Have you decided what you want to call her?"

"I like the name Mabel. Is that okay with you?"

"Whatever you want to call her is fine with me."

"Then it will be Mabel Anna."

After a few moments, Mabel began to squirm, causing Brodie to feel anxious. "Here, I think she wants her mother."

Once the baby was back in Martha's arms, Brodie walked to the other side of the bed and lay down next to his wife. With the help of the alcohol, he was able to relax, and almost immediately fell asleep.

Thankfully, Mabel was a happy and healthy baby. She nursed well and, with the help from Martha's family, Brodie was able to return to work. But, as well as his wife and baby were doing, work was a different matter.

In late 1874, Washington had come to Durham and built a large building for his tobacco business. He had specifically divided the building into two parts, one side for Brodie and the other for his half-siblings. Both sides had agreed to work independently on the tobacco manufacturing, and to support each other with the sale of their products.

At first, sales were slow in comparison with the William T. Blackwell Company, located in a large building across Main Street. Buck and his other partners tried to tolerate the sound of the train whistle, as the bull sound emphasized the success of their competitors and was a clear indication of how the Bull was thriving.

Many of the small tobacco factories in Durham had closed, overwhelmed by the success of the William T. Blackwell Company, but quitting wasn't in Buck's blood. Instead, he used the sound of the train whistle as a way to fuel his determination to become the best tobacco factory in the town, and maybe the state.

Washington was gone most of the time, crossing the country trying to sell their tobacco, and leaving Buck in charge. In the beginning, it appeared that everyone wanted Brodie's opinion about how the tobacco business worked in Durham, but after a few months, his view on the business was downplayed altogether.

As time went by, Brodie felt like an outsider as he observed how Benjamin, Buck, Washington, and Mary Elizabeth, worked together. Mary Elizabeth spent most of her time preparing the bags that the tobacco was sold in. Benjamin used his business sense to understand more about the product and how to obtain the best tobacco. Washington spent time training Buck on how to sell the brand and compete against the other tobacco companies. This left Brodie with very little to do at the management level, which caused him to feel less and less significant.

Many days, Brodie would leave home and head toward the office, only to be distracted by the desire for a drink. Carrington Bar was one of his favorite spots, a place where he found others who enjoyed his company and even cared about his opinion. As the days turned into months, Brodie spent less time at the office, and more time sitting at Carrington Bar with a drink in hand.

Over the next three years, Martha gave birth to a son named Lawrence, and a second daughter by the name of Pearl. Just as Brodie's family was growing, the family business was also expanding. In 1878, the W. Duke, Sons and Company was incorporated, demonstrating to the business world that this family was serious about the expansion of their particular brands of tobacco. But, even with this growth, the family knew that, in order to expand, they needed to hire someone with a better educational background than any of the Duke men had obtained.

George Washington Watts was born and raised in Baltimore and attended the University of Virginia, where he received a degree in business. After graduation, he returned home to work with his father in his tobacco wholesale company. Soon afterward, his father, wanting his son to use his degree, invested $14,000 to buy a fifth interest in the W. Duke, Sons and Company.

George was a hardworking man with a quiet demeanor and a strong business sense. He had a solid faith in God and never took a drink. He worked with Benjamin Duke in the front office, responding to correspondences and calculating ways to increase tobacco sales. George stepped right into his role and, by all accounts, was just what the company needed in order to move forward.

Everyone in the Duke family, except one, was ecstatic over the new hire. Right off the bat, George rubbed Brodie the wrong way. Maybe it was the high moral standard George kept or the way he bonded with Washington and his half-brothers. But, whatever it was, Brodie didn't like the man who seemed to have taken over his position.

In 1880, after Washington came back from one of his trips out west, he called the family together. Brodie rarely spent much time in the office and was surprised that his dad asked him to join them. When he entered Washington's office, he noticed Buck giving him a strange look. He was tempted to say something, but didn't think this was the time to begin an argument.

Washington waited for Brodie to sit down and then stated, "As you all know, I'm going to turn sixty years old this coming December."

Buck called out, "Dad, you're looking good for your age."

"Well, thank you, son. But, as good as I might look, my body is telling me otherwise."

Brodie sat up in his chair. "Dad, are you okay?"

"Yes. And that's why I've made a decision. As you all know, I've worked hard my entire life and I believe I'd like to do some other things with my time, outside of the office."

Buck spoke up. "But, Dad, you're the best salesman we have. If you aren't out selling our brand, who will?"

"I've been watching Richard Harvey Wright do business with his *Wright's Genuine Durham Smoking Tobacco.*"

Buck spoke up. "What makes him different from all of the other small tobacco business owners here in Durham?"

Washington lit his pipe, breathed in the smoke, and let it out. "Richard has the work ethic that, I believe, will carry this company far. We've been crossing paths for some time. When I was in Kansas City, every store I went into had already purchased Richard's tobacco. We met up at my hotel and talked. Come to find out, he's doing well with the sales end of his business, but hasn't been able to keep up with the demand."

Brodie listened as Benjamin asked the most important question. "So, what did Richard say about joining our company?"

"He told me he had to think about it and would get back to me when he returns to Durham."

Brodie spoke up. "So has he returned?"

Washington looked around the room, creating a suspenseful feel, which caused Brodie to lean in. "Well, we met yesterday and discussed the terms, but it'll depend on what all of you think, given we are all equal partners."

Buck looked at his father. "We need a strong businessman, and one that is willing to live in Chicago until we get the new plant up and running. I'm busy working in New York and I know Benjamin, you, and George, are needed here in Durham."

Brodie didn't like the way his brother had said nothing about his contribution to the company. Yes, he knew he hadn't worked as hard as the others, but Brodie also knew that some of his ideas were worth mentioning. Instead of giving in to his anger, he turned his attention toward his father. "So, Dad, when are we going to be able to sit down with Richard?"

"Well, it just so happens that he's coming over as we speak."

Just about that time, there was a knock at the door. Washington looked in Brodie's direction. "Son, can you please let Richard in?"

Brodie stood and opened the door. He looked at the man who was only a couple of years his junior. As he surveyed his attire, he could tell from the way Richard was dressed, and how he carried himself, that he was a man to be reckoned with. Brodie couldn't help but smile at the thought of Richard and Buck butting heads.

After Richard sat down at the large table, Washington spoke. "I'm sure everyone has seen Richard around town and heard of his fine smoking tobacco. If not, Richard has created *Wright's Genuine Durham Smoking Tobacco,* a product that has become known all over the country. Richard, we've discussed your excellent sales skills and would like to ask you to become a partner."

"Sir, I'd be honored to become a partner. But, I have to tell you that I don't have any capital. I've been putting my profits into property."

Washington paused, clearly thinking about Richard's words. "I think we can work out something. We believe the partnership is worth about $23,000."

Richard leaned forward, looking directly at Washington. "I do have one piece of property that has been appraised for close to that amount. I'm still paying off a loan on it. If that works for all of you, I'll continue to pay the mortgage until it's paid off."

Brodie was ecstatic about Richard joining the firm. He had a feeling that he would give Buck a run for his money. It might be nice to have another strong-willed man to help balance out Buck's domination of the company. "I'm fine with that. I also have property in and around Durham. I believe, like you, that the value will only increase as the population grows."

Buck spoke up next. "I believe we can work with that. Benjamin and George, do you have any thoughts on the matter?"

Benjamin and George shook their heads and remained silent. Washington looked over at Richard and then at his youngest son. "Well, Buck, I'd appreciate it if you would get the paperwork together. Also, the rest of you need to carve out some time in your schedules to fill Richard in on how we run our business. And while you're doing this, I plan on spending more time with my grandchildren and helping out at the Methodist church."

Washington stood up to signal that the meeting was over. He leaned over to Richard and shook his hand. "Richard, I hope we have a long and prosperous partnership."

Richard replied, "Yes, sir. I hope we'll all prosper and, most importantly, push the bull out of the limelight."

"Now, that's what I like to hear!" Buck stated, as he reached over and shook Richard's hand.

13

1880-1884

Brodie stumbled through the door and closed it behind him, unaware of the loud thud it made when it hit the doorjamb. He laughed to himself, oblivious to the commotion he'd created. The room seemed to spin as he slipped across the space that led to his bedroom. Just as he thought he was in the clear, the screeching cry of a baby rang through the air. "Shoot," he proclaimed out loud.

The door to the baby's room was open and he could see Pearl sitting up in her crib. He hesitated, not sure which direction to take. His body screamed for his bed, but his conscience told him to check on Pearl. Brodie walked into the nursery using the light from the moon to direct his path. "Shh, it's okay."

Pearl continued to cry, raising her arms to be held. At this point, Brodie knew he had no option but to pick up his daughter. He reached his hands over the crib rail, trying to get a good grasp of the baby when he was overtaken by the odor of a full diaper. Brodie's first thought was to place the baby down and go to bed, but knew it wouldn't be a productive course of action. "Now, Pearl, you're going to have to help your Papa. You know I'm not good at this."

"You're so right about that." Martha stepped up beside him and took Pearl from his grasp. "If you would please hand me the clean towel and water basin, I'll take it from here."

"Martha, have I told you how beautiful you are?"

"Brodie Duke, I know you've been drinking."

"Just a little. Anyway, I was working on a business deal."

"That's a very weak excuse."

Brodie walked over and leaned in to kiss Martha on the cheek, but before his lips could touch her soft skin, she moved out of the way, causing him to stumble. "Brodie, you know I don't like the smell of rye whiskey, and I particularly don't want you to come near me after you sneak in the house at this God forsaken hour!"

"I'm sorry. I don't know why I can't stop drinking." Brodie sat down on a loveseat that was situated near the crib. He placed his hand in his pocket and reached in, retrieving the wooden fox. "Did I ever tell you about what a good brother Sidney was?"

"Yes, many times."

"I just don't understand why everyone I love is taken from me."

Martha placed the dirty diaper in a pail, closed the lid, and reached back into the crib to pick up Pearl. "Move over. I need to nurse Pearl."

The warmth of Martha's body next to him made him feel safe. He loved her so much and didn't understand why he couldn't be the man he needed to be. He didn't want to move and ruin the moment, so he sat in silence, rubbing the fox and hoping he could be better. "I know it has been years, but I still feel so guilty about being alive. And now that we have three children, money to spend, and a nice home, I feel even guiltier."

For a few minutes, the only noise that could be heard was Pearl sucking Martha's breast and the ticking of the grandfather clock. "Brodie, I can't understand what you went through during the war. I have known death, but not in the way you have. I wish I could help you, but I just don't know how."

Martha rose, placed Pearl back into her crib and took Brodie by the hand. "Let's go to bed. It's been a long day for both of us."

The next morning, Brodie woke to the sound of Martha stirring. A dim light filled the room, allowing him to see his wife lying beside him. Her eyes were closed and curls of hair surrounded her head like a halo. Brodie reached over to capture one of the curls and twist it lightly between his fingers. An intense emotion welled up inside him, causing him to pull his fingers back. How could this woman tolerate him, when he behaved so poorly?

Martha blinked and opened her eyes. "Good morning, Brodie. I hope you slept well."

"I did." Brodie leaned back onto the pillow, crossing his arms.

Martha sat up and looked at Brodie. "What's wrong?"

"I just don't understand how you can forgive me so easily, when I'm such a mess."

There was a pause before Martha spoke. "Brodie, we're all flawed. I guess I'll never know the burden you've carried with you since leaving Salisbury, but I do know that God loves you and created you to be my soulmate."

Brodie struggled with believing that this woman could care so deeply about him, particularly since he had been so selfish. "Martha, I'll try and do better. I do love you and our children so much."

Martha took her finger and traced around his ear and down to his chest. He knew this was an invitation to take her into his arms and, as he leaned over to kiss her, the door opened and Mabel and Lawrence came running into the room. Mabel smiled, ran up to the bed, and climbed up beside Brodie. "Daddy, you're home. Can you play with us today?"

Brodie smiled down at the little girl with her soft auburn hair and fair face. "I'd love to spend time with my children today. How about a ride into the country?"

The small children jumped up and down on the bed. "Yay! Lawrence, did you hear that? Daddy is going to take us to the country."

That afternoon, Brodie placed all of his children into his buggy and rode out toward the old Duke homestead. Once there, he led his children toward the creek bed where he had spent so many hours fishing with Sidney. On the way back up the hill, they passed the fields where his brother had been overcome with typhoid fever. Once or twice, he thought he saw a young boy running into the woods, but knew it was just his imagination. He tried to suppress the memories that appeared so vivid in his mind, but as hard as he tried, they couldn't be shut off.

As time went by, and the W. Duke, Sons and Company expanded, Brodie began to feel his role become more and more insignificant in the decisions that were being made. George and Benjamin were running the front office, while Buck and Richard were heading up the New York and Chicago factories. Whenever he had a chance, he shared his opinion, but as time went by, no one seemed to care, shutting him out altogether.

People were beginning to enjoy smoking tobacco in the form of cigarettes, which Buck believed was going to change the dynamics of the tobacco business. He had hired a large number of Jewish men from New York to come to Durham to hand roll each cigarette. The public enjoyed the flavor of the hand rolled cigarette and how easy it was to smoke over the pipe. But even so, during the early 1880s, the Dukes were one of only a few companies producing tobacco in the form of cigarettes.

There were many people trying to compete in the tobacco business, but only a few could contend with companies like Allen & Ginter, Kinney Brothers, Kimball and Company, and the William T. Blackwell Company. Even though there was strong competition, Buck had his sights on destroying his local competitor. He was determined to put an end to the bull that was painted all over town and, for that matter, most towns he had visited. More times than Brodie could remember, Buck could be heard screaming about how he was going to put the bull down.

Instead of being so concerned about competing in the tobacco business, Brodie had taken his profits and invested in real estate in and around Durham. The oldest son of Washington Duke was not the only person who was purchasing land and building other industries in and around Durham. Julian Shakespeare Carr loved Durham and cared about its growth benefiting all the residents, white and black.

Julian had been a partner with William T. Blackwell, until William sold his interest in 1883 to a Philadelphia firm. Julian had tried to persuade him to stay, but William was eager to move into the banking industry, a decision he would later regret. Once William exited the company, most of the decisions pertaining to the tobacco business were placed in Julian's hands. Under Julian's leadership the business prospered and from all perspectives, it appeared that the W.T. Blackwell Company would continue to thrive.

Brodie enjoyed speaking with Julian, the small man with huge aspirations. He approached business in a creative manner and wasn't so aggressive toward his rivals. Brodie believed that the

W. T. Blackwell Company was successful because of Julian's flair for advertising the bull everywhere he could. Most large baseball fields had a bull painted on the wall where the pitchers warmed up and this area of the ballpark began being called the bullpen. Brodie had even heard that a bull had been painted on the side of a pyramid in Egypt, ingenious marketing by most accounts.

So, one day, with very little work to be done in his office, Brodie walked across the railroad tracks and entered the large factory that faced their business. Coming through the door, he could hear the sound of voices singing an old gospel song. The workers appeared happy, almost joyful. He spotted Julian at the front of the building and made his way toward him. "Brodie Duke, what do I owe this visit to?"

"I heard you had some land you were considering selling. I'm interested in any land north or west of the city."

"Are you now?"

"I'd like to extend the railroad and build houses for all the people moving to Durham."

"That sounds like a good idea. Let's step into my office to discuss this further."

Once the door was closed, Julian went over to his desk and sat down. "So, Brodie, I've heard that Buck has located a machine that can roll cigarettes faster than the Jewish men he's hired."

"If you can call it a machine. A man in Virginia by the name of James Bonsack invented it, but it requires someone who can fix it every couple of minutes to keep it running. Buck is working with the company to try it out. William O'Brien has been hired to work on it. I must admit, William is doing a phenomenal job keeping it running."

Julian sat back in his chair, took his pipe out of the ashtray, filled it with a pinch of tobacco, and lit it with a match. "I personally enjoy smoking out of a pipe over a cigarette, but I do know that times are changing, and cigarettes are becoming extremely popular."

Brodie leaned in toward Julian. "I don't know what will come from the use of the Bonsack machine, but I do believe if we can get it working up to capacity, we'll have something special."

"Well, I know you didn't come here to share all your company's secrets. There is some land north of Main Street that's for sale. I believe it might be just what you're looking for."

"Julian, if you can get me more information, I'd greatly appreciate it."

"I'll be glad to. Is there anything else I can help you with?"

Brodie looked down toward the floor. He was hesitant about bringing up the past, but believed Julian might be one of the only people who could understand his suffering. "I know you are active in the affairs of former Confederate soldiers. I also know you witnessed some horrendous things while you served."

Julian sat back and remained quiet for a moment. "Yes, it was an awful war."

Brodie shook his head at the thoughts of what he experienced. "I know you and everyone else in Durham know about my issues."

"Brodie, I did go into battle, but I didn't get anywhere close to the brutality that you witnessed. I do wake up many a night to the sounds of men screaming or shots being rung out. But, for some reason, thanks be to God, it doesn't haunt me. I've met many a Confederate at our meetings that can't get past the suffering they endured. I'm sorry you're going through this."

"Thanks, Julian. People have been talking about how much I drink, and I admit, I do drink more than I should. But it's the only thing that keeps me from being so obsessed with the guilt."

"I wish I knew what to say to you. Liquor isn't the answer, but to be honest, I don't know what is."

| 14 |

1884-1886

Brodie stood at the open grave, peering around the Durham residents to take note of who was present. This was the third funeral for the same family in less than two months. It was damn twisted of God to take a father and two daughters in such a short time. Each of the Exums were kind-hearted people who'd only brought good into the world. But, even so, being good didn't keep you out of the web of death.

An eerie feeling drifted through the small city of Durham in the late spring of 1885. Death had come a-calling and one family would bear the brunt of it. The first death could have been predicted, given Mr. Exum's age and health, but no one would've guessed that his two daughters would follow him into death in only a matter of weeks.

William T. Blackwell was blindsided by his wife Emma's death, so soon after their daughter, Mary, had passed. Brodie would never forget the sight of this broken man standing frozen under the magnolia tree in Maplewood Cemetery with his son, W.T., clinging to his leg. William could barely raise his eyes to the mourners as they came forward to pay their condolences.

As horrendous as William appeared, Richard Wright's response to his wife's death was outright bizarre. Mamie had been the only woman Richard had ever loved, and everyone knew he must be devastated. Word had reached Durham less than two weeks after her sister's death that Mamie had died moments after delivering a baby girl.

It was well known that Richard rarely showed any emotion, but no one thought that he would be outright rude during the funeral proceedings. To begin with, Richard didn't even look up while the preacher went on and on about eternal life. He visibly shook as the man of the cloth shared how Mamie was now with the Lord. Brodie noticed Richard staring down at his shoes, clenching his fists, and mumbling something to himself. Once the preacher's final words were spoken, Richard whispered something into his sister Nannie's ear, rose from his chair, and left.

Richard's sister, Lucy, screamed out, "Richard, you can't just leave!"

Richard ignored the outburst and continued to walk toward his coach. He stepped inside and, before anyone could stop him, he was gone. Brodie walked up beside Nannie and asked, "So, what did he whisper in your ear?"

Nannie was taken aback by Brodie's forthrightness. "That is between him and me."

"I'm sorry, but don't you find his behavior a little unusual?"

"Under the circumstances, no, I don't. And, by the way, Mr. Duke, you have no idea how it feels to lose a spouse."

"You're right about that, Miss Wright, but I do know something about grief."

Martha placed her hand in the crook of Brodie's arm. "Come over with me to speak to Benjamin and Sarah." She gently led him over to where they were standing.

"Sarah, how's Angier doing? I heard he wasn't well."

"He still has a cough, but other than that, he's doing okay."

Brodie turned toward Benjamin. "So, is there any more news about Richard's attempt to sell his partnership?"

"No. I heard he asked George to buy his interest, but George refused. I also heard from several other tobacco companies how he tried to get them to buy out his partnership."

Brodie looked over at Nannie, who had turned away and was speaking with several women. "Why do you think he wanted to get out of the partnership in the first place?"

Benjamin laughed. "He and Buck are too much alike. Also, I think that when I sent him the letter back in December asking for more money, he became perturbed and wanted out."

Brodie chuckled. "He sure isn't one who likes to hand over his money without a fight."

Benjamin sighed. "We sure did mess up when we didn't renew the contract for the partnership in January."

Benjamin paused and, with a defiant voice, proclaimed, "What bothers me the most is the fact that the property that Richard gave Dad for his interest in the partnership still has a mortgage. It's like he's taking us not only once, but twice."

Brodie shook his head. "That's so true."

Benjamin waited a moment and then said, "But, in the scheme of things, he's the one who is going to lose the most from leaving the company. I believe our cigarette-rolling machine, along with

William O'Brien's expert mechanical skills, will provide us with more money than we could ever imagine."

"Well, brother, I hope you're right."

Martha, who had remained silent, looked right at Sarah and Benjamin. "I hope we can get together soon. It would be nice for our children to get to know their new cousin."

Sarah extended her hand to Martha. "Let's do it."

A few days after the funeral, Brodie was called into the office. He knew there was a lot going on and was eager to hear the news for himself. Brodie opened the large doors that led to the factory floor and noticed William O'Brien working on the cigarette-rolling machine. He looked in the direction of the men who continued to hand roll cigarettes while gesturing toward the contraption that had come to a standstill. They appeared happy at the breakdown as they continued to roll the cigarettes and place them in a bin. Brodie turned, walked up the stairs that led to the second floor, and entered Buck's office.

Brodie noticed his brothers, George Watts, and his father, in a serious conversation. Benjamin rose from his seat. "Brodie, let me fill you in on what we're discussing."

Everyone looked toward Benjamin as he summarized what had just been stated. "Well, to start with, we just received a letter from John Hinsdale, Richard's attorney. He's bringing a lawsuit against us, requesting Richard's fair share of the profits as of the day he left the company."

Brodie responded, "I'm not surprised that Richard would sue us. I believe he's determined to create his own successful company and, if bringing a lawsuit against us helps his cause, he's going to try and milk us for all he can."

Benjamin interjected, "I'm just glad he's decided to move to Lynchburg and away from Durham. He's a smart man, so it doesn't surprise me that he's taken over the Lone Jack Cigarette Company."

Buck spoke up. "I believe Richard thinks he's going to get an inside deal on the use of the Bonsack machine, given that D.B. Strouse and others that sit on the Bonsack Machine Board are also on the Lone Jack Cigarette Company Board."

George Watts chimed in. "I can't imagine D.B. Strouse being willing to give him a better deal than what he gave us."

Buck rose and started pacing. "I wish I'd never told Richard about the deal I made with Strouse. He knows we're paying twenty-four cents for every thousand cigarettes. He also knows that Strouse agreed to charge all other companies at least twenty-five percent more."

Brodie gazed around the room. "I think we're all fools if we believe Richard won't try and persuade Strouse to give him a better deal."

Buck stopped pacing and slammed his fist down on the table. "He better not! I believe the use of the Bonsack machine is what's going to keep us on top, and I'll be damned if some weasel comes in and keeps us from our goals!"

Washington took out his pipe, lit it, and watched as the smoke ascended up toward the ceiling. "Buck, you know that we have the advantage here. First of all, William O'Brien is, by far, the best mechanic and has been doing an excellent job of keeping our machines going. Second, you've purchased the machines faster than any other company, eliminating their chances of getting their hands on one of them any time soon. Not to mention, George has done a nice job persuading Strouse that all future machines need to come to us. And, if that isn't enough security, we had our lawyers write up contracts stating that no one can receive a machine in the United States without going through us first."

Everyone in the room sat in silence as Washington took another toke of his pipe. "If Richard wants to go to the far ends of the world to sell the machines, let him. Meanwhile, we'll be increasing production of our cigarettes, and have the security of not only owning the majority of the machines, but also having the best mechanic to keep them working properly."

Benjamin spoke next. "Now that we have Richard out of the way, we need to discuss how we can protect ourselves from him, or others who want to break up this partnership. I was speaking to our lawyers, and they believe we need to move away from a partnership and move to a joint stock corporation."

Brodie spoke up. "Tell me what that means in layman's terms?"

Buck sat back down, leaned back in his chair, and stared back at Brodie. "We're going to dissolve W. Duke, Sons and Company, and become incorporated under our new name, American Tobacco Company. Each of us will receive the same number of shares of stock." Buck paused a moment and then looked directly at Brodie. "We'll be asking you to contribute a percentage of your income due to the fact that you're working primarily out of the office."

Everyone looked at Brodie, waiting to see how he would respond. "I'm good with that." Brodie then looked at his father. "What are your thoughts?"

"As we all know, Richard was hired to take over my responsibilities here at the company. But given that he's now left, I've decided to become more involved with the philanthropy aspect of how some of our profits are spent. Recently, I've been involved with the relocating of Trinity College to Durham. I believe it will speak highly of us if we continue to donate to the college, as well as to the Methodist Church."

Benjamin spoke up. "Dad, I think that's an excellent decision. I'd like to make sure that the citizens of Durham know we're not only invested in our company, but also in our city."

Buck got up, took his hat off the hook, and looked back at the men seated at the table. "I'll be spending the majority of my time up in New York. Now that we have a clear plan to keep us from being bamboozled in the future, I have work to do to make the American Tobacco Company the largest tobacco company in the country, if not the world."

| 15 |

1887-1888

MAYOR OF
NORTH DURHAM

With the production of cigarettes increasing at a rapid rate, Brodie, along with the other partners of the newly named American Tobacco Company, were beginning to experience sizable profits. Every time he received a large check, Brodie would use this income to purchase property or spend it on building the infrastructure of Durham. The citizens of Durham were so elated with Brodie's willingness to invest in their city that many started referring to him as the Mayor of North Durham.

It was during this time, when Brodie was striving to fill his days with business deals that Martha began to feel sickly. Instead of being up and around for most of the day, she began retreating to her bed for extended periods of time. Thankfully, Brodie had hired help for Martha and, instead of his wife dictating what needed to be done around the house, the responsibilities of the home went to their hired help.

Martha's illness was very difficult for their three children, particularly Pearl. Pearl was the youngest and Martha had always treated her as such. The two had been inseparable, which made it challenging now that Martha was spending the majority of her day in bed. Pearl would come into the room with her dolls and find a place at the end of the bed to play. Many nights, when Brodie came home from work, Pearl would be found curled in a ball and sound asleep.

One night, in early April, Brodie came home, after spending time at the Carrington Bar, to find his daughter sitting up at the end of the bed, staring at Martha. Brodie was tired and wanted to go to sleep, but his daughter barred his way. "Pearl, you need to go get in your own bed."

"Daddy, Mommy is going to leave us soon."

"Now, Pearl, your mother is going to get better."

"No. She's going to be with Jesus."

"Now, how do you know that?"

"I just do."

Brodie paused a moment. He didn't know what to say. His daughter was so certain and it bothered him that she was so calm about it. It was like she really believed that Jesus was going to take care of Martha, something he hadn't been able to do. No matter the size of his bank account or portfolio, Brodie didn't have any idea of how to save his wife. So many doctors had come and gone, some with outlandish ideas of how to make her feel better, while others just left, leaving Brodie burdened with guilt.

As he stared at his young daughter, he so wanted to make everything right. But he just didn't know how. He knew his words would fall flat so, instead of trying to convince his daughter that her mother would be okay, he turned and walked out of the room. His first thought was to go back to the bar, but he thought better of it. He walked into the parlor, picked up a blanket off the couch, laid down, and fell asleep.

The next morning, as the sun was beginning to shine through the window, Brodie felt a tap on his shoulder. At first, he thought it must be a dream, but the tapping continued. Once he opened his eyes and looked into Pearl's face, he instantly knew.

Brodie stood up, threw the blanket on the floor, and walked into the bedroom. Mabel and Lawrence were lying on the bed, tucked close to Martha. He looked over at the scene that was unfolding before him, unable to process the truth of the situation. His beautiful wife, with such a pure heart, was gone. The mother of his children, as well as his very best friend, had left, just like all the others he had given his heart to.

Brodie was overtaken by a burning anger that brewed within his soul. He wanted to flee, but knew he had to stay calm for his children. After taking a couple of deep breaths, he reached over and placed one hand on each of them. "Mabel, Lawrence, I'm so sorry. Your mother loved you very much."

Mabel looked up and asked, "Why, Daddy? Why did she have to leave us?"

"I don't know. I just don't know."

The following days were a blur to Brodie. He wanted to avoid drinking, but it was the only thing that took the edge off of the pain. He kept his flask close by, sipping the burning liquid every chance he could. When Brodie arrived at the church for the funeral, John McMannen met him at the door. "John, I don't know what to say."

His father-in-law stared at him, aware that he had been drinking. "Brodie, I know how much you loved my daughter, but please try to stay away from the whiskey. This service is about Martha and not you."

Brodie looked down, knowing John was right. "I'll try. It's the only thing that keeps me going forward."

"You may think that, but I can assure you, it's not. Please, for my daughter's sake, hold back on the drinking. Your children need you and I'll not tolerate it if I hear that you are neglecting them or worse, abusing them."

"I know. I promise you I'll try to refrain from drinking."

John turned and uttered some words as he left. "We'll see."

The two men walked into the church, and down the aisle toward the front row. Friends and family filled the pews, all staring at him as he shuffled to his seat. The open coffin was situated right in front of Brodie, where he could see Martha's body in full view. Gut-wrenching feelings caused him to reach for the flask. But knowing he was in church, with everyone staring, he kept the flask in his pocket.

Brodie's three children could be heard moaning from the pew behind him. Sarah, Benjamin's wife, had her arm around Pearl, trying her best to comfort her. He was tempted to look back to offer his own sympathy, but just didn't have the words to express his sorrow. He looked down at his feet when John stood up and began to share about his daughter. Brodie's breathing quickened and his heart began to race. He wasn't sure how to calm himself down, so he decided to focus on the cross that hung on the window above John. His thoughts drifted away from the words John spoke and, when the minister got up to preach, he decided it was best to focus on something; anything but what was happening around him.

After what seemed like an eternity, the congregation stood, as the pallbearers took their positions around the coffin. Everyone began to sing *Amazing Grace,* Martha's favorite hymn. Brodie walked behind the coffin with his head down, trying to avoid the stares of the parishioners. The words of the hymn drummed into his ears, convicting him of his selfishness. All he wanted to do was flee, but knew that, for Martha's sake, as well as his children's, he had to go through the motions of a mourning spouse.

Once the congregation was out of the church, they walked behind the carriage that held the coffin and proceeded to Maplewood Cemetery. Magnolia, oak, and maple trees provided a canopy overhead. There was a small mound of dirt next to the grave, marking the site where Martha would be laid to rest. Brodie stayed close to his children, holding Pearl's hand, as they gathered around the grave. Somehow, the faith of his daughter gave him the strength to get through this moment in time.

After the minister said a few words, the coffin was placed inside the freshly dug hole. As the mourners waited, Brodie took a handful of dirt and tossed it onto the top of the coffin. Mabel was next, followed by Lawrence, and then Pearl. As the little girl took the handful of dirt into her small hand, she looked down at the coffin and muttered something under her breath. Brodie looked at her, wondering what she had spoken, but knew it wasn't the right time to ask.

Brodie had hoped to slip quietly away, but his friends and family all came up to him, wanting to share their condolences. At the back of the line, unnoticed by many, stood Nannie Wright. She had waited until everyone was gone before approaching Brodie. "I just wanted to tell you how sorry I am about Martha. I never thought, when I spoke to you at Mamie's funeral that you also would lose your wife."

"I appreciate it."

Nannie stood still, not making any attempt to leave. "Brodie, I also want you to know how sorry I am that it didn't work out with Richard and your company. I hate the fact that he feels the need to bring a suit against you and your brothers."

"That's okay. Richard and Buck are too much alike, both wanting to lead the ship. I've heard he is spending a lot of time traveling around the world. There's talk that he's discovered a machine in Gainsborough, England, that makes a package for cigarettes."

"Yes. He's hoping it will be a huge breakthrough for the cigarette industry. We write every now and then. Most of the letters concern his daughter, Little May. She's very sick and he's been trying to find someone to help her get better."

"I'm sorry to hear that."

"Anyway, I just wanted to let you know I'm praying for you and your children."

"Thank you. We sure can use some prayers."

Nannie turned and walked away, leaving Brodie standing beside the covered grave. He took a handful of the loose dirt and sifted it through his fingers over the mound where his wife laid. "Martha, I sure am going to miss you. I'm sorry I wasn't the best husband for you. I don't know what I'm going to do. You were so wonderful with the children. I wish I could promise you that I'll be a good father, but I just can't."

16

1888-1890

The months that followed Martha's death were a blur to Brodie. The American Tobacco Company was producing more cigarettes than any of the competition. To encourage people to purchase their brand, the company began to insert beautifully colored portraits of great Americans such as John Adams, Benjamin Franklin, and Thomas Edison, into their packages. One of their greatest competitors, Allen & Ginter, issued a fifty-card set of American Indian chiefs, while the Kinney Brothers produced a twenty-five card set of portraits of great historical people.

All of the major tobacco companies were doing everything in their power to win over the public with their specific brand. Advertising was only one aspect of the business that needed constant tweaking. Buck Duke worked very closely with D.B. Strouse, president of the Bonsack Machine Company, to keep the cigarette-rolling machines out of the hands of all the small tobacco companies, particularly the Lone Jack Cigarette Company.

Little did Buck Duke know, Strouse had made a secret deal with Richard Wright. Buck thought that his deal with Strouse for twenty-four cents per thousand cigarettes produced by the machine was, by far, the lowest royalty any company paid. But, to his dismay, Buck found out that Richard had signed a contract with Strouse to pay only fifteen cents per thousand cigarettes.

In addition to deals between companies, there was also discussion that the four major tobacco companies were considering consolidating. But Buck was hesitant about the move. He was afraid that his age of thirty-two might cause the other companies to push him aside for an older, more experienced leader. So, instead of consolidating with the other companies, he made the decision to stay independent and demonstrate his abilities to lead his company to the top of the industry.

Brodie tried to stay away from the office as much as possible. He knew he had no voice in the company and no matter what he suggested, Buck, Benjamin, and George Watts, usually had an objection. He particularly found George difficult to converse with. George was constantly trying to convert him and convince him to accept Jesus as his Lord and Savior. This infuriated Brodie, making him feel insecure and guilt-ridden.

One day, when Brodie arrived at the factory, he walked by George's office and heard him speaking with his father. "Washington, I'm very concerned about Brodie's children. We all know that he hasn't stopped drinking. I've heard from some of the regulars at Carrington Bar that Brodie stays there drinking until the doors close. You know that's no way to raise his three children."

"George, I have to admit I'm also concerned about him. I just don't know what to do anymore. I wish I knew."

"I've tried to talk to him about Jesus, but he doesn't seem to be interested in religion."

Washington leaned back in his chair and clasped his hands. He appeared to be lost in his thoughts as Brodie made his appearance. "Pa, I heard you wanted to talk with me."

"Yes, son. Can you please sit down? George, if you don't mind, can you leave the two of us alone? And please close the door behind you."

Brodie sat down in front of the large walnut desk that his father had purchased when they first moved to Durham. He remembered how he and his brothers brought it up the stairs and placed it in Washington's office. It was extremely heavy and all three of them struggled to hold onto it. Once it was in place, Buck took a seat and acted the part of president. It was in that moment, that Brodie knew his brother would never give up that position.

Washington took his pipe out of the ashtray, filled it with some ground flecks of tobacco, and lit it with a match. "So, Brodie, how are the children?"

"They're well. Why do you ask?"

"Word is you've been spending a lot of time out at night and I want to make sure your children are getting the attention they need."

"They are. I've hired several competent nannies, as well as a cook and butler. I believe they are getting along as well as could be expected, given the death of their mother."

Washington paused a moment before speaking. "Brodie, do you remember when Sidney passed?"

"Of course, I do. How could I ever forget losing the one person I felt a true connection with?"

"I can't stop thinking about those days. I knew you were hurting. I wanted to be there for you, but I guess I was overwhelmed with my own grief. And then, for Artelia to die so soon afterward. I was so wrapped up in my own pain. As I think back now, I know I didn't give you the attention you needed from me."

"Dad, why are you bringing this up?"

"I've felt so guilty about not being there for you."

"Dad, you did the best you could. I understand why you felt the need to spend more time with Mary, Buck, and Benjamin."

"I assumed, since you were older, you didn't need me as much as they did. But as the years have gone by, I've felt I failed you."

Brodie became quiet, thinking back on the anger he'd felt when Sidney died. He always justified his father's actions due to the circumstances. "I guess I did need you more than I thought I did."

Washington rubbed his arm across his face. "I'm so sorry that I wasn't there for you when you returned from Salisbury. To this day, I can't imagine the hell you went through. I was so focused on getting a business started that I neglected to understand how the war impacted you."

"Dad, it's okay. I know you were doing what you thought was best."

"I just can't help but feel responsible for your drinking. If I had been there, maybe you wouldn't feel so inclined to numb yourself with alcohol."

Brodie fell silent. He'd never considered how his father's actions could've contributed to his drinking. "No. I'll not allow you to take responsibility for my poor choices. Yes, maybe if I was able to somehow talk through the nightmare I experienced, I'd be different. I just don't know. To this day, I'm still awakened by the scenes I witnessed in Salisbury. I just don't know how a man is supposed to process the injustice of so much unnecessary suffering."

Washington stood up and walked around the desk, stopping in front of Brodie. "Stand up."

Brodie felt awkward, not knowing what was going to come next. He slowly rose and looked in his father's eyes. "What?"

Washington extended his arms. "Now, give me a hug."

Brodie barely leaned in. Washington released the hug and looked at Brodie. "Now let's do that again, and I want you to lean in hard."

"Why?"

"Because I'm your father and I want you to know it."

This time, Brodie pressed into his father and, for the first time in a long time, he allowed his pent-up emotions to flow. As he cried, Washington kept a firm grip on him. After a few minutes, Washington released Brodie and sat down in a chair next to him. Brodie took out his handkerchief and wiped his eyes. "Son, I have a favor to ask."

Brodie looked at Washington. "Sure, Dad, what do you need?"

"There is some tobacco in Gadsden, Alabama, I want to purchase."

"Okay. So, why don't you send one of your brokers?"

"No, I want you to go. I think a trip will do you some good. Anyway, Henry Woodward is a good friend and I don't want just anyone working with him."

"Alright. When were you thinking I'd go on this trip?"

"I've told Henry you'll be down there in a couple of days. Now, I'd love to spend some time with my grandchildren and have plenty of room in my house to accommodate them."

Brodie was puzzled by his father's request, but thought it might do him some good to get away. He hadn't left Durham since Martha's death and found the idea of going to Alabama intriguing.

Days later, as his carriage crossed the bridge over the Coosa River, Brodie looked at the water below, noticing how different it was from the landscape in Durham. He spotted several wooden structures in the distance and was relieved to finally reach his destination. Once the horses stopped in front of a large building, he got out and stretched. An older man walked over and extended his hand. "You must be Brodie Duke."

"Yes, and you must be Henry Woodward."

"I'm so glad you came. Your father and I are friends from the war. We were both taken prisoner in Richmond, where we spent our days talking about our lives back home. He told me a lot about your childhood and couldn't stop telling me how proud he was to have you as his son."

Brodie didn't know what to say. The man seemed very sincere about his father's words and he knew he needed to reply. "Well, thank you."

"He also told me in his letters about your time in Salisbury. I'm so sorry you had to experience that hellhole. I was in the battle at Fredericksburg, which still haunts me to this day." The older man paused a moment and then continued. "Anyway, that's not why you came."

"So, where is this tobacco that my father sent me to purchase?"

"How about I get my daughter to take you to my house first? You can freshen up and have some lunch. Then she can bring you back here this afternoon and we can talk business?"

"That would be nice. I have to admit, after such a long trip, I am a little hungry."

"Good." Henry turned and walked inside the large building. Moments later, he returned with a young woman following close behind him. Brodie turned toward the woman, but the sun hit him in the eyes and he couldn't see her features.

The woman walked into the shade where Brodie could clearly see her. She was about the same size and height as Martha, but her hair was darker. She had a dimple when she smiled and appeared to be close to a decade younger than him. Brodie was immediately drawn to her and glad to have such an attractive woman escorting him to Henry's house. "Mr. Duke, I hope you had a pleasant trip."

"Yes." Brodie had a difficult time taking his eyes off of Henry's daughter. "I'm sorry, I didn't get your name."

"My name is Mary, but people call me Minnie."

Brodie reached for her hand and held it for a moment. "Minnie, people call me Brodie."

"Well, Brodie, if you will follow me, I'll take you to our home so you can wash up."

Minnie turned away from the large building and began walking down the dirt road that ran through the center of town. Brodie picked his bag up off the ground and quickened his step in order to catch up to her. People began to stare at him, apparently not used to seeing a strange face. There were several dogs that were lying in the middle of the road, sound asleep. Given the weight of his bag and the dress shoes he wore, Brodie had trouble keeping up with Minnie. "Minnie, can you slow down a bit. I'm not used to walking far in these shoes."

"Mr. Duke, I can't imagine a man your size having trouble keeping up with a young woman."

Brodie chuckled. "I haven't had to chase a woman in a long time."

"Oh, so that must mean you're a kept man."

Minnie slowed down and Brodie began to walk in sync with the attractive woman. "No, I'm a widower. My wife died last year."

Minnie stopped and looked right at Brodie. "I'm so sorry."

"Thank you for your sympathy. I must admit it has been more difficult than I imagined. Martha was such a wonderful woman."

"So do you have children?"

"Yes, I do. I have two girls and a boy. They have adapted, but I know they miss their mother very much."

"I can relate. I lost my mother when I was only five. Dad has been so attentive, but he can never replace my sweet loving mother."

As they reached the house, Brodie noticed how bright and cheery it was. "Is this where you and your father live?"

"Yes. He had it built right after my mother died. He just couldn't stay in the old house and, anyway, he needed a place for his business acquaintances to stay."

As they entered the house, an older man greeted them at the door. "Miss Woodward, will you be staying for lunch?"

"Yes, and can you set another place for Mr. Duke?"

Minnie began walking through the foyer and called out, "Brodie, please follow me and I'll take you to your room."

Brodie followed Minnie until she stopped in front of a door at the end of a long hallway. "This is your room. You should find everything you need." She paused a moment before turning. "Lunch will be in about thirty minutes."

"Thank you. I appreciate the hospitality."

"You're welcome. I'll see you in a little bit."

Brodie wasn't sure what he thought of Minnie. She was very attractive and appeared confident in herself, but he knew he wasn't ready to become emotionally involved with someone so early after Martha's death.

Over the next few minutes, Brodie placed his clothes in the drawers and washed his face, removing the dust that came from traveling. After he finished, he was tempted to lie down when he heard a knock on the door. "Mr. Duke, lunch is now being served."

When Brodie opened his door, he could hear the voices of small children coming from down the hall. For a moment, he thought one of the voices could be Pearl's. The sound of the child's voice caused him to wince with the pain of knowing how he had neglected his children. He shook his head to wipe away the thought of his youngest daughter.

When he reached the large dining room, Brodie was taken aback by what he saw. Henry was seated at the end of the table, Minnie on one side, and two small children on the other side. "Come in, Brodie. Take a seat next to Minnie."

Brodie pulled the chair out and sat down. He looked across the table at the young children and then glanced at Minnie. "Brodie, this is my niece, Emma, and my nephew, Thomas. My sister is visiting friends in Birmingham and they are staying with us until she returns."

Brodie wasn't sure how to respond. He rarely ate with his own children and he found it unusual to see small children at the table. "Hello."

Emma and Thomas sat very still as Henry said grace, then the food was served. Everyone was quiet for a moment as they began to eat. Henry finally looked up at Brodie and stated, "We've had a good tobacco crop this year. I believe you'll be pleased with the quality. After lunch, I'd like to take you to the warehouse and show it to you."

"Yes, I'd like that very much. It's been awhile since I've been given the opportunity to purchase tobacco. Believe it or not, I ran my own tobacco business for a while. I moved to Durham in 1869 when there was only a couple of buildings. Gadsden reminds me of what Durham looked like back then."

Minnie looked at Brodie with a puzzled expression and then returned to her meal. For some reason, Brodie felt the need to fill the silence. "Yes, Durham has grown by leaps and bounds since tobacco has become so popular. And now, with the demand for cigarettes, Durham has become a place where people are arriving in droves looking for jobs."

Brodie took a bite of his food, and then looked over at Minnie, wondering what she was thinking. "Would you like to visit Durham?"

"Well, it does sound like an intriguing place."

Henry looked directly at Brodie. "Now, maybe Minnie and I could come visit your tobacco factory in the near future. It's always good to see where our tobacco ends up."

"Aunt Minnie?" Emma spoke up.

"Yes?"

"Can you help me with my reading this afternoon?"

"I'd love to help you."

The little girl smiled as she looked across the table. "You're the best aunt in the whole wide world."

"And you are the best niece in the whole wide world."

Brodie noticed how Minnie began to blush as she and her niece bantered back and forth. He found himself intrigued by the interaction and, in that moment, he thought of how she'd be a wonderful person to have around his own children.

For the next few days, Brodie spent a great deal of time at the warehouse with Henry. But in the evening, he found himself enjoying Minnie's company. The last night of his visit, Minnie went out to the front porch and sat down in a rocking chair that adorned the deck. Brodie followed her. "Is it okay if I sit with you?"

"Of course." A few minutes passed in silence. The humidity hung heavily in the air and lightning strikes could be seen in the night sky. Thunder rumbled in the distance, along with the sound of a stray dog barking. Brodie had begun to ponder something, but was nervous about bringing it up. Finally, he asked, "Minnie, have you ever wanted to move away and start over?"

"What do you mean, start over?"

"When the war was over and I made my way home, I didn't know what I wanted, but I knew I couldn't return to my previous life. So, when I got back to Durham, I moved in with my uncle. It was difficult to start over, but I'm so glad I did."

"Do you think I should start a new life?"

"Minnie, there is so much more to this world than this small, rural town."

"But, this is where my family lives. I feel needed here."

For a moment no one spoke. Brodie was preoccupied with his thoughts. Should he explore the idea of having her move to Durham? He found this woman attractive and so good with children. Even if he didn't feel a deep profound love for her, he believed she'd be exactly what his children needed. "Minnie, I know we haven't known each other for long, but I truly believe I was meant to meet you. I'd like it if you would consider being my wife?"

Brodie heard Minnie gasp. "If you would just consider it, I really think we would be good together."

"That really isn't the kind of marriage proposal I was hoping to receive one day."

Brodie lowered his head, thinking that maybe he shouldn't have been so presumptuous. Minnie appeared very intelligent, as well as self-assured. She definitely deserved a good man who loved her, but where in the world would she meet him? Definitely not here in Gadsden.

Then, to his amazement, Minnie spoke the words he wanted to hear. "Okay, I'll marry you."

"You will?"

"Brodie Duke, if you belabor this, I might change my mind."

Brodie stood up and walked in front of Minnie. "You won't regret this."

"I surely hope you're right. Now, let's ask my father what he thinks before we go forth."

At first, Brodie could tell Henry had mixed feelings about the news. He knew the proposal had come quickly, but believed Henry would be happy to have his daughter move away from such a small town, where there were very few suitors. Brodie also had the finances to provide for Minnie in a way that wouldn't happen if she stayed in Gadsden.

Two days later, the three of them rode to Birmingham where Brodie and Minnie spoke their vows in front of a justice of the peace. It was a short service with only a few people in attendance. Once the service was over, the three headed to the train station. When they stood on the platform, Henry embraced his daughter and, with tears in their eyes, said their good-byes. Henry then turned to Brodie, and spoke in a stern voice. "Brodie, I want you to promise me to take care of my daughter. And I don't mean just providing for her with the things you can purchase. I want you to know that she means everything to me and, if I hear that you are treating her poorly, you will have me to answer to."

Brodie's heart was beating rapidly and the reality of what he had just done began to sink in. He was close to telling this man and his daughter that it was all a mistake, but felt he couldn't go back and undo it. He needed a mother for his children and, hopefully, over time, would fall in love with her. With a broken voice, he responded, "Yes, sir. I promise I'll take good care of Minnie."

Both men shook hands and then Brodie escorted Minnie up the steps onto the train. And, as the train left the station and headed down the tracks, all Brodie could do was pray that he had made the right decision.

17

1890

After their wedding on May 6th, Brodie took Minnie on an extended honeymoon. The first stop the couple made was to New York City. Brodie had visited the large city for business in the past and thought it would be nice to enjoy several evenings attending the theatre, along with visiting the many sights New York had to offer.

Once they left New York, they headed west to Chicago. The weather was spectacular as they walked hand in hand along the shore of Lake Michigan. In the evenings, after having several drinks and eating a meal from one of the upscale restaurants, the couple made their way back to the hotel room where they made love. Minnie had never been with a man before and was very shy at first. But, as time went by, she began to enjoy the intimate moments with her new husband.

St. Louis, Missouri, was their next stop before heading home via Chattanooga, Tennessee. In early June, with work that needed to be addressed and a guilty conscience over leaving his children for so long, the couple returned to Durham. One night, as they cuddled together in their train berth, Minnie said, "Brodie, please tell me about your children. I want to know everything about them so I can make a good first impression."

Brodie placed his weight on his elbow and smiled as he spoke. "Mabel has just turned fifteen and is growing into a beautiful young woman. Lawrence is fourteen and loves playing baseball. Pearl is eleven going on twenty. She's very inquisitive and will probably ask you lots of questions. If she does, please don't become upset."

"How have they taken the death of their mother?"

"At first, all of them were devastated. For months, they moped around the house. I couldn't say or do anything without them becoming defensive. As time has gone by, they've adjusted. My sister-in-law, Aunt Sarah, has been wonderful. She comes over almost every day or invites them to her house. I'm not sure what I would've done without her. I'm very excited about you meeting her, as well as my brother, Ben."

"Have you heard from your father?"

"No. I sent him a telegram about our wedding, but haven't heard back from him."

"Do you think he'll be okay with you marrying so soon after Martha's death?"

"He knows what it's like to lose a wife. He married Artelia a couple of years after my mother died. After she and Sidney died of typhoid fever, he never considered marriage again. There was just too much to take care of with the war and all."

Brodie placed a blanket over Minnie's lap and kissed her on the forehead. "I do believe he'll love you very much once he meets you."

"I sure do hope so."

The next morning, the train pulled into the Durham station, and a buggy with a driver was there to meet them. On their brief ride to his home on Duke Street, Brodie pointed out the different businesses and landmarks that made Durham unique. When they came to a halt before his house, he noticed the expression of disbelief on Minnie's face. "Is this your house?"

"No, my darling. It's our house."

As she looked around, men were tending to the yard and cutting back debris. A stable was set back behind the house. Several horses were grazing in a side yard. A man walked up and took their bags from the carriage. Brodie took Minnie's hand and helped her down. When they approached the front door, a butler appeared and directed them to the dining room where the three children were seated. It had been such a long time since Brodie had been home. He wasn't sure how they would receive him but, when he entered the room, all three children rose and came over to give him a hug.

After the children greeted their father, Mabel and Lawrence returned to their seats, while Pearl stood peering at Minnie. Brodie noticed the young girl's expression and coaxed her back to her chair. "Now, Pearl, you know it's rude to stare."

Pearl didn't move, which caused Brodie to become anxious over his decision to bring Minnie home. He looked right at Pearl. "Minnie is a very nice woman and I hope you will all come to like her as much as I do."

Pearl stood still. "Why are you here?"

Brodie looked at Minnie, wondering if he should intervene or let Minnie answer the question. Before he could decide, Minnie responded, "Pearl, your father and I were married last month. He asked me to be his wife and come here to live. What do you think of the idea of me living here with you, your brother, and sister?"

"I don't know."

"Well, I can understand your hesitancy to have another woman in your house. If it's okay with you, I'd like to get to know you better. What do you like to do for fun?"

"Play the piano."

"I also like to play. I find it to be very relaxing. What's your favorite song?"

Pearl peered upward, thinking, and then responded, *"Evening Bells and Silver Threads of Love."*

"I don't know that one. Can you teach it to me sometime?"

Lawrence was the next to ask Minnie a question. "Do you ever watch baseball?"

"I've watched baseball games between teams at church."

"We actually have several good teams here in Durham. Maybe you can come watch me play sometime."

"I'd love that. And how about you, Mabel? Do you have any questions for me?"

"I like the dress you have on. Did you make it or buy it?"

Minnie looked at her dress before answering. "I made this. Do you know how to sew?"

Mabel appeared annoyed. "Yes. I thought every girl knows how to sew."

"Well, maybe we can sew something together."

Brodie wasn't sure if Minnie had made a good impression and was concerned that she might be feeling intimidated. "Okay, everyone. There will be plenty of time in the future for questions."

Pearl looked right at Brodie. "Why did it take you so long to come home?"

Brodie had known that Pearl would be likely to question his absence. "I didn't intend to stay away so long. After I met Minnie, I wanted to get to know her, with hopes that she'd agree to marry me. Once we were married, I took her on a honeymoon."

All three children looked away, clearly upset over the present circumstances. Brodie wanted to somehow bridge a gap between Minnie and his children and proclaimed, "I know this is hard to understand, but my hope is that each of you will come to love and respect Minnie as much as I do."

Pearl appeared angry as she stared at Brodie. "Well, she's not mother and never will be!"

Minnie walked over and kneeled in front of Pearl. "Oh, Pearl, I'd never want to replace your mother. You see, I lost my mother when I was a little girl and I totally agree that no one could replace her. I just hope we can start by being friends."

Pearl looked at Minnie and, in a quiet voice, responded, "I guess we could be friends."

In early June, Sarah and Benjamin hosted a party to celebrate Brodie and Minnie's marriage. The June 11th edition of the Durham Daily Globe included an article describing the event.

An Evening to Be Remembered: The Most Recherché Reception that Durham Ever Witnessed

"The reception at Mr. and Mrs. B. N. Duke's last evening, from 9 to 12 o'clock, to meet Mr. and Mrs. B. L. Duke, was a most brilliant affair. The guests were almost numberless, and during the time mentioned, a continued throng poured in and through the house. Carriages almost locked wheels as they came and went. The vestibule was filled with a mellowed light that was most enchanting, while the salon was all a glory of illumination. On the very threshold, a most hearty welcome was tendered the visitors, and then they were escorted to the reception room where they were most graciously received by Mr. and Mrs. B. N. Duke. Next, the guests were presented to Mr. and Mrs. B. L. Duke and the hearty hand-

shakes lacked everything of formality and showed genuineness as the words, 'I am glad to meet you,' were said. Mr. Duke's dignity and cheery smile were very becoming to him while Mrs. Duke, in her elegant toilet, looked just as pretty and happy as could be.

As each couple filed by to make room for others, a merry conversation filled the rooms, and the beaming faces gave plain evidence that all were enjoying themselves. In due time, each guest found his way to the refreshment room, and a thing of beauty it was, too. In the center of a large table was a miniature lake, around the edges of which, ferns and water lilies seemed to grow. This was the feature of the room, but the other decorations were of corresponding richness. Here ribbon water ices, cream, and other delicacies were served in the cutest souvenirs. All this time. grand strains of music filled the whole house, and made all hearts joyful.

A look over the crowd showed scores and scores of middle-aged ladies wearing neat evening caps and becoming dresses; those younger yet, wearing lovely bonnets and costly garments of finest texture; and blooming maidens, with uncovered tresses, wearing gowns of rarest beauty. A pleasing picture to look at. The gentlemen were there in great numbers also, and each man wore his best clothes.

But all things earthly must have an end, and so this entertainment had its termination. Mr. and Mrs. B. L. Duke, Durham greets you, welcomes you, and wishes you long life and happiness."

18

1892

Long life and happiness were all Brodie ever envisioned as he started his new life with Minnie. But Brodie knew happily ever after only happened in fairy tales. At first, Brodie believed that he could be happy with Minnie. She was wonderful with the children and, not long after they had arrived in Durham, she realized she was pregnant.

Brodie couldn't put his finger on the reason why he wasn't satisfied with his life. He had all the nice things money could buy, and Minnie was very attractive and easy to be around. But none of it seemed to be enough. For some reason, he still couldn't get past the demons that haunted him, screaming words of doubt and guilt, never allowing him the sense of peace he so desired.

The only way Brodie could shut the voices out was through drinking and the constant pursuit of building his legacy. This started with the purchase of land and the building of a railroad that wrapped around Durham. Given Brodie had an equal share of the American Tobacco Company stock, he received an equal share of the profits. With enormous amounts of money coming in, he didn't hesitate to purchase buildings, businesses, and land.

One day, while sitting in his office, drinking from the bottle that he hid from plain sight, he heard a knock on the door. "Yes, who is it?"

"It's Julian Carr. I'm here with Richard Wright. We have a business deal I believe you may be interested in."

Brodie rose from his seat and walked across the room. Upon opening the door, he was greeted by two finely-dressed men. Julian wore a beard that was beginning to show signs of gray strands. Richard was clean-cut and holding a cane.

Brodie extended his hand, first to Julian and then to Richard. "Come in. What a pleasure to see both of you. Richard, it sure took some guts for you to show your face around here."

"You know me well enough to know I'm not going to let your brothers or George Watts get in my way of a deal."

"Richard, I'm so sorry about your accident. It appears you are adapting well."

"Ever since the horse accident, my leg has hurt like hell. But I refuse to be thought of as an invalid. And, to be honest, I believe the best medicine for me is to be active. Anyway, enough about me. Julian and I have a proposal we think you'll be interested in."

"Julian, what's this deal you two believe I'd want to hear about?"

"Well, we have our hands full with the Durham Consolidated Land and Improvement Company. Not long ago, we purchased two mills that we believe will do well. The problem is that we're too busy, but most importantly, we believe you have the capital to make them prosperous."

"Now you've piqued my interest."

Richard spoke up. "Last year, we purchased the Commonwealth Manufacturing Company, along with another mill. We know you've been interested in investing in the textile industry and both of us thought you were the first person we should approach."

Brodie leaned back in his chair, took the bottle out of his drawer, took a swig, and looked back at the two men sitting in front of him. "So, what kind of deal are you thinking about making me?"

Richard responded, "We're eager to get these two properties off our books, so Julian and I are willing to sell them for twenty-five percent off of their appraised value."

"So, why such a good deal?"

Julian took a puff of the cigar securely lodged in his mouth. "To start with, you helped us out with the sale of the land we purchased around Trinity College. And, to be honest, Richard has been busy traveling around the world selling his packaging machine, and I have my hands full running the W.T. Blackwell Company. I've also bought some property in Orange County and I've come to realize that I can only do so much without overextending myself."

"I've heard there's money in the mill business. Let me think about it and get back with you."

Richard stood, leaning on his cane to gain balance. "Don't think too long. We have a few other people who are interested."

Julian remained seated. "Richard, I know you have other business to tend to before your train leaves for New York. I'll talk to you soon. Go ahead. I'd like to speak with Brodie concerning another matter."

Brodie stood, shook Richard's hand and waited until he left the room. Once he sat back down, he took another swig from his bottle. "Julian, what do you want to talk with me about?"

"To be honest, that bottle that you keep drinking from."

Brodie was speechless. Benjamin and George had both been harassing him about his drinking. Just last night, even Minnie brought it up, which didn't go well. He knew everyone had his best interest at heart, but he wasn't ready to give it up. Now Julian, a man he respected, had noticed. He realized it was impairing his judgment, but damn, he believed it was the only thing that kept him sane. "Julian, you were in the war. How do you keep a level head after watching so many senseless deaths?"

"Brodie, we both know most people have no idea what it's like to be a part of such brutality, but there has got to be a better way of dealing with your problems. Look, I just heard from a friend of mine who's been drinking heavily for years. I saw him the other day and he's been cured."

"Cured of what?"

"Alcoholism."

"What are you talking about? I've never heard anyone refer to alcoholism as a disease. Everyone thinks it's a habit that I can quit at any time. But what you're saying is that alcoholism is a disease with a cure?"

"That's what I'm saying. Listen, my friend just came back from Dwight, Illinois. A doctor by the name of Leslie Keeley has discovered a cure. He swore that it was a miracle for him."

"Let me think about it."

Julian leaned in. "Brodie, I consider you a good friend and I hope you think the same of me. There are three children and a baby on the way. If not for you, try it for them."

Julian stood up, placed a piece of paper on the desk in front of him, and walked out of the room. After a few minutes, Brodie picked up the paper and looked at the advertisement for the Keeley Institute. Then, in that moment, he thought out loud, "To hell with it. What do I have to lose?"

Several days later, Brodie arrived in Dwight, Illinois. He was exhausted from the trip and only wanted a drink. He thought it best to try and stay sober, but it was harder than he expected. He was irritable and unpleasant to everyone who spoke to him. When he exited the train, a man standing on the platform approached him. "Are you Brodie Duke?"

"Yes, I am."

"Dr. Keeley asked me to give you a ride to the institute. I hope you had a pleasant trip."

"No, not really."

"I'm sorry about that. Here, I'll take your bag."

Brodie stepped into the carriage, leaned his head back, and wondered what he was doing here. He dozed off as the carriage rolled down the sandy road. When it came to a stop, Brodie looked up to see a large Victorian-style house to his right. The man tied the leather lead to a hitching post, picked up Brodie's bag, and walked toward the house.

Brodie took a deep breath and made his way to the entrance. He opened the door to a spacious foyer that reminded him of his own home. A man wearing a lab coat approached him. "You must be Brodie Duke."

"Yes."

"I'm so happy to meet you. My name is Dr. Leslie Keeley." Dr. Keeley pointed to an open door off the foyer. "Come into my office."

Brodie followed Dr. Keeley into a stately room with several large windows that overlooked a massive back yard. People were sitting in chairs, some reading, others smoking, but all seemed content.

"Before we begin the treatment, I'd like to go over the process and answer any questions you may have."

With a skeptical tone, Brodie said "So, I was told that you believe alcoholism is a disease that can be cured."

"Yes, I do. I've been working on my cure for over a decade and have had remarkable results. I also believe you'll be an excellent candidate."

"So, when do I begin the treatment? I've gone three days without a drop of alcohol and all I can think about is getting my next drink."

"Well, you're in luck. We're going to start your treatment by letting you consume as much alcohol as you can tolerate. We're going to house you at the Dwight Livingston Hotel, which you should find to be very comfortable. In a couple of days, you'll receive four injections, along with several glasses of tonic. The treatment usually takes about four weeks before you begin losing your desire for alcohol."

Brodie looked right into Dr. Keeley's eyes. "You mean to tell me that I'm going to be given as much alcohol as I can consume?"

"Yes, I am. The combination of the alcohol with the medicine creates a reaction in the body which leads to sobriety."

"Well, hell, that sounds like my kind of treatment."

"Your bags will be delivered to your room at the hotel. In the meantime, we'll conduct a physical, and after all the consent papers have been signed, you're welcome to go to the bar and drink as much as you desire."

That night, Brodie had to be escorted back to his hotel room. The next morning, he woke to a splitting headache. He stayed in bed much longer than he was accustomed to, but given that he had no responsibilities to attend to, he slept until almost noon. Once dressed and shaved, he went down the stairs and spotted a pot of hot coffee and muffins on a large table. He walked over and poured himself a cup of the brew and picked up a muffin. As he was searching for a place to sit, he heard a woman's voice. "You must be Mr. Duke."

"Yes, I am. And who are you?"

"Elizabeth Broadbeck."

Brodie noticed a vacant chair situated next to Elizabeth. "So, is this seat taken?"

"No, it isn't. Please join me."

"How did you know my name?"

"Mr. Duke, everyone knows who you are. Your tobacco company is ruffling a lot of feathers all over this country. I heard you might come here and, I must admit, you are far more attractive than I thought you'd be.

Brodie felt a little uncomfortable by this woman's straightforward nature. Before he could respond, she continued, "Anyway, we have something in common."

"And what is that?"

"I've been smoking Duke's Cameo cigarettes for quite some time."

"Why do you smoke that brand?"

"I like the picture on the package."

"So, Mrs. Broadbeck, why are you here?"

"For the same reason you are. Alcohol."

"So, where are you from?"

"Kansas City."

"How long have you been here?"

"I just arrived yesterday. I saw you in the bar. You were pretty intoxicated, and I thought I'd wait until you were sober before introducing myself."

"Was I very obnoxious?"

"Do you want the truth?"

Brodie hesitated a moment before responding, "Yes."

"Well, you were singing and I even saw you dance with a chair."

"I'm sure that was entertaining."

"If I hadn't been so intoxicated myself, I would've joined you."

"So, Elizabeth, are you married?"

"I was, but my husband left me when I refused to stop drinking."

"I'm sorry to hear that."

"Thanks, but it was for the best. Anyway, enough about me." Elizabeth leaned in. "So, I heard that you're married."

"Yes, I am."

"So, what does your wife think about you coming here?"

"Minnie is happy that I agreed to come, but she doesn't seem to have a lot of faith in me." Brodie hesitated a moment before going on. "I really don't blame her."

Brodie looked off, thinking about Minnie and the children. He wasn't sure why he married her. She was an incredible woman and he respected her deeply, but he couldn't say that he loved her, not like he had loved Martha.

A man in a white coat walked up, holding two glasses of a red-colored liquid. "Mr. Duke and Mrs. Broadbeck, please drink this. I have to warn you, it has a bitter taste."

Brodie picked up a glass and, before drinking it, raised it and touched Elizabeth's glass. "This is to us."

As Brodie swallowed the liquid, he was appalled by the taste. He looked over and had to laugh as Elizabeth grimaced. "Mr. Duke, what's so funny?"

"I'm sorry, I just wish you could've seen your expression."

Elizabeth stood up and looked in Brodie's direction. "Why don't we take a walk around the grounds? I've heard it's beautiful this time of year."

Brodie jumped up from his seat and walked toward the door. "I'd love that."

The two walked to the far end of the property where a bench was placed under a weeping willow tree. It was an isolated spot where no one could see them as they talked. At first neither spoke as they sat only inches apart. Puffy clouds drifted across the sky and several birds could be heard in the distance. It was almost like a dream.

In that moment, Brodie knew he shouldn't spend time alone with another woman, but there was something special about Elizabeth. It was like she could see into his soul, accepting him with all his inadequacies. When he told her about his childhood, and the hurt he continued to carry from Sidney's death, she responded in a manner that no other human had ever done before. Instead of brushing it off, she reached over and touched his face. She spoke no words. She didn't have to. Her expression said it all. Tears fell from her eyes and down her cheeks.

Brodie reached over to brush her tears away and a feeling rose from deep within. He gasped at the mere emotion that welled up as Elizabeth took his hand and, ever so lightly, traced each finger. He reached over to kiss her but, to his dismay, she pushed him away. In a calm voice full of assurance, she spoke. "Brodie, there is nothing I want more than to be with you, but this isn't the time. Let's stay strong and fight for our sobriety."

Brodie pulled back, feeling rejected. Anger stirred under the surface and all he wanted to do was leave. But, before he could stand, Elizabeth smiled into his eyes. "Brodie, I want the best for you. You have to believe me. These next couple of weeks are going to be difficult enough, without having a relationship that may only cause more guilt. Once we get through this program, we can discuss the possibility of being together. I couldn't live with myself if we were to become sexually involved and our relationship is the reason you don't get sober."

"I've never met anyone like you. I wish I hadn't been so impulsive when I married Minnie."

"Brodie, I'm not sure why you married her but we have to remember the fact that you did marry Minnie. This is hard for me. It would be so easy to be with you, but it's just not the right time. Be patient. I can't promise you what will happen between us, but I can promise you that I'll be right here going through it with you."

Elizabeth was there with Brodie for the next four weeks. They both received four injections daily and drank bitter tonics throughout the day. Over the course of the weeks, they kept themselves busy reading, walking the grounds, or visiting a nearby spring. During the evenings, instead of drinking, Brodie and Elizabeth played card games or participated in events set up by the institute.

Toward the end of his stay, Brodie was amazed at how well he felt without drinking. He slept well and his conscience was clear. He never wanted to admit that Elizabeth was correct, but knew in his heart that she was.

On the day of his departure, Brodie packed his bag and went out into the lobby to wait for his carriage. He glanced around, hoping to see Elizabeth one more time, but she was nowhere to be found. He approached one of the workers. "Have you seen Elizabeth Broadbeck this morning?"

"She left before dawn. She gave me this envelope to give to you."

Brodie lifted the flap on the back of the envelope and pulled out a note card that smelled of the scent Elizabeth wore.

Dear Brodie,

I'm sorry I wasn't here to tell you good-bye. I just couldn't look into your beautiful blue eyes, knowing I wouldn't be able to touch you and hold you close. I'm so proud of you and how you won this battle. I know that each of us will have our own wars to fight when we return to our homes, but I want you to know I will be thinking of you often, hoping you find what you are searching for.

I'll always have a special place in my heart for you. You are an incredible man.

Love,

Elizabeth

Brodie took a deep breath in, exhaled, and placed the envelope inside his coat pocket. He wanted to scream out, but remained quiet, as he picked up his bag and walked out of the door, a sober man.

19

1892-1893

As hard as he tried, Brodie couldn't stop thinking about Elizabeth. He'd hoped that, now that he was home with Minnie and the children, his memories of her would fade, but they only intensified. Many nights, he awoke from a vivid dream: a dream of Elizabeth standing in front of him, holding his hands, and drawing close, encouraging him to brush his lips upon her blushed cheek. But, as often as he had the dream, it would stop abruptly with Brodie dangling on and desiring more.

When Brodie had first arrived back home, Minnie approached him with a sincerity that caused him to pull back. "Brodie, it's so good to have you home."

"Hello, Minnie."

He knew his answer was stale, void of emotion. But how could he pretend to have feelings for this woman when his heart ached for another?

"How are you feeling? You must be exhausted from such a long trip."

Brodie took his hat off and placed it on a nearby rack. He looked toward the open doors, hoping someone would come and interrupt their conversation. "Yes, I'm exhausted. It was a very trying time, but you'll be happy to know that I'm sober at last!"

Minnie leaned in to give Brodie a hug, but his arms went limp, speaking volumes. "What's wrong, Brodie? I thought you'd be glad to be home and see me."

"I'm just tired." Trying to change the subject, Brodie asked, "So, where are the children?"

"Woodward is asleep and the others are out riding. They should be returning any time now. I know they'll be glad to see you."

Brodie walked past Minnie and headed to the back porch, sat down in an old rocking chair, and lit a cigarette. He gazed out over the wooded acres he had recently acquired, hoping to feel some sort of fulfillment from his achievements. He just couldn't understand why he felt so empty. His first instinct was to reach for a drink, but he knew better of it. He had been sober for over three weeks and wanted to try and stay that way. Minnie followed him and sat down in a chair a few feet away. He initially felt annoyed by her presence, but didn't say anything.

"Brodie, I'm happy you were able to stay sober while you were in Illinois. I guess I thought that, maybe if you were sober, you could look at our relationship from a different perspective." Minnie paused a moment for a response but, when none came, she spoke in a broken voice. "But, I guess I was wrong."

The loose boards on the porch made a creaking noise as Brodie rocked back and forth. Unsure of what to say, he remained silent.

"I know we both had our reasons for getting married. I wanted to move away from Gadsden and you wanted a mother for your children. I love your children and Woodward is such a sweet baby. I have no regrets."

Brodie could tell by the sound of her voice that she was trying to believe her own words. He wanted to encourage her, but just didn't have it in him to say anything. Just about this time, he saw Mabel, Pearl, and Lawrence, ride up on their horses. They rode up to the porch, dismounted, and climbed up the steps. Pearl approached him first, flinging her arms around his torso. "Daddy, it's so good to see you. How are you?"

Brodie rose and, for the first time since leaving Illinois, felt the blood rushing through his veins. "I'm doing well. The place was very nice and I feel rested."

Lawrence reached out his hand for his father to shake. "Hello, Father."

Brodie looked intently at his son. "It seems like you've grown two inches since I last saw you."

Lawrence responded, "It does seem like a long time since you were here. Are you going to stay home for a while?"

"That's my plan. I need to attend to the new mill that I recently purchased." He looked down at his daughter. "Pearl, I hope it's okay, but I'd like to name it after you."

Pearl, who was appearing indifferent to her father, looked at him with a new-found respect. "I would like that."

"What about me? Are you going to name a building or road after me?" Mabel asked.

"I'll definitely consider it. Lawrence, what can I do for you? Do you want to work in one of my mills?"

"That's okay. Uncle Benjamin has been taking me over to the American Tobacco Company and introducing me to the different people who he does business with."

"Do you think you want to work there one day?"

"I do."

"Well, if you decide to help me with the cotton mills, I'll be glad to show you around."

"Thanks, Dad. I'll definitely give it some thought."

"It sure is nice to be at home with all of you."

Pearl spoke up. "Daddy, I like you like this."

Brodie sat back and absorbed his daughter's words. She was always brutally honest. He looked around at his family and smiled. "I like being this way as well."

The first few months after Brodie returned home, he kept himself occupied with building up North Durham. He had made a deal with a local contractor to build homes for the employees of his different enterprises. He paid to have the railroad line, called the Beltway, expanded around Durham. His willingness to invest so much in his hometown, particularly North Durham, brought him the respect of many of the locals. It was when he was out and about in Durham that he could feel like his life had a purpose, one that mattered to the citizens of the city he had grown to love.

One day, as he was entering the post office, he noticed an older gentleman sitting at a desk with a headset on his head, writing something down. He'd never seen anything like this before and approached him. The man noticed Brodie and lowered the headset. "Can I help you?"

"I've never seen a contraption like this before."

"It's a telegraph machine. We just had it installed."

"How does it work?"

"Each letter is a pattern or code. The operator on the other end sends me a message using the code. I write it down, then deliver it to the person the message is intended for."

"So, if I want to send a message to my brother, who lives in New York, he could receive it much sooner than if I sent him a letter?"

"Yes. The telegraph operator will write it down and have it delivered to him almost immediately. It has a lot of purposes, but I'm finding a lot of people using the telegraph system to purchase commodities."

"I never thought about that before. So, if I wanted to purchase cotton, you could find out what cotton is trading for on the Chicago exchange?"

"Yes."

"Can you do that for me?"

"Sure."

As the telegraph operator was checking the price of cotton, Brodie began to think about the implications of purchasing and selling commodities. Adrenaline began to rush through his veins as he thought about the money he could make.

After working out the logistics of the process, Brodie visited the post office almost on a daily basis to either buy or sell commodities. The more often he went, the more he became consumed with the thought of making money. Over time, Brodie developed an obsessive passion for trading.

One day, as he was going to the post office, he looked into a local restaurant and spotted Nannie Wright sitting at a table with her brother, Richard. His eyes were drawn toward Richard as he abruptly got up, placed his cane on the floor, and walked out the door, passing Brodie without acknowledging his presence.

Brodie's curiosity was piqued and he decided to enter the restaurant and approach Nannie. Once he was at her table, he noticed her sad demeanor. "Nannie, I saw Richard leave. Is everything okay?"

"He's irritated by his leg. Ever since the doctor cut his leg off, he's been agitated. I know he's in pain, but he won't let me help him." She shook her head in dismay.

Brodie looked around the room, wondering if people would gossip about seeing the two of them sitting alone at a table. He didn't know why it bothered him, but he didn't want people interpreting a purely innocent situation in the wrong way. He decided to sit down across from her, putting distance between the two of them. "Nannie, I'm sorry he treats you so poorly."

"I've gotten used to it. Anyway, enough about me, how are you?"

"I went to Illinois a couple of months ago and have been sober ever since."

"That's wonderful! I'm assuming you've had to stay very busy to keep your mind off the bottle."

"I have." Brodie intentionally kept his answer short, not wanting to tell her about his new passion for trading.

"I've heard about all the building you've been doing in North Durham. You're really making a name for yourself."

"I don't know about all that. Anyway, Durham needs people to build up the city. That's one reason I appreciate your brother and Julian Carr. Both of them have invested in land and are building large structures in the heart of the city."

"You're right about that. Even with the amount of time Richard spends traveling around the world, he seems to make time and finances available to build on Main Street."

"With all the building and purchasing I've been doing, I'm most proud of my recent purchase of the Bennett Place."

"It does seem like a long time ago that the Civil War ended and the treaty was signed right here in Durham. I do appreciate how you've been willing to spend your money to preserve our history."

"Well, if someone doesn't, the people in Durham will soon forget the significance of the Bennett Place."

"Speaking of significance. I spoke to Sarah Duke the other day and she was sharing how her husband, Benjamin, and George Watts are investing in the Keeley Institute."

"I heard that. I don't know why they feel it's such a big deal that I was able to get sober." Brodie felt anger build up inside him. "I've always felt like George Watts is judging me. He seems so self-righteous at times. He just rubs me the wrong way."

Nannie didn't respond. It was clear she didn't want to step into that muddied water. After a moment of silence, she looked up. "Brodie, I think we have a lot in common. We both have two brothers and a sister. Your brother, Buck, is a very driven man, just like Richard. We can sometimes feel like we don't have value when our siblings are so successful. But, I want to tell you, that I'm proud of how much you've done for Durham."

Brodie took a deep breath and exhaled. "Buck and I have never been close. He was so much younger and he couldn't understand what I went through in Salisbury. He also has no idea how it feels to lose a brother. When George became a partner in the W. Duke, Sons and Company, it felt like he pushed me out and took over my role."

Nannie wiped her mouth with her napkin and set it down. "Brodie, I spoke to Minnie the other day. She asked me to be part of a group that she's forming. I think she's lonely."

"While I was in Alabama, I really thought that it would be a good idea for the two of us to be married. I just didn't realize how different we are. I want to make her happy, but I just don't know how."

"I can't give you advice on that. I've never been married or had a serious relationship. Ever since Richard's wife died, I've given up my life for him. At first, when I was taking care of his baby girl,

I had a purpose. My entire life was wrapped up in taking care of Little May. Then, when she died, I was devastated. It felt like I had no reason to go on, but I knew I needed to be strong."

"I'm so sorry."

"Brodie, don't worry about me. I'll be okay. But Minnie is more fragile. She needs you more than you probably realize."

Brodie lowered his head and didn't respond. He knew he should be more attentive toward Minnie, but his passions and desires were directed elsewhere. Even though it had been months, he still couldn't get Elizabeth off his mind. And if he wasn't thinking about her, he was focused on purchasing commodities and checking on his investments. He loved the feel of adrenaline rushing through his veins when he was purchasing or selling commodities. And, so far, he had done well. But little did he know, that everything was getting ready to change, and not for the better.

20

1893

Brodie had difficulty keeping his eyes open as the train car rolled down the track. He looked at Minnie, who had already succumbed to the motion of the train and had fallen into a deep sleep, leaning in and using his shoulder as a pillow. Benjamin was sitting in front of him, speaking in a hushed voice to his father. He wanted to hear the words being spoken, but thought better of trying to interfere.

Washington, visibly upset, brushed his eyes with his handkerchief. Brodie wanted to provide some sort of comfort, but knew there was nothing he could say to ease his father's pain. After a few minutes, Washington leaned back into his seat, disappearing from Brodie's sight.

The last couple of weeks had been difficult for all of the Dukes, but it was clear that Washington was inconsolable. He had loved his daughter so much, doting on her from birth. Some may have thought it had to do with Mary's poor health, but Brodie knew better. He had witnessed the bond his half-sister had with his father and knew it went beyond the typical father-daughter relationship.

Out of all his half-siblings, Mary was the one who Brodie had found to be sincere and compassionate. She never seemed to judge him, even when he was judging himself. She always had a smile on her face and a kind word for everyone she met. Given her poor health since birth, it was amazing to observe her push through her personal pain to lift the spirits of others. But, what stood out the most to him, was the relationship Mary had shared with their father, Washington.

One particular memory stood out in Brodie's mind that embodied his thoughts about Mary. It was from the day Washington learned that he had to go to war. Washington was sitting in the old cabin at the same table that Sidney had used as his workshop for whittling his animals. Nine-year-old Mary was sitting next to Washington, with her hand held firmly on his arm. Neither spoke, nor did either look up, when Brodie walked into the room.

Observing the situation, Brodie felt like he was intruding and turned to walk outside, but Mary's sweet voice stopped him. "Brodie, don't go. Please, come and sit with us."

"What's wrong?"

Washington looked up and it was clear that he had been crying. "Brodie, you need to know I received my orders. I'm headed off to Charleston."

Brodie wasn't sure what to say. He looked over at Mary who continued to keep her hand placed on Washington's arm. Mary turned toward her father. "Tell him."

Brodie was puzzled. "Tell me what?"

"Those weren't the only orders we received."

"What do you mean?"

"You've been ordered to go to Salisbury to serve as a prison guard."

Brodie fell into a chair across from his father and Mary. He was so young and never imagined that he would be called up to go to war. As he sat in a state of shock, Mary reached over and touched his hand. "I'll pray for you, Brodie."

Brodie kept that memory in the forefront of his thoughts during the horrors of Salisbury, and the years that followed. Even when his faith in a loving God waned, he couldn't help but remember the love he felt from his sister.

When the men had returned from war, it was Mary who rallied her siblings and father to look beyond the devastation the soldiers had imparted on their farm. And it was Mary, with her sewing needle in hand, who stitched the small bags for the Duke's first brand, *Pro Bono Publico*. In all the years that followed, she never complained about the long hours, or sore fingers, as she leaned into the light of the fire to create the needed number of bags.

There were times when Mary's health would get the best of her, causing her to be bedridden but, even then, she never complained or said a harsh word. No matter how bad she felt, she always made sure Brodie knew how much he meant to her.

Brodie would never forget the day his sister walked down the aisle of Main Street Methodist Church with Washington at her side. The older man was clearly elated by her choice of husbands, but tears still welled up in his eyes as he handed his only daughter to Robert Lyon. He was mesmerized by his father's nervous hands as the two hugged, and by how they smiled at each other before Washington took his seat in the front pew.

After Mary's first baby was born, Washington took an active role as a grandfather. This wasn't surprising given his role with Brodie's children, but there was something different. It was as if he was preparing Mary's children for the inevitable. With each additional child Mary birthed, her health deteriorated further. But, even though her pregnancies were difficult, she loved being a mother and gave birth to five beautiful children. Each time a new child came into the world, Washington was there to greet them in a way that only a grandparent can.

Brodie was tempted to be jealous of the relationship Mary had with their father, but he just couldn't. She was such a sweet person, who had suffered so much in her lifetime. If anything, he felt like she was someone who could understand the demons that haunted him. Many times, since he had returned from war, he found solace in her company.

Daylight faded into darkness as the train made its way to Durham. As much as everyone had hoped the doctors Buck had hired would cure Mary, in the end their hopes were futile. After a week of her family being by her bedside, she finally succumbed to death. In the moment that she took her last breath, everyone inhaled, hoping and praying for Mary to overcome the dreaded tuberculosis that had ravaged her young body. But it was not meant to be.

Minnie stretched and opened her eyes. She was clearly disoriented. "Where are we?"

Brodie whispered, "We just went through Richmond."

"How is your father?"

"He's clearly upset. I don't know what to say to him."

Minnie placed her hand on Brodie's arm. "Just being here for him is all you can do."

Brodie looked at his wife, and thought about how beautiful she was and how she didn't deserve being treated so poorly. He turned away from Minnie, not wanting to admit his feelings.

"Brodie, what's wrong?"

"Every woman I've ever cared about has died. First, my mother, and then Artelia. Then, Martha, and now Mary. I guess, sometimes I try and hold back my feelings. I guess, I'm afraid something might happen to you."

Minnie squeezed Brodie's hand. "My dear husband, nothing is going to happen to me."

But, as much as Brodie wanted to believe the words Minnie spoke, he just couldn't. He truly wanted to be sober and attentive to his wife, but just didn't know how. He felt cursed and everyone who came too close suffered for it. As he thought through the situation, he dozed off and was awakened by the screeching of the metal wheels coming to a halt in Durham. He looked up to see Benjamin and Sarah walk through the narrow opening between the train cars. His father followed with his head bent downward. Brodie reached up, took his hat from the overhead bin, and made his way toward the entrance, then down the stairs to the platform.

Several women were huddled together nearby, watching as the family came out of the train. Brodie couldn't help but notice how upset they were as they hugged Sarah and Minnie. Nannie Wright stood alone to the side, looking in his direction. He thought of her as a friend and wanted to approach her, but thought better of it. Instead, he stood to the side as many of Mary's grief-stricken friends approached the family. And, in that moment, he felt around the inside of his coat pocket for the carved fox, and placed it in his hand, rubbing the smooth wood between his fingers.

| 21 |

1893

Brodie felt the December wind penetrate through his coat and pulled the collar up tight against his neck. It had been a horrific day and the last place he wanted to go was home. There was only one place he believed he could receive some solace so, instead of walking north, he turned and headed west. He approached the large door without hesitation, taking hold of the wooden handle and pulling it open.

"Well, well, look who the cat drug in."

Brodie stepped into the dark, smoky room and looked around to see familiar faces staring in his direction. It had been almost a year since he had last visited Carrington Bar and, by the looks of the place, nothing had changed. He walked up to the bar, sat down on an empty stool, and waited for the bartender to approach him. He had recently begun drinking again and was tired of hiding the fact from his family and friends. Anyway, he missed the regulars, who could be found either here or at Mangum's Tavern.

Thomas Wright sat down on the stool next to him and called out, "S.R., can you pour me a beer and also pour one for my friend?"

Brodie smiled. "Well, thank you, Thomas. The next one will be on me."

"So, what brings you to Hickstown?"

"What do you think?" Brodie paused a moment as he surveyed the room. "I wanted a drink and, since Durham has adopted prohibition, I walked a couple of blocks to the west side to enjoy a cold beverage."

Thomas chimed in. "It'll be interesting to watch how people like Richard Blacknall, J.W. Brooks, and J.W. Swift, fight the incorporation of Hickstown. They need to keep themselves and their well-to-do beliefs in their churches and away from us."

The two men clinked their glasses and sat back for a moment. Thomas wiped his lip with his sleeve. "So, Brodie, I heard your assets are now being held by your brother, Benjamin, and George Watts."

Brodie shifted his position on the barstool. "News sure does travel fast around here."

"Well, anyone known as the Mayor of North Durham will be talked about. Also, as much as you don't like it, you and your family will always be fair game for Durham Daily Globe's gossip column."

Brodie stared at his drink and gulped down the last little bit of beer. "Is there anything in your life that gets your blood pumping? For some reason, just the thought of trading commodities makes me excited. And, for a long time, I've been making good money. But now, with the price of cotton plummeting, I had to pay up, and it's cost me almost everything I had."

Thomas laughed under his breath. "Well, I wouldn't know what having money to buy commodities is like. When I moved to Durham, my brother, Richard, made it out like I was going to be rich, but that is the furthest thing from the truth. I feel like I have to beg him for every penny I get."

"I can relate. Just recently, I had to give up my cotton mills to my brother, Benjamin. That wasn't so bad, but to have to get help from George Watts was an entirely different matter."

Brodie ordered two more beers. Once they were placed in front of him, he slid one over to Thomas and took a swig of his. "So, Thomas, I see William Blackwell in that booth over there. I think I'm going to go speak with him. If anyone understands what I'm going through, it should be him."

"You're right about that. He's definitely a riches to rags story." Thomas patted Brodie on the shoulder. "It was good seeing you."

"Likewise. Oh, and please tell your sister, Nannie, hello from me. I sure don't understand why she hasn't been married by now."

Brodie stood and walked over to where William Blackwell was sitting. He couldn't help but think about how important this man used to be. He and Julian Carr had built the William T. Blackwell Company from the ground up. Over time it had become the top-selling tobacco company in the country. But then, in 1883, William sold his interest to a Philadelphia firm for a mere one hundred thousand dollars.

Brodie would never forget the time that Richard Wright was speaking in front of a group of businessmen, blasting William for his poor negotiation skills. Richard believed that the Philadelphia firm should've paid William at least three hundred thousand dollars, if not more.

After receiving the buyout payment for the tobacco company, William made the worst mistake of his life. He used the money to open up The Durham Bank. Someone with a good business sense of how to run a bank might've succeeded, but not William. William was just too sympathetic to the needy. He lost all of the bank's money by offering loans to people who had no way of paying them back.

To make matters worse, when William realized his bank needed capital, he applied for loans from several Northern capitalists. The first loan, for thirty thousand dollars, was granted, followed by a second one for thirty-five thousand dollars. About this time, a local election was being held. A man by the name of Mr. Jordan, one who believed in the rights for all men, black and white, ran for office on the Republican ticket. The day after the election, a mob of conservative Democrats approached Mr. Jordan's home and successfully forced him and his family out of Durham. When word of the violence against a fellow Republican reached the Northern capitalists, not only did they refuse to give the second loan to The Durham Bank, they also demanded repayment of the initial loan. This was the final nail in the coffin that permanently closed the bank.

Brodie looked down at William who was sipping on a beer and spoke. "William, can I join you?"

William pointed to an empty chair. "Sure."

Brodie sat down and didn't speak for a moment. He knew William might not want to talk about his poor financial decisions, so Brodie decided to speak about his own personal failures. "So, I guess you've heard about my misfortune."

"Yep, I did. Sorry to hear about it."

"I was just wondering if you have some advice for me."

"You want advice from me?" William chuckled.

"Maybe not so much advice, but some empathy. Most don't know what it is like to have so much money at your disposal, and then you wake up one day and it's gone."

"Well, I don't see it that way. You see, I didn't have a family who could back me up when I lost the bank. No, instead, I made a lot of enemies. I really thought I was doing a good thing when I helped the ordinary man. I didn't ask questions when people needed a loan. But then, when the bank no longer had the funds to back what was owed, we went down and took half of Durham with us."

Brodie waited a moment before speaking. "Well, I just received a letter from Julian Carr blaming me for the downfall of the Durham Consolidated Land and Improvement Company, because of the failure of my supply company."

"I wouldn't worry about Julian or Richard. Both of them have enough money to get by. But let me tell you, don't think about asking Richard for money. I asked him for five hundred dollars to get started in a venture with Theo Allen, but he never responded. Nothing. Just left me hanging."

"I wish I had some money to lend you, but if you read Durham's daily newspaper this morning, you would have seen everyone I owe money to. It took up the entire front page. It sure doesn't feel good to know everyone is aware of my shortcomings.

"I'm sorry about that." William took a sip of his beer and shook his head. "I'll never forget reading the newspapers in November of 1888. Just like you, everyone knew who I owed money to, but unlike you, I had no way of ever returning their money to them." Brodie lowered his head and then muttered under his breath, "That was a miserable Christmas for so many Durham families."

Both men sat in silence for a couple of minutes until William said, "So, I thought you'd been cured of alcoholism."

Brodie leaned back and laughed. "Well, I guess not."

"I was sorry to hear about the death of your sister, Mary. I heard that your father has Mary's children living with him. Given the size of Fairview, he definitely has room. I also heard that Artelia's sister, Ann, is working for him as a housekeeper. It sure would be nice to have some help at my house on the corner of Chapel Hill and Duke Streets. My son, W.T., has moved out and I can't afford to pay anyone to clean."

"I'm sorry about that."

William took a sip of his beer and stared out into space. "Anyway, I hope your father is enjoying his grandchildren."

Brodie fumbled with his glass of beer. He began to speak, more for himself to hear the words than for William. "My father is a good man. He never judges me like Buck or George do. He's decided to put my profits from the American Tobacco Company in a trust. I can understand, given the reckless use of my funds. I believe he's trying to protect me from myself."

"Back when I was running the bank, I wish I had had someone like your father to protect me from myself. Losing my own money was bad enough, but I hated the thought that I was personally responsible for the financial losses of so many good people right here in Durham."

"I'm sorry about that." For a moment, neither spoke, then Brodie broke the silence. "Well, I believe that this present depression our country is going through is one of the causes of my losses, but I also believe I'm going to somehow rise again. You just wait and see."

William raised his glass. "Let's drink to rising up again!"

"Amen to that!"

22

1895-1899

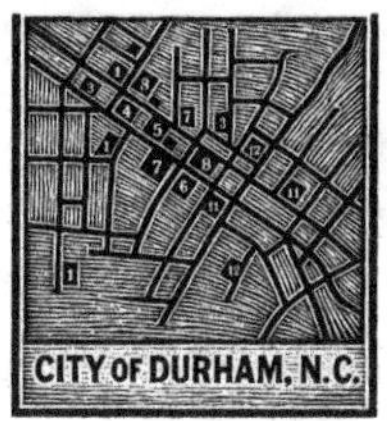

"Damn it!"

"Brodie, please do not use foul language at the table in front of the children."

"If you'd read this article in the Durham Daily Globe, you'd understand why I'm upset." Brodie made a loud huffing noise. "And, it's not like they haven't heard words like this before."

"So, what has you so stirred up?"

"Two years ago, when I had to turn over my assets to my brother, Benjamin, and George Watts, I did so, believing that I'd be able to recover them once I was financially secure. Benjamin kept his word and I was able to pay him for the Commonwealth Manufacturing Company and return to my position as president. But, George Watts, on the other hand, refused to sell Pearl Mills back to me."

"Yes, I remember this conversation," Minnie said, in a calm voice.

"Of all the assets I lost, Pearl Mills is the one I wanted to buy back the most. Shoot, I named the mill after my own child."

"Darling, I'm sorry you're so upset."

"Upset! I'm furious! You should read this article. It speaks of George Watts like he is an angel from heaven and is the only person who has contributed to this town. Yes, he was the major contributor to building Watts Hospital, but it was me who's built streets and houses. If it wasn't for me, we wouldn't have the railroad system that everyone enjoys."

"Now, Brodie, there's no sense in getting all worked up."

"If it wasn't for our family, George Watts would be a nobody, living somewhere in Maryland."

"Well, we know all of you, including George, have been very generous with your money. I know the Presbyterians are happy with the new church he built on Main Street."

Brodie stood up and began to pace. "The last thing Durham needs is another church."

"Some might not agree with you."

"Now I'm not big on contributing toward religious or educational philanthropies, but I've done a lot for this city."

"Honey, no one can disagree with that. Speaking of adding to our city, I'm starting a new club with your daughter, Pearl."

"Don't you have more important things to tend to than starting all these clubs?"

"Brodie, when I moved here five years ago, I had no friends. I spent a lot of time with your children and was ecstatic when Woodward was born. But, just like you, I've wanted to contribute something to this wonderful place I now call home. So, I decided to start a club that could include women and their daughters. That's why Pearl and I started the Up-To-Date Club. And then, when we started traveling, I wanted to share with other women about the places we've visited. So today, I'm going over to Sarah's house for the first meeting of the Tourist Club."

Brodie couldn't find fault with Minnie. He had been spending most of his time away from home and didn't blame her for wanting to make friends. Anyway, he had more important things to think about. One, being how he was going to let the city of Durham know how he felt about George Watts.

That day, when Brodie went into his office, he took out a map of Durham and laid it out flat on his desk. As he was studying the map and trying to figure out a plan to put George Watts in his place, William Branson, the manager of the Commonwealth Manufacturing Company, knocked on his door.

"Yes, William, come in."

Brodie, totally absorbed in the map, didn't look up.

"Mr. Duke, I wanted to go over some next steps I'd like to take for the expansion of the mill."

Brodie didn't respond, but continued to stare down at the map of the property he owned.

"Mr. Duke, can I ask you what you're thinking about?"

Brodie huffed as he looked up at William. "I'm very disturbed by George Watts. He makes me so angry."

"I'm sorry about that. So, what does the map have to do with anything?"

Brodie pointed to the drawn lines that represented how Duke Street ran parallel to two unnamed streets. He looked up and, with a grin on his face, proclaimed, "I've got it! William, do you see how Duke Street is here, and then there are two other streets that I haven't gotten around to naming yet. Well, I just figured out what I'm going to name them."

William looked down at the map, curious to hear what Brodie was going to say. "What are you going to name them?"

Brodie pointed to Duke Street and then to the ones that ran parallel to it. "This street is going to be called Hated and this street is going to be called Watts."

William stood quiet as Brodie continued. "That's exactly what I'm going to call them. I want everyone to know how I feel about George Watts, and what better way than to have the streets declare it to the citizens of Durham."

William turned and walked out of the room, but Brodie didn't even notice. He was too preoccupied to care.

As soon as the streets were named, Brodie had maps produced and circulated around town. None of his family members appreciated what he had done, but it wasn't until Buck came home from New York that all hell broke loose.

One night, when Brodie was in Carrington Bar, circled by a cluster of his cronies, the door opened and a hush fell over the large room. Brodie had his back toward the door and continued to cackle with the group of men, who appeared highly intoxicated.

"Yep, last month I was able to take my profits from the American Tobacco Company and use it to cover my losses from trading commodities."

One of the men standing in front of Brodie could see Buck walking in their direction. As Buck neared, he moved out of the way. Before Brodie saw Buck, he declared, "I'm sure George Watts and my brother, Buck, would be appalled at how I spend my money."

Suddenly sensing the heat of his brother walking up behind him, Brodie turned and found himself face to face with Buck. "What are you doing here, little brother?"

"I'd appreciate it if you don't refer to me as your brother. If I had my way, you'd be out in the streets with nothing."

"Well, that's not going to happen. Anyway, I didn't ask you to come in here and interrupt my discussion with my friends."

Buck scanned the room and looked back at Brodie. "That is part of the problem. The people you choose as friends."

A man within earshot of Buck, called out in a slurred voice, "Hey, what's wrong with Brodie's friends?"

Buck paused before going on. "It's disgraceful for a man with the last name of Duke to lower himself to such poor standards."

"I know you didn't come in here to give me a lesson on how to keep the Duke name pure and above reproach. Why did you come here?"

"I saw the map you made and I'm here to demand that you change it."

"Why? And, if it's so bad, why doesn't George come to me instead of sending you to defend his name?"

"He's too much of a gentleman to waste his time on you."

"You and George would have nothing if it wasn't for me. I'm the one who came to Durham in 1869 and started a very successful business."

"I doubt that very seriously. You might've been the first to start manufacturing tobacco, but it was our father, with the help of the rest of your family, that has made this business into what it is today."

"Okay, so you came and said what you wanted to say. Now, I'll ask you politely to leave before I ask these fine people to escort you out."

Buck turned and headed toward the door. Before he reached it, he raised his fist in the air for all to see. "Brodie, you're not worthy of the Duke name!"

Brodie's voice began to crack as he spoke. "I'm not going to ask you again. You need to leave!"

Buck turned around and made his way toward the door, tossing chairs and slamming his fist on a table as he left. Several men stood up ready to come to Brodie's defense. Once his brother had closed the door behind him, Brodie announced, "Thank you, everyone, for being willing to come to my aid. As a way to thank you, S.R., the next round is on me."

As much as Brodie didn't want to let Buck's appearance bother him, he couldn't rid himself of the feeling of not being worthy. And the only way to get rid of the feeling was to drink. And Brodie did just that. So much so, that the last moment before Brodie passed out was spent in a mud puddle in Hayti. He remembered looking up into the sky, with the full moon shining so brightly that clouds appeared to race across the star-filled night. Then everything went blank.

23

1899-1900

There was something familiar about the light-skinned black man who stood peering down at him. Brodie's head was throbbing and an intense feeling of nausea swept over him. As he turned his head to the side to vomit, the soft-spoken man held a bowl under his chin to catch the contents of Brodie's stomach. Once the last of the spew hit the bowl, Brodie looked up again into the eyes of this man, who he still couldn't identify.

"Mr. Duke, are you okay?"

"I'm not sure." Brodie paused and continued to think of where he had seen this man before and, more importantly, where he was.

"Mr. Duke, you may not remember me, but my name is Aaron Moore, Dr. Aaron Moore."

As he processed this information, he realized exactly who this man was. He and his friend, John Merrick, had recently visited him and Julian Carr. They had been to his office to discuss plans for a religious school for the black citizens of Durham. At the time, Brodie didn't feel compelled to help them and had told them so.

"Where am I?"

"John found you about a block from here, in the middle of the road. He was headed to his barbershop and came to get me. We carried you here to his house. He asked if I would make sure you were okay."

The realization of where he was, and how he got here, caused Brodie to twinge with remorse. "I'm sorry to cause you such trouble."

"Well, it's not every day that we discover a white man in the middle of the street in Hayti. Do you have any idea of why you came to our parts last night?"

"I remember having an argument with my brother, Buck, at Carrington's Bar. Once he left, I must admit, I had quite a few drinks. But, how I got to Hayti is beyond me."

"Do you feel like sitting up?"

Brodie rested his weight on his elbows to determine if he was going to become nauseated. He took a deep breath and sat up, leaning his body against the headboard. He looked around the room and noticed a picture on the wall that was directly in front of him. It was a picture of Jesus, with dark skin and a halo around his head. Brodie had never seen a picture of Jesus portrayed in this way and it intrigued him.

Dr. Moore smiled at Brodie and asked, "By the way you're looking at that picture, I'm assuming you've never seen a picture of Jesus with dark skin?"

"No. To be honest, it's been awhile since I've even seen a white Jesus. After my first wife, Martha, died, I didn't feel the need to go back to church."

Brodie watched as Dr. Moore moved the bowl to the other side of the room. He then came over and sat down in a chair that was placed next to the bed. Brodie could taste the remains of vomit in his mouth, but ignored it. Given his situation, he believed he should return to the conversation that Dr. Moore had started in his office awhile back. "Tell me more about this religious school you're planning to build?"

Dr. Moore sat taller in his chair and a smile formed across his face. "Shaw University is one of the only institutes of higher learning for blacks in the state. You may not know this, but there are several very intelligent black men right here in Hayti, who are eager to attend school. Many of them to become preachers and teachers."

Brodie felt like he could be honest with Dr. Moore and began to share his own thoughts on the matter. "You know, my father, Washington, was always against slavery. When he purchased Caroline, it bothered him. So much so, that he later let her go, even before the war. I was upset when she wasn't there one day. Not so much because he let her go, but because we had become friends. She learned to read in no time. She was also good at arithmetic."

Brodie looked over at Dr. Moore who was listening intently. "And then, there was Elijah. He came from the Stagville Plantation and worked for my uncle for several years. We became close friends during those years on my uncle's farm. He was the only one who seemed to understand the suffering I had endured in Salisbury. Elijah didn't know how to read or write when he came to my uncle's."

Dr. Moore sat still as Brodie continued to speak. "Every night, before we went to bed, I would bring him books and a writing tablet." Brodie smiled to himself as he continued. "Elijah was desperate to learn to read and write. And, for me, being able to give him the gift of education was one of the only ways I've ever been able to turn my attention away from myself, and actually help someone else."

With Brodie lost in his memories, Dr. Moore waited a moment before speaking further. "Mr. Duke, would you like something to eat? Martha, John's wife, sure does fix a good breakfast. I can ask her to fix you some toast and see if you're well enough to get home."

"That would be very kind."

Dr. Moore got up, walked quietly across the room, opened the door, and walked out, leaving Brodie with the picture of Jesus looming over him. For a moment, he thought the black Jesus had smiled at him. A strange feeling swept over him. He blinked his eyes and the picture returned to its original form. Dr. Moore returned with two pieces of toast and a cup of hot coffee. "Here, now don't eat too fast."

Brodie took small bites of the toast and a sip of the hot brew. "So, what do you need for this religious school to be built?"

"We're having a meeting next week. If you could come, and bring Julian Carr, we would greatly appreciate it."

"Why Julian Carr?"

"We've had a couple of conversations about the education of black citizens in Durham. He's been involved in the development of Trinity College and, even though he might say some racist things, I do believe he wants our city to be a place where all people can be educated."

"I'll ask him, but I can't make any promises." Brodie tossed the blanket off and sat on the edge of the bed. "I think I'm feeling better now. I truly appreciate your care. I know you've been a doctor here for a long time. I've even heard that some white people in Durham ask for your help."

Dr. Moore pressed his glasses closer to his face. "The Lord called me to help others, no matter their color or their beliefs. Mr. Watts asked me to work at his hospital, but I declined. We'd like to have our own hospital, where black men can practice medicine and our women can be nurses. Right now, we've been working out of my house, but believe, one day, we'll have our own hospital. We already have a name for it."

"What are you going to call it?"

"Lincoln Hospital."

Just about that time, John's wife, Martha, appeared in the doorway. "Mr. Duke, is there anything else I can get you?"

Brodie liked the sound of her voice and was taken aback by how kind everyone had been. "No, I think I'm feeling well enough to walk home."

"We have a buggy and would be glad to take you."

Brodie placed his feet on the side of the bed and lifted himself up. He waited a moment to make sure he was going to be okay. Once he rose, he looked back at Martha. "Thanks, but I think the walk will do me good."

"If you insist."

"And, Dr. Moore, I can't promise you that Julian Carr will be at your meeting, but I can promise you that I will."

Later that day, Brodie returned home looking disheveled and smelling of vomit. He hoped he could sneak inside and upstairs before Minnie noticed him. As he entered, he heard Minnie wheezing as she sat in the parlor. He had noticed lately that she had been having trouble breathing. Even though he didn't want her to see him this way, his concern for her outweighed his embarrassed state. He walked over to her and placed his hand on her arm. "Are you okay?"

Minnie wheezed before speaking. "Where have you been?"

"That's a long story. I'm worried about you. I've noticed you've been having trouble breathing lately."

"The humidity in the air makes it difficult for me to breathe. I've been to the doctor, but they tell me that I won't get better here."

"What are you talking about?"

"The doctor told me that the air in California is much better for people with my condition."

"California!"

"I'm sorry." Minnie couldn't continue to speak due to her inability to breathe.

Brodie knew he had been harsh and felt bad. He had made it clear to Minnie that he didn't love her in the same way he had loved Martha. And as bad as he had treated her, she stayed with him. So, instead of trying to argue with her, he sat down and waited for her to catch her breath. Once she seemed a little better, he spoke. "Minnie, I'm the one who needs to be sorry. I've given you such a hard time about things. You deserve a better life and, if moving to California will improve your health, then I want to support that."

"Really?"

"Yes, really. So, is there a specific place in California you were thinking about?"

"My doctor has referred me to a doctor in Pasadena."

"So, when were you thinking of going?"

"I was hoping to go in the next few weeks. I'll be taking Woodward and I'd like Pearl to come with me."

"How about we travel as a family? I've heard California is beautiful and, if it turns out to be a place where you can feel better, then I'll support your living there."

"Thank you, Brodie. I hate to leave Durham, but I'm getting worse, not better."

Brodie sat back and thought of the benefits to this arrangement. He had always wanted to travel to California and this would give him the perfect opportunity. He also wanted Minnie to feel better and, hopefully, find some relief. But deep down, he also had a sinful motivation; for them to live apart. He still couldn't keep his mind off of Elizabeth and had recently heard that she had moved to Washington D.C. With Minnie gone, he could easily take the train up to Washington to, hopefully, kindle the fires that burned inside.

| 24 |

1901-1902

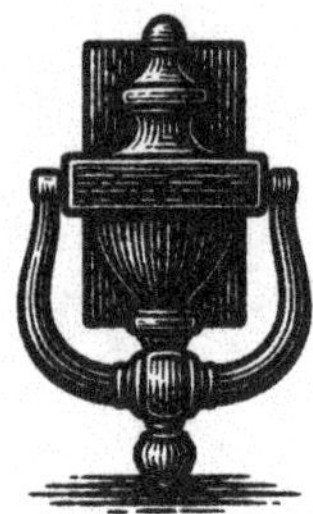

"Nannie, what is going on? I thought I'd been a good father to Mabel, but now she's gone behind my back and married Henry Goodall. I told her I wouldn't give her my blessing. And what does she do? She rides right by me on the way to the train station to catch a train to Raleigh, where Henry's father officiated their ceremony."

"Brodie, I'm not sure why you're asking me. I don't have children of my own."

Brodie had been walking toward his office and spotted Nannie coming from Trinity Methodist Church. He didn't know why he felt comfortable speaking to this woman, but he did. It might've been her willingness to give her honest opinion, no matter how hard it was to swallow. He thought of her as a sister and, now that Mary Elizabeth was gone, he enjoyed sharing his concerns with her.

"You might not have your own children, but I've seen you on the front porch of the Parrish house with your sister-in-law and her brood."

"That's true. Ever since Thomas suddenly died, I've definitely been pitching in."

"I'm sure you and Bettie have done a wonderful job with the children."

"Well, if you asked my brother, Richard, he might not agree with that assessment."

"Ever since Minnie moved out to California, neither of my daughters seem to listen to me. Woodrow is a momma's boy and Lawrence is living in Charlotte. I love Mabel, but believe Henry's family is too religious for my liking."

"Mabel is a grown woman with a mind of her own. I know you men think you know what is best for us, but I have to side with your daughter. She's an educated woman, with her own financial means. I'm sorry you placed her in this situation. If you had listened to what she wanted, you might've been walking down the aisle with her, instead of being left in the dust."

Brodie used his shoe to smooth out a clump of clay on the dirt road. He looked up and noticed the number of small wooden structures with slanted roofs. He counted the number of buildings he had built and took pride in his accomplishment. It seemed so easy to build a store or house but, when it came to women, he was lost. He was so irritated that Mabel would go off and elope. Who did that? All he could think of was how women should be kept in their place, and that particularly meant his wife and two daughters.

"So, how's Minnie doing in Pasadena?"

"She definitely is feeling better. I can understand why she wanted to move there. I just wish it wasn't so far away."

"Well, when you see her next, please let her know the women in her Tourist Club miss her. She always had an interesting story to tell about the places she had visited."

Just about this time, a shadow darkened the spot where they were standing. Brodie looked up and noticed a 120-foot steeple blocking the sun from their view. "Why did the Methodists feel the need to build such a tall steeple?"

"I'm not sure, but I believe the Methodists wanted to stand out from the Baptists."

"What is this town becoming? First the Baptists, then the Methodists and, just recently, the finishing of First Presbyterian's massive structure. Next the Catholics will be coming here from the north."

"Brodie, I know you haven't been a churchgoer since Martha's death, but it might do you some good."

"No, thank you. I have enough guilt without having self-righteous religious nuts telling me what a bad person I am."

Nannie sighed and shook her head. It was clear she wanted to change the subject. "Brodie, now that Mabel is married and Minnie is in California, what are your plans?"

Brodie thought a moment and then answered, "I don't know."

But Brodie did know. He had received several letters from Elizabeth Broadbeck and was communicating with her on a regular basis. They had even discussed the possibility of him visiting her in Washington.

Several months later, Brodie found himself walking toward Dillard Street to catch the train headed north. As he drew closer to the tracks, he had to smile as he glanced over at Julian Carr's Somerset Villa. The train station, located at the back edge of Julian's property, with its small simple building and odd-shaped roof, was such a contrast to Julian's Queen Anne Victorian-style home. As he looked over toward the manicured lawn and trimmed shrubs, Brodie wondered how many people, waiting for a train, were tempted to sneak into Julian's yard and climb the large turret that was capped with an ornate copper weathervane.

His thoughts were interrupted by the loud steam whistle as the train pulled into the station. He waited a moment to allow the arrivals to make their way out of the train and onto the platform. Just as he was getting ready to enter into his train car, he brushed up against a man balancing his weight on a cane. "Richard Wright, how are you?"

"I'm tired and ready to be home for a while."

"So, have you been off on one of your global trips?"

"I have. This time I spent time in Egypt and South Africa."

"I can't imagine traveling to those God-forsaken places with two good legs. I have to admit, I admire your willingness to travel with only one good leg."

"Well, given that your tobacco company holds the rights to selling the Bonsack machine here in America, I have no choice but to go to the ends of the earth, even when I have only one good leg."

"Well, I sure can't argue with that."

"So, where are you headed?"

"Washington, D.C."

"I didn't know you had business dealings there."

"Richard, I need to get to my seat, but maybe, when we're both in Durham, we can have a meal together. Now that Minnie is in California and my daughters have moved out, I'm free to come and go as I please."

Brodie turned and walked up the stairs, then down the narrow aisle, where he found a seat. Looking out the window, he saw Richard hobbling across the platform and thought to himself,

"That is one determined man on his way to make a fortune, no matter where he has to go to obtain it."

Brodie hadn't felt so excited about seeing someone in a long time. It had been eight years since his time in Illinois and he knew that he had aged. His beard was beginning to show signs of gray and his waistline had expanded. But, even so, he thought he looked good for a man in his mid-fifties.

Once the train finally stopped in Washington, D.C., Brodie made his way from the train station to the address Elizabeth gave him. As he walked, he began to question why he had come. He had just explained to Nannie that he couldn't figure women out, so why did he want another woman in his life? Also, he hadn't seen Elizabeth since their time in Illinois and, for all he knew, she may no longer be appealing. But, even with all the reasons why he shouldn't pursue this woman, he continued in her direction.

When Brodie arrived, he looked up at the large brownstone building with its ornate details. His hands began to shake and he felt his heart pound in his chest. But, as nervous as he was, he was determined to see if he still had feelings for Elizabeth. He took a deep breath, walked up the steps, and raised the doorknocker in his hand. After knocking several times, with no response, he turned to leave. He began to feel like a fool for coming and was just about to walk away, when the door opened.

| 25 |

1903

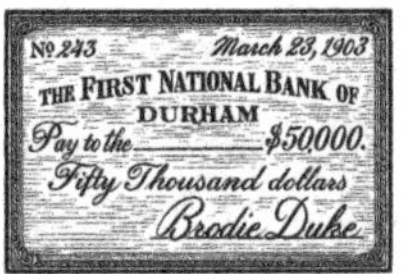

As Brodie reflected back over the previous year, he couldn't recall a time that he'd felt so drawn to another human being. He was possessed by the emotional rollercoaster he had been on since Elizabeth's door had opened. It wasn't necessarily her beauty that had captivated him, or the way she had looked into his blue eyes and, with a soft voice, told him to enter. It wasn't the smell of her perfume or how she had her hair pinned up with a couple of loose curls touching her exposed skin.

If Brodie could define what attracted him to this woman, it would be her aura. Plain and simple. Her distinctive and pervasive character pulled him in and captured his heart. And from the moment he saw her standing in the doorway of her Washington brownstone, he was like a puppy dog wanting only to please this woman, whom he had come to believe was his soulmate.

The first meeting started off with both Elizabeth and Brodie trying to keep their distance. But after only a few minutes, they realized that this time, there would be a physical relationship. Unlike the homes Brodie occupied, there were no maids, servants, or children around. Elizabeth, now a divorced woman, had sent her maid home early, allowing them the freedom to discover the intimacy they both hungered for.

Brodie promised himself he would never forget the feelings of satisfaction as he lay bare on the white cotton sheets. Elizabeth had turned and fallen asleep on her side. He glanced over to see the way her hips sloped downward toward her small waistline. The curls, that had been bound, were now flowing over her pillow, creating a desire for him to catch a lock and twist it in his fingers.

The large clock in the hall ticked away the seconds as clouds raced across the sky. He thought for a moment of how he should feel guilty for sleeping with this woman, but the feelings didn't come. Instead, he believed he had found what he had been searching for his entire life.

Several days went by and Brodie never left the brownstone. The two spent most of their days in the bed or sipping bourbon until late into the night. They talked incessantly about the years that had separated them, making promises of finding a way to be together for the rest of their lives.

When the day finally came that Brodie knew he must return to Durham, his mood was somber. He sat at the small table they had occupied to sip their coffee, wishing he could figure out a way to stay. As he stirred a spoonful of sugar into the cup, he looked up to see Elizabeth smiling at him. "Why are you smiling?"

"Brodie, I've loved every moment you've been with me and hate the thought of you leaving."

"But I don't want to leave. There is nothing about my life outside of this brownstone that means anything to me."

Elizabeth ran her finger along Brodie's cheekbone. "There is something that I haven't told you."

"What?"

"Well, when I left my husband, he stopped supporting me."

"So, how were you able to move here and have such nice things?"

"That really doesn't matter now. But." Elizabeth hesitated a moment.

"What? You can tell me. I'll do anything to help."

"I'm being evicted from my home, and have no choice but to move back to Kansas City."

"Darling, what can I do to help?"

Elizabeth lowered her head and didn't speak. Finally, after an intense fear of losing her swept over him, Brodie said, "Elizabeth, it doesn't matter. What do you need? I can help you."

"I never meant to bring you into this mess. I thought the matter would be resolved, but it hasn't."

"What mess? Please tell me."

"Let me just say, I've made some bad decisions in the last few years. I was resigned to leave and go back to Kansas City. It was at that moment that you contacted me."

"Elizabeth, I love you, and am willing to provide whatever you need."

"No. Go back to Minnie. She's your wife."

"You're the only one who I want to be with. Let me know what you need and I'll get it for you."

Elizabeth looked up and, with a soft voice said, "Brodie, I need fifty thousand dollars."

Brodie gasped.

Elizabeth quickly responded. "I meant it. Go back to Minnie. I'll be okay."

Brodie reached for Elizabeth's arm. "No! I'm not going back to Minnie. If you need fifty thousand dollars, I'll get it. I can sell my stock in the Durham Belt Line. It's worth about that."

Elizabeth's eyes welled up with tears. "You would do that for me?"

"Yes, I'll do that for you. I love you and want to be with you. And, if you need fifty thousand dollars in order to stay here in Washington, I'll get it for you. I'll need my attorneys to have Minnie sign the papers and then, once I sell my stock, I'll get you the money. Until then, I can write you a check for a couple thousand dollars."

Brodie looked over at Elizabeth who was now crying. "You would do that for me?"

Brodie rose and took Elizabeth in his arms. He kissed her on the lips. She placed her arms around his neck and they stood there for a moment.

Knowing it was time to leave, he pulled out his checkbook, wrote a check for two thousand dollars, and placed it on the table. "Now, Darling, I'll return in a couple of weeks. I love you and want to be with you forever."

Brodie did return with a check in hand. He never questioned Elizabeth about why she needed the money. He didn't care. All he wanted was to be with this woman.

| 26 |

1903

"Brodie, Pearl and I traveled across the United States in order to spend time with you. Ever since we've been in Brooklyn, you've been preoccupied and downright mean."

"I didn't ask you to come. Anyway, if I remember correctly, you were coming for the restaurants and shows."

"Dad, I came to see you. And Minnie is right, you haven't been your usual cordial self. What is wrong?"

Neither Minnie nor Pearl knew what Brodie was thinking and he intended to keep it that way. Even though he had given Elizabeth the fifty thousand dollars, she was still threatening to leave Washington. Just the thought of her going back to Kansas City made Brodie even more determined to spend time with her and, somehow, figure out a way to get out of his marriage. At this point, he really didn't care what Minnie, or any of his family members, thought about his strange behavior.

"Pearl, darling girl, I'm sorry if I've been rude. It's just that I have a lot on my mind and some important matters I need to tend to."

"Dad, if you could share with us what is going on, we might be able to help."

Just then, there was a knock on the hotel room door. Brodie, thankful for the interruption, called out, "Yes?"

A voice from the other side of the door could be clearly heard. "There is a telegram for Mr. Duke from Washington, D.C."

Brodie quickly got up from his chair and walked over to the door. He opened it wide enough to see a young man with a piece of paper in his hand. He pulled out a couple of coins from his pocket and exchanged them for the neatly folded telegram. "Thank you."

Brodie opened the paper and quickly skimmed the contents. He turned toward Pearl and stated, "I need to go."

Minnie responded, "Go where?"

"I'm leaving for Washington. I'll pay for this room for two more days. Then I expect you to return to California."

Minnie slumped back in her chair. Pearl stood up to confront her father. "Dad, what are you doing? We aren't stupid. We know there is someone in Washington who you're seeing."

"Yes. You're correct. Minnie, you know as much as I do, that we are married for all the wrong reasons."

"I don't agree. We have a beautiful son and I know your children have benefited from our marriage."

"I'm not going to argue with that. But, it's time for our marriage to end."

"No, Brodie. I'm not going to stand by and allow you to end our marriage."

Brodie picked up his briefcase and coat, turned, and walked out of the room. "We'll see about that!"

As Brodie slammed the door behind him, he could hear Pearl's voice pleading with him to stay. Even though he didn't want to disappoint his daughter, he knew he needed to see Elizabeth. So, feeling a strong desire to reach the woman he loved, he walked down the steps, passed the doorman at the front door, and headed toward Grand Central Station, where he caught a train to Washington.

For the next couple of months, Brodie spent a great deal of time in the brownstone apartment that felt more like home than his own house in Durham. Just like drinking, or gambling with commodities, Brodie couldn't get enough of Elizabeth. He was willing to do anything for this woman, and the first thing on his list was to divorce Minnie.

One day, as Brodie and Elizabeth were lying in bed, he brought up his idea. "Elizabeth, I want to marry you."

Elizabeth rested her elbow on the bed and looked at Brodie. "Now, Darling, how can that be possible? You're married to Minnie."

"I've been doing some thinking. I'm going to hire a private detective to go to California to search for Minnie."

"But you know where she is."

"I believe, if I can make people think that she deserted me, I'll have a case against her."

Brodie sat up and looked right at Elizabeth. "That's what I'm going to do. I'm going to put an article in the Los Angeles Express asking people to help locate Minnie."

"Oh, I see where you're headed. Given that she's been in California for the last two years, it can definitely appear like she deserted you."

"After I place the article in the newspaper, I'll have my attorneys publish a summons for her to be present in court. This way it'll look like she has willfully refused to live with me."

In November 1903, Brodie published this notice in the Durham Daily Sun.

North Carolina Superior Court, Durham County, November 2nd, 1903, Notice of Publication of Summons

B.L. Duke vs. Minnie W. Duke

The defendant above named, Minnie W. Duke, is hereby notified that an action has been brought against her entitled B.L. Duke vs. Minnie W. Duke, returnable to the December term of Durham Superior Court to be held at the Court House in Durham, North Carolina, on the thirteenth Monday after the first Monday in December 1903, the object of which action is to wholly exclude the said defendant from any interest in the lands of said B.L. Duke, which lie in said county and state of North Carolina, and the counties of said state, and to remove the cloud which her said claim has cast upon the title to said lands and enable him to sell or dispose of said lands freed from any claim of her and she is hereby duly notified to appear at the above time and place to answer said complaint as required by law, otherwise the prayer of the plaintiff's complaint will be granted. C.B. Green Clerk Superior Court.

Once Minnie saw that Brodie was determined to make it look like she had abandoned him, she called in a Los Angeles reporter to give her side of the story. On November 12th, this article appeared in the Los Angeles Times.

Mrs. Duke Speaks Out Against Her Husband.

Pasadena Woman Declares She Will Fight in Court.

Wife of Eastern Tobacco Man Makes Flat Denial of Sensational Hiding. Tale Published by Los Angeles Express—Her story.

Pasadena. Office of the Times No. 26 South Raymond Avenue. Nov. 12—Mrs. Brodie L. Duke, a charming woman living on South Orange Grove in Pasadena, has been brought into sensational prominence by an article published in the Express Tuesday night, which she claims to be absolutely false. The article asserted that hotel registers had been searched for months by detectives and attorneys in an endeavor to find her and that it was presumed that she was somewhere in Southern California under an assumed name and that she had left her husband about a year ago, voluntarily, and that she has repeatedly refused to live with him.

"Much as I regret to be discussed in the newspapers," said Mrs. Duke last night, "I feel that the time has come to speak plainly and that, in justice to myself and my son, I should tell the straightforward facts about this matter. Mr. Duke has been living with me on South Orange Grove the greater portion of the first part of this year. He did not go East until almost the last of July, and has been corresponding with me ever since. I received my last letter from him three weeks ago. The detectives have known where I lived, for one of them came to the house during my absence and tried to force the maid to allow him to enter. His intention was to get certain papers, which I have in keeping there. I have never left my husband and I came to California for my health. The statements are false and I consider the whole matter published in the newspaper from beginning to end as simply a subterfuge on the part of my husband and his detectives, attorneys, etc., to endeavor to force me to sign certain papers. It is alleged that a suit is to be brought against me by Mr. Duke to quit title on the property which I have refused to sign away, and that he is to introduce divorce proceedings. These two statements are probably true, and I am going to leave for Durham very shortly and will fight both proceedings in court."

Brodie Duke is the eldest son of W. Duke, founder of the great American Tobacco trust. His brothers are J.B. Duke, president, and Ben Duke, treasurer. Brodie is a large stockholder, but has not taken an active interest in the business for several years. He married Miss Minnie Woodward of Gadsden, Alabama, who was a handsome southern girl well known throughout Tennessee and Alabama. Mr. Duke was a widower and had two little girls. During the time that these children were growing up, and while they needed the care of their new mother, the husband was most devoted to his wife. But, as soon as they reached the age when her care was no longer necessary, he endeavored to thrust her aside and devoted his attentions elsewhere, she asserts.

Mrs. Duke, breaking down in health, was brought to California, her stepdaughter, Miss Pearl Duke, accompanying her. They spent a season at the Casa Grande, where Mr. Duke joined them, and then Mrs. Duke, becoming infatuated with California, bought a beautiful residence at No. 1045 South Orange Grove Avenue, where she has since been living until a week ago when she moved over to the Maryland, expecting to remain there for the winter and lease her house. Now her intentions are to go East, at once, and fight the cases in court.

"Within the past two years," said Mrs. Duke, "my husband has forced me to sign my name to deeds worth over $150,000. He sold the Durham Belt Line railroad for $50,000 and I signed the paper. Real estate to the amount of $35,000 has gone, my signature having been placed on the deeds, two mortgages, amounting to $40,000, stocks and other things. The last demand was only for a property amounting to $17,000, a small sum in comparison with the others, but I felt that the time had come to call a halt, and I sent the papers back unsigned. Now, he has resorted to the disappearance story to attempt to force me to sign this paper."

As to the claim that Mr. Duke did not know where his wife was in California, E.H. Groenendyke, who has had charge of Mrs. Duke's affairs, said yesterday: "Mr. Duke was here at the time of the buying of the property on South Orange Grove and he was most persuasive in his endeavor to get Mrs. Duke to remain out here. He had other interests in Washington, D.C., and wished to be unencumbered. When Mrs. Duke went back East, after spending the season here, she was to meet her husband in Brooklyn. He came and visited with Mrs. Duke and Miss Duke for two days and then had a sudden call to Washington. The day after he left, a packet of letters arrived from his private secretary in Durham, the letters having been written by a woman in Washington, and it is these letters which will be introduced in court as evidence, and it was these letters which the private detective endeavored to obtain from the maid at the house on Orange Grove."

The following telegram was sent to the Durham Daily Sun, wherein the substance of the report in the Express was published: "Publish in Durham and Raleigh. Any person wishing to communicate with Mrs. Brodie L. Duke of Durham, N.C., will find me at my home, 1045 South Orange Grove Avenue, Pasadena, California, or by applying to my husband, Brodie L. Duke, now in Durham, having returned East after several months visit with us in house here, and who has been in constant communication with me until he went to the Durham Hospital three weeks ago." Mrs. Brodie L. Duke signed the telegram.

Mrs. Duke has the article published in the Durham papers and says Duke was in Durham at the time of the publication. Mrs. Duke is in receipt of a letter from Mrs. Rivers Goodall, Mr. Duke's daughter (Mrs. Duke's stepdaughter), inviting her to stay with her upon her arrival at Durham and expressing the deepest sympathy for the sad state of affairs. A portion of the letter reads: "We were all shocked beyond expression by the account in the morning papers of Papa's proceedings. I write at once to tell you that if you should come home to fight it, I shall certainly expect you to stay with us and we should be hurt if you stayed with anybody else. I am truly, heartily sorry that such a thing has happened but, of course, none of us can help it. Papa is a queer creature and I don't suppose anyone on earth ever knew him."

"I would not contest the abominable business, except for my children's sake, and you may be sure that no divorce will ever be sought by me and I shall fight it," said Mrs. Duke last night.

Mrs. Duke has made many warm friends during her stay in Pasadena, who are highly indignant over the injustice which they assert has been done her.

The newspaper article was published all over the country and was talked about by everyone with a desire to speak poorly of the wealthy tobacco family. People from all walks of life were taking sides over what should happen next. But all the gossip didn't bother Brodie. He was determined to be with Elizabeth, no matter the financial cost or damage it would do to his character. Nothing was going to stop him. He would take Minnie to court and be free of her. Free to be with the woman he loved.

But little did Brodie know, that, as powerful as he was, he had no control of what was to happen next.

| 27 |

1903

When Brodie was summoned to Fairview, Washington Duke's residence, he felt in the pit of his stomach that this visit was going to be difficult. Everyone, including his father, had seen the newspaper articles that had circulated across the country, placing a black smudge on the Duke name. But what transpired on this particular day, set off a series of events that would eventually sever his relationship with his family, particularly Buck.

"Good afternoon, Mr. Duke."

Brodie took off his hat and coat and handed them to James.

"Your father and brothers are in the office. Is there something that I can get you?"

Brodie walked by the butler. "No, James. I don't think I'll be here very long."

He walked through the foyer to the back of the house, noticing the expensive paintings that hung on the walls and the classy chandelier that sent a prism of light across the room. It was clear that Washington had recently hired a decorator to refurbish the house. Brodie had always thought of his father's style as conservative, and he found the changes to be strange and out of character.

As he approached the back office, he heard Buck speaking loudly. "Now that we have finally put that bull to death and bought out the W.T. Blackwell Company, I would like to expand the building on the corner of Pettigrew and Blackwell Streets. Of all the companies we have acquired, I must admit that this one brings me the most pleasure." Brodie couldn't help butimagine his brother's smirk as he continued. "I never thought, back in the early 1880s, that we would acquire almost every profitable tobacco company in the world."

Washington looked in Brodie's direction. "Son, come in. We're having a discussion about what Buck plans on doing with the old Blackwell building."

Even though they hadn't seen each other in months, Buck, who was lighting a cigarette, made no attempt to greet him. On the other hand, Benjamin, who was sitting in a leather-bound chair, rose and extended his hand. "Brodie, it's good to see you."

Buck took a drag off of his cigarette and placed it in the ashtray. "Well, now that Brodie is here, I'd like to get to the point. I have several important meetings to attend before going back to New York."

Brodie couldn't help but feel all three men looking in his direction. Washington cleared his throat. "Brodie, we wanted to have this family meeting to discuss the recent events that we keep reading about in the newspaper."

"What? Do you mean the articles pertaining to the termination of my marriage with Minnie?"

"Yes."

"I believe that is between the two of us."

Buck took another drag from his cigarette and blew the smoke in Brodie's direction. "I must disagree. We have a reputation to keep and you, and your foolish behavior, are tarnishing it."

"Well, at least I am open about my affairs. You, on the other hand, have been keeping your relationship with Mrs. Lillian McCredy from father."

Buck's face flushed with color, and his hands clenched tightly, as he walked in Brodie's direction. Washington stood up and spoke in a stern voice, "There will be no violence in my home."

Brodie was elated when he realized the attention was now being placed on his younger brother. He was tired of everyone thinking Buck was perfect. Yes, he was an excellent businessman, but he also had his faults and it was great to be able to share some of them with their father.

Washington sat back down and looked at Buck. "Is this true? Are you having an affair with a married woman?"

"No, it isn't. Lillian is a widow. But, yes, we have been seeing each other and enjoy each other's company."

Washington shook his head. "Buck, you're forty-eight years old and I can't tell you what to do, but you have been raised in the Methodist Church and you know what the Good Lord thinks about sexual immorality."

Buck lowered his head and softly answered, "Yes, Father."

Washington appeared very upset by the news. The older man remained silent for a moment, then looked toward Buck, and responded, "I hope you can make it right in the sight of the Lord."

Buck gave Brodie a disapproving look. "I'll consider it."

Benjamin, trying to be the peacemaker, said, "Father, I did know about Buck's relationship and I do believe he'll try and do the right thing. Now can we change the subject?"

Buck stood up. "Yeah, let's get to the point of why we're here."

Brodie looked around and noticed that everyone was staring at him. "What are you all looking at me for?"

Washington cleared his throat. "Just the other day, I ran into a clergyman asking if he could hold prayer meetings in the tobacco warehouse."

Brodie looked around the room. "So? What does this have to do with me?"

Washington replied, "He told me he used to know you before he was saved for the clergy. He specifically told me that we need to pray for you."

A feeling of anger swept through Brodie's veins. He was sick and tired of people judging him. He knew he had been making some bad decisions, but he had never intentionally hurt anyone.

"So, what do you want me to say?"

Buck practically screamed. "You are making a mockery of our name. If you weren't my half-brother, I would cut you off from every dime you have received since I made this company what it is today."

Brodie felt his hands clench and was overtaken by a strong desire to stand up and hit Buck, but he knew that would accomplish nothing. So instead, he took a couple of deep breaths and, in a calm voice, spoke. "Oh, now the truth is coming out."

Benjamin was the next to speak. "Now, Brodie, you can see how it pains Pa to discuss how your misconduct is impacting our family. Your behavior has attracted attention from the press all over this country. For me, I'm concerned for your safety." Benjamin paused a moment, turned, and placed his attention onto his younger brother. "We all know how much effort you have put into this company, and I, for one, appreciate it. But I also know that it hasn't helped Brodie to have you always breathing down his neck."

The room went silent. Brodie wanted to defend himself, but when he looked over at his father, slumped in his chair, looking small and vulnerable, he decided to refrain from speaking. Instead, he walked over to his father, leaned down at eye level and, with all the sincerity he could muster, hugged him as he spoke. "Pa, I'll try. That's all I can do."

And before anyone could say another word, Brodie turned, walked out of the room, grabbed his coat from James, and made his way out into the streets of Durham.

28

1904

Press from as far as New York City had come to make sure their readers wouldn't miss out on the court proceedings that were going on in the Durham County Courthouse. The buzz around town was that the court proceedings would last at least a couple of days and that neither party was going to back down.

Every seat in the courthouse was taken. People were jammed outside on the courthouse steps, waiting to hear from anyone who would come out to report what was happening. Thankfully, the proceedings had been postponed to March and it was neither too cold nor too hot. The windows were open and the backs of people were visible from the crowd down below.

Everyone stood as Judge Cook walked into the courtroom. Once the bailiff called the court to order, people settled in, hoping for a juicy story of infidelity and a woman's pursuit of her husband's wealth. But, little did anyone know, the proceedings wouldn't go in the manner the press had predicted.

Brodie was called to the stand to share his side of the story. He looked around the courtroom and was surprised at the number of people in attendance. He then focused his gaze on the twelve people sitting in the jury box. His attorney began the questioning. "Mr. Duke, can you please let us know what has transpired between you and your wife, Mrs. Minnie Woodward Duke, to provide the evidence needed for the court to grant your request for a divorce."

Brodie sat up as straight as he could to project an attitude of confidence. He knew what he was about to say was a lie, but being with Elizabeth was more important to him than being morally righteous. He cleared his throat and began speaking. "I met Mrs. Duke in Gadsden, Alabama, over ten years ago. When we married, we had agreed that this was not a marriage based on love, but for what was best for my children, as well as for her to be able to enjoy a prosperous lifestyle."

Several people began to murmur from the back of the courtroom. In order to retain order, Judge Cook spoke up. "There will be order in my courtroom. If you can't remain silent during Mr. Duke's testimony, I will have you escorted out."

Immediately, the murmuring stopped. Judge Cook paused a moment, making sure everyone was silent before speaking. "Mr. Duke, you can continue."

"As I was saying, Mrs. Duke and I agreed to this marriage, knowing that there was a possibility that one of us may try and put an end to it. Anyway, two years ago, Mrs. Duke told me that she was moving to California. I didn't support this decision, but she left me anyway. She took our son, Woodward, with her, keeping him from me. But even so, I want the members of the jury to know that I have dutifully continued to provide support for him."

Brodie looked over at Minnie to gauge her reaction to his words and noticed her shaking her head in disbelief. He continued. "A year ago, I had an offer to sell some property at a good price. Given that Minnie's name was on the deed, I asked her to sign the property over to me. And she promptly refused. I also had several other properties that I wanted to sell, but couldn't, because I didn't know where she was living. It was as if she and Woodward had vanished. It was at this point that I hired a private detective to search for her, and it was then that she was located in Pasadena, California."

As Brodie finished his testimony, he spotted several of Minnie's friends in the audience. They were shaking their heads, trying to convey to the jury that he was lying. He then turned his attention to where his daughters were sitting. Both Pearl and Mabel were directly behind Minnie. As he looked at them, Pearl reached over and placed her hand on Minnie's shoulder. He was surprised at his feeling of anger toward his daughters. They seemed to have turned on him in support of this woman.

After Brodie finished speaking, his attorney sat back down. Judge Cook looked over at Minnie's attorney and asked, "Do you have any questions for Mr. Duke?"

It was at this point, that the people leaned in, ready to catch Brodie in a lie. But Brodie didn't flinch or display any emotion. The attorney stood, looked at Minnie, and then stated, "No, Your Honor, we have no questions for Mr. Duke."

Shockwaves ran wild in the courtroom. People who had been summoned to testify on Minnie's behalf appeared stunned. The audience began mumbling and then voices were heard shouting out to the people on the streets. Judge Cook banged his gavel onto the walnut desk. "We will have no more talking in my courtroom!"

Once silence prevailed, Judge Cook continued, "Mr. Duke, you may leave the bench."

Brodie stood up and walked to the table where he and his attorneys sat. Once he was seated, Judge Cook looked toward the jury box. "At this point, given the evidence you have heard, I am going to ask you to answer the following questions to determine if a divorce should be granted."

Judge Cook looked down at a piece of paper and asked, "First. Were plaintiff and defendant married as alleged?"

The jury responded, "Yes."

"Second. Did defendant willfully and, without cause, in the month of February 1901, abandon the plaintiff, and has she lived separate and apart from him since said date?"

The jury responded, "Yes."

"Third. Has plaintiff been a bona fide resident of the state for the past ten years?"

The jury responded, "Yes."

"Fourth. Has defendant willfully, and without just cause, abandoned him and refused to live with him, as alleged in the original complaint?"

The jury responded, "Yes."

"Fifth. Has defendant any right of estate of her husband?"

The jury responded, "Yes."

"Sixth. Does defendant claim an estate, or interest in, the real property of plaintiff adverse to him, and does such claim cast a cloud upon the title of said property?"

The jury responded, "Yes."

"Seventh. Ought the cloud, which such claim of the defendant casts upon said property be removed by this court?"

The jury responded, "Yes."

Once the final question was answered, Judge Cook stated, in a loud and clear voice, "The following order shall be recorded in the docket. The court doth here now, upon the consideration of the complaint, and the amendment to the complaint, and in answer of the defendant filed to complaint, and the amended complaint, consider, order and adjudge upon such verdict, that the bonds of matrimony, heretofore existing between the plaintiff, B.L. Duke, and the defendant, Minnie W. Duke, be, and the same are hereby dissolved, and the court doth further consider, order, and adjudge, that the said, Minnie W. Duke, has no right of estate in the property of B.L. Duke, the plaintiff, which the defendant has made adverse to him, causes a cloud upon the title to the real estate of the plaintiff, and that said cloud ought to be removed, and this judgment and decree should operate, and does hereby operate, to remove all such cloud from the property of said plaintiff."

The decree was signed by the Judge and docketed. He turned toward the jury. "Thank you for your service." He then rose, banged his gavel on his desk, and proclaimed, "Court is now adjourned!"

Many of the audience sat in silence, trying to process what had just transpired. Several women flocked around Minnie, letting her know that they believed her name had been slandered. On the other hand, men who had benefited from Brodie's wealth came over to shake his hand and pat him on the back.

Brodie felt a bit guilty over the ease of the proceedings, but was elated at the thought of being with Elizabeth. Earlier in the day, he and Minnie had argued over the terms of the settlement. Minnie had initially demanded $75,000, but Brodie felt $25,000 was sufficient. Finally, they had agreed she would receive $30,000.

After the finances were settled, they discussed the custody of Woodward. As much as he loved his son, Brodie knew that Woodward would be better off with Minnie and her family. So, Woodward was sent to Gadsden, Alabama, to stay with Minnie's brother until the details pertaining to his custody could be settled.

When Brodie turned to leave, every person had their eyes fixed in his direction. Several women near Minnie pointed at Brodie. One spoke up. "You should be ashamed, Brodie Duke. Minnie is a good woman and did nothing to deserve such horrendous treatment."

Brodie walked behind his attorney, through the massive crowd, out the door, and down the stairs. He ignored the angry words that many yelled in his direction. They could yell all they wanted. He was free and could now openly pursue the woman of his dreams.

29

1904

The sound of the train whistle woke Brodie from his deep slumber. He wiped his beard of the moisture that had seeped out of his mouth while he slept. Looking out the window, he saw that a dense fog had settled in overnight. He heard the squeaking noise of steel on steel as the brakes grinded to a halt.

His first thoughts revolved around the latest events and his new-found freedom. A feeling of elation swept over him as the train pulled into the Washington, D.C., station. It had been several weeks since he had seen Elizabeth. He had decided it was best to keep her off of the front-page news while he finished up the proceedings that would finalize his divorce from Minnie.

During their last visit, Brodie had given Elizabeth the last large sum of money he had in order for her to invest in an upscale apartment in Alexandria, right outside of Washington. He had no regrets that his money was being spent on her, the love of his life. Just imagining her inside their new home was almost too much for him to bear.

Once the train stopped and the doors were opened, Brodie grabbed his bag and walked out into the cool March air. The fog was still dense and the air was wet and cold. He pulled his coat closer to his body and began walking through the throngs of people scattered around the train station. He had made this walk many times, but this time was different. This time he was a free man.

Brodie reached the apartment building and approached the doorman. "Good morning, Charlie."

Charlie, who had greeted him many times, displayed an expression of surprise on his face. "Good morning, Mr. Duke." The older man, with the neatly pressed suit and shiny shoes, paused a moment.

"Charlie, is everything okay?"

Brodie began to feel nervous and wondered why he was not being greeted in the manner he had become accustomed to. "Charlie, you're making me nervous."

"I'm just surprised to see you."

"Why would that be? I told you that I would be returning to Washington after my divorce was finalized. Now that I am finally divorced, I plan to make a life with Mrs. Broadbeck."

"Mr. Duke, I have something to tell you."

"Is Elizabeth well?"

"Yes. She's fine."

"Charlie, you're scaring me. What do you want to tell me?"

"Mr. Duke, Mrs. Broadbeck is gone."

"What do you mean gone?"

"She left about two weeks ago."

"Where did she go?"

"Mr. Duke, she wouldn't tell me. Wherever it was, she left in a hurry."

"I'm going to go up and see for myself." Brodie moved past Charlie and walked up the two flights of stairs that led to the third-floor apartment. He could hear Charlie calling something behind him, but wasn't sure what he was saying. All he knew was that he had to find Elizabeth.

When he reached the door, he took out his key and tried to open it, but found it locked. He tried again, but it wouldn't turn. Suddenly, the door opened and a strange man was standing in the entryway. The man, wearing a stern face asked, "Can I help you?"

"Who are you?"

"I own this apartment. Who are you?"

"What happened to Elizabeth?"

"Oh, you must be the man that she warned me about. She said you may come looking for her."

Brodie could feel heat rising in his veins and a sudden sensation of fear pounding in his heart. He pushed past the man and screamed out, "I have to find Elizabeth! Where is she?"

"Mister, you can see that she is gone and this is no longer her residence. I paid her good money for this apartment, and now I'm going to ask you to leave."

At this point, Charlie was hovering in the hallway. "Mr. Duke, you'll need to leave. Mr. Stagg is correct. Mrs. Broadbeck sold this apartment to him a few weeks back. Neither he nor I know her whereabouts. Apparently, she did not want you to find her."

Brodie wouldn't, nor couldn't, believe these words. Elizabeth was not the type of woman who would betray him. She was sensitive and loving and had spoken often of the life they were going to have together. She had never given off the impression that she wanted anything from him but his love.

He looked up at the two men standing in front of him and ran out of the apartment, down the stairs, and into the street. The fog had cleared and large, puffy clouds raced above him. The early morning sun blinded him as he walked east. He wasn't sure where he was going. All he knew was that he had to find Elizabeth.

Two days later, he was back sitting in his office in Durham. He had contacted the same private detective he had used to locate Minnie. But this time was different. This time he truly didn't know where Elizabeth was, while he always knew where Minnie had been.

"John, I need to find this woman."

"Mr. Duke, I'll do the best I can. But, as you know, this can become complicated. First, we don't know why she has left and if she wants to be found."

"She would never betray me. She loves me!"

"You may not want my thoughts on the matter, but it looks like she was using you for your money."

Brodie ignored the statement. "Hell, John, all I want is to find Elizabeth. I love her and want to spend the rest of my life with her."

"So, let's consider the worst scenario. What if she doesn't want to see you? What if she was only after your money?"

Brodie slumped back in his chair. "I cannot accept that. I want to talk with her." Brodie stood up.

"Mr. Duke, I'll do my best, but I don't have high hopes."

Brodie glared at John. "All I know is that I love Elizabeth and believe she'll have a plausible explanation as to why she left." Then, as if he was trying to convince himself to believe everything was going to work out, he yelled at John, "I don't give a damn what you have to do! Just find her!"

John walked out of his office and Brodie laid his head down on his desk and began muttering to himself. "I have to find her. I just have to. I'm supposed to be with Elizabeth and live happily ever after."

| 30 |

1904

Ever since his return to Durham, Brodie had avoided his family. He knew they were disturbed by his treatment of Minnie and didn't want to hear their reprimands. But, as much as he wanted to avoid them, he knew he needed to see his father. Washington's health had been failing for several months and Brodie didn't know how much longer his father would be around.

Brodie knew his father usually took a nap around 1:00 pm and arose around 3:30, so he decided to walk over from his office to the home that had become a landmark in Durham. It always amazed Brodie how well the landscaper kept his father's yard. Every inch of the property was covered with lush, green grass except for the well-manicured flower beds. This time of year, the daffodils had begun to spring up and the yellow flowers served as a striking backdrop to the beautiful Victorian-style house.

Looking out over the stunning green lawn, he thought about a story he had recently heard. Apparently, one of the students from Trinity College had walked by one day and spoke to his father, commenting about his beautiful yard. Washington had responded by telling the young man that he was welcome to come over any time and lie down on it. And sure enough, one day, his father had looked out the front window and there was the young man lying down in the middle of the yard.

Today, as Brodie walked up to the entrance of Fairview, he began to feel anxious about how his father would respond to his recent divorce. He never intended to hurt his father and would never do anything to jeopardize his health. When he reached the porch, he took the large knocker in his hand and banged it up against the walnut door. He waited a moment and, when there was no response, he knocked once more.

Ann, Artelia's sister, answered the door. She had become Washington's housekeeper several months ago and was a welcome addition to the household. Brodie looked at the petite woman whom he had known since his childhood. "Hello, Ann. I hope you're doing well."

"Thank you for asking. I am. It has been so nice to work for your father. He treats me very well." Ann smiled. "It is so good to see you. I know your father will be so happy that you came for a visit. He's been asking about you." Ann hesitated a moment before continuing. "Brodie, I think he's concerned about you."

"Well, he has nothing to worry about. I'm doing okay. By the way, how is he doing? If he's unwell, I'll be glad to come back another day."

"Nonsense. He's sitting in his study. I'm sure he'd love a visit." Ann leaned in and whispered, "He's been feeling pretty low lately."

"Thank you, Ann. I'll go and seek him out."

Brodie walked through the foyer to the back of the house where the study was located. He stepped into the room that was decorated with dark furniture and large windows covered with heavy drapes. He saw his father slumped over in a large chair that appeared to swallow him up. Brodie couldn't remember his father ever looking so frail. "Pa, can I come in for a visit?"

Washington slowly raised his head and, in a quiet voice, responded, "Brodie, of course, you can."

"I just didn't know if you would want to see me."

"Now, Son, there isn't anything that you could do to keep me from loving you."

Brodie sat down in a chair diagonal from where his father was seated. He sat quiet for a moment, not sure how to respond to this man who had been so kind to him. He knew Washington was torn about the love he had for him and his two youngest sons. None of them were perfect, but Brodie knew that he had caused a lot of unnecessary grief. "Pa, how are you feeling?"

"I'm okay. I've been trying to stay busy at church and, on days when the weather is nice, I've been going on buggy rides. There's nothing like escorting young women around Trinity College."

"Now, Pa. You old rascal."

Washington grinned for a moment and then his expression changed. Brodie knew his father wanted to have a discussion, but he wasn't sure if he wanted to hear what he had to say. "Son, I'm sorry it didn't work out between you and Minnie. I always liked her. She seemed to have a good head on her shoulders."

Brodie didn't know how to respond. He couldn't deny his father's words, but didn't have any true regrets. He wanted to share with Washington about his love for Elizabeth, but knew it wasn't what his father wanted to hear. So, he decided to talk business. "I heard that Benjamin and William Erwin have done well with the mills. It won't be long before Durham will be known as, not only a tobacco town, but also for textiles."

"William Erwin has a good sense for business. I know it took a while to get the mill running but, after all the research he did up north, he's been able to get the business off to good start." Washington looked down and, in a quiet voice, said, "Brodie, I want to share something with you."

Brodie had an uneasy feeling that he wasn't going to like what he was about to hear. "Okay."

Washington cleared his throat. "As you know, I'm not much longer for this world and I've been trying to get my affairs in order."

Brodie quickly interceded. "You aren't going anywhere. Maybe you should spend more time outside."

"Brodie, I've had a good life. Better than I would've ever expected. When I returned from the war, I only saw hard work ahead. But, when you came to Durham and started your tobacco business, and later when your brothers and I joined you, I felt a sense of hope that I could finally retire and enjoy spending time with my family. I really thought that when Richard came into the business, I wouldn't have to think about it again, but we all know how that turned out. It was probably best that he left the company. It just makes me sad how he felt the need to keep dragging us through the courts over all these years."

"I know what you mean."

Washington cleared his throat. "Anyway, as stockholders in the American Tobacco Company, we all have made more money than what one man should ever possess. That's why I felt the need to give money to the church, as well as Trinity College. But, as you know, I've also given a great deal of my wealth to my family."

"Yes, I do appreciate what you have given to me over the years."

"Well, given your financial decisions over the past twenty years, I've decided to put any future money for you into a trust. The interest on the money should bring you and your children about $28,000 a year. Half of it will go to you and the other half will go to your children."

Brodie sat back and thought about what his father was telling him. He could allow it to upset him but, in reality, he knew that he hadn't made good choices. And, if his father knew what he had done with all the money that Minnie had been forced to sign over to him, he would be even more adamant about the course he was taking.

"Brodie, do you understand what I'm saying?"

Brodie paused a moment before speaking. "Yes, I do."

"Well, I appreciate you taking this so well." Washington looked directly into Brodie's eyes. "You know, I do love you."

"Yes, Pa, I do, and I love you as well."

The two men sat in silence for several minutes, neither sure of what else to say to each other. Brodie could hear the sound of Mary Elizabeth's children playing in the backyard. He looked out the window to see a boy running with a ball. Several others caught the boy and tackled him to the ground. Washington slowly arose from his chair. "I need to go and check on the children before someone gets hurt."

Brodie stood and looked at his father. "I don't understand why you took in all of Mary Elizabeth's children."

"Brodie, I hope one day you'll see that wealth alone can't make a man happy. Giving our time and using money to help our loved ones is what makes us happy. The Good Lord has blessed you with four wonderful children who need to know you love them."

"You're right. I do have some work to do regarding my children. I hated when Mabel ran off to Raleigh to get married. But I was glad that Pearl allowed me to pay for her wedding at my house back in January. Nathan seems to be a fine man, but I hate that they now live in Chattanooga."

Washington grew quiet and appeared forlorn. "I hope you can have Woodward come and stay in Durham for a while. I really like the young boy."

"Pa, I'll see what I can do."

The two embraced before Washington shuffled to the back door. Brodie heard the door close and the sound of Mary Elizabeth's children running up to meet the frail, old man. He looked out the window and saw Washington sitting down on a bench, with the children huddled around him.

Brodie stared at the scene that was being played out in front of him and, for the first time in a long time, began to feel regret over how he had treated his own children. As the feelings dug in, tears began to form in his eyes. He turned to leave and found himself staring straight at Ann.

Embarrassed at his open emotions, Brodie wanted to flee, like he had done so many times. But as he looked at this woman, he thought of her sister, Artelia, and the last words she had spoken. Ann reached her arms upward and Brodie allowed this older woman to embrace him. At that moment, all he could think about was the way he had felt when he was a young boy and the love he had for the woman who had loved him like a mother.

31

1904

For the next few months, Brodie was preoccupied with trying to find Elizabeth. He was able to sell property to the American Tobacco Company for $20,000, which gave him enough money to pursue his search. John, his private detective, had gone to Kansas City to make sure Elizabeth hadn't returned to her home. He had also gone to Washington, D.C., and walked the streets where her apartment had been. But no matter how much money Brodie spent to search for the woman he loved, it appeared she had vanished into thin air.

Brodie continued to spend a lot of time over at Carrington Bar. Now that there was no one at home to give him grief about his drinking, he didn't see any reason why he shouldn't enjoy a cold drink with his friends. Brodie understood that many of the men only hung out with him because of his willingness to pay their tabs, but Brodie didn't care. All that mattered was their willingness to listen to him go on and on about Elizabeth or his grudges against George Watts and his brother, Buck.

One afternoon, he entered the dark room and made his way up to the wooden bar. He looked around and noted how barren the room was, except for an older man who was asleep in a corner booth. The bartender came around the corner, spotted Brodie, and walked toward him. "What can I get you today?"

"My usual."

"So, what are you doing here so early?"

"Why not?"

The bartender poured whiskey into a glass and placed it in front of Brodie. "I'd think the Mayor of North Durham would have work to do."

"Now, I didn't come here for a lecture. I get enough of those from my father and brothers."

"Speaking of your brothers, how's Benjamin?"

"He's enjoying New York City. I never thought he would leave Durham, but he just doesn't care for the conservatives around here. He doesn't want to give his good tax money toward a government that denies the rights to people of color."

"Well, I'm not going to get into politics. That's the easiest way to lose my customers. What have you heard lately from your brother, Buck?"

"Hell, he never contacts me. He has his mind set on believing that I'm giving our family a bad name. Ironically, he's going to get married in November and my father has summoned me to appear."

"I know him getting married will make your father happy."

"I'm sure it will." Brodie took a swig of his whiskey. "How about let's change the subject. I'm interested in knowing if the new textile mill has impacted your business."

The bartender wiped down the counter and leaned in. "Some of the new employees have made their way over here. The problem is they work at least sixty hours a week. Some work even more. Your brother, Benjamin, and William Erwin are the only ones making the big money. The employees are just barely surviving. I heard that some are planning to unionize."

Brodie wasn't sure what to say. He knew, even with all of his poor financial decisions, he'd always have enough money to get by on. The days when he felt poor were long gone. "That probably isn't a good idea."

"You're right about that. Word has spread that Erwin is going to close the store to people who unionize. Without the store, they won't have anything."

Just about this time, the doors swung open and John, his private detective, walked in. "Brodie, I thought I'd find you here."

Brodie raised up in his seat and, for the first time in a long time, felt some hope that Elizabeth might be found. "Do you have some information for me?"

"I think Elizabeth was sighted in New York City. I need to go up and check my sources, but wanted you to know that it's likely that she's residing there."

"So, what are you waiting for?"

"I need some money to cover my charges."

Brodie pulled out his checkbook and wrote John a check. "Now, I want to make sure you're going to keep me informed. If you find her, don't approach her. I don't want anything to scare her off."

"I won't."

With the excitement of knowing that he might soon be with Elizabeth again, Brodie paid his tab and walked out into the bright fall sun. The leaves had begun to change color and the oak trees were starting to lose their leaves. He decided to walk home and, along the way, he spotted William Blackwell.

"William, how are you?"

"Not as good as I was when I was running my tobacco company. As much as I wanted to sell out back in the 1880s, I now wish I had stayed with it."

"I know what you mean."

"I heard your brother has finally taken over all of the major tobacco companies. It was in the paper that the Consolidated Tobacco Company and the Continental Tobacco Company have all merged and elected your brother as the new president."

Brodie thought a moment and then said, "I can remember, back in 1884, we were concerned that Allen& Ginter was going to win a lawsuit that would've put us out of business. And now, today, Buck has taken over their company along with the bull."

William shook his head. "Things sure haven't changed around here. The rich are getting richer and the poor are just plain poor. At least, now, I've got a job with the post office. It doesn't pay a lot, but it pays the bills."

"Well, William, I hope the best for you. We both have our own personal regrets, but nobody else in this town has been referred to as the father of Durham and for myself, the Mayor of North Durham."

William chuckled. "That's so true. Take care of yourself, Brodie, and try to stay out of trouble."

"I'll do my best."

But, little did Brodie know, he was headed right into the depths of trouble; the kind that would change his life forever.

| 32 |

1904

Brodie sat in the back of the room observing his brother as he recited his vows. He avoided arriving early by taking the red-eye train and entering the home of Mrs. Lillian McCredy's aunt in Camden, New Jersey, only minutes before the ceremony began.

Once he was seated, Brodie looked out over the room that was decorated with a multitude of ferns, along with countless vases of different kinds of flowers. He knew his brother preferred spending his money on plants and horticulture exhibits over expensive paintings, which explained the extravagant number of floral decorations. Lillian, dressed in a light-blue suit and a string of pearls, appeared pale in comparison to all the flowers. Buck wore a tailored, dark-blue suit with a flower on his lapel. Neither seemed overly happy about what they were doing.

Brodie had heard from Benjamin that neither Buck nor Lillian had wanted to get married, but were willing to go through the formalities for Washington's sake. And, judging by the expression on his father's face, the ceremony was bringing him much-needed joy. Brodie watched the scene taking place in front of him and wondered if he could ever make his father as happy as his younger brothers had.

His thoughts were interrupted when Rev. Marshall Owen pronounced Buck and Lillian man and wife. Buck leaned in and kissed his bride. Everyone clapped and then Lillian threw the bouquet into the air. Brodie saw the flowers coming in his direction and instinctively reached out and caught them. Everyone laughed at the sight of a man catching the bouquet. Brodie quickly handed them to a woman sitting next to him. The woman laughed as she handed them back. "I believe these are intended for you."

"I hope not. I just got divorced."

The woman smiled back at Brodie. "Well, you never know."

A butler came around handing out glasses filled with bubbly champagne. He reached for a glass when Buck approached him. "I'd appreciate it if you would try and refrain from getting drunk."

"Well, brother, it's nice seeing you, too. Congratulations on finally making your relationship legal."

"Just try and not make a fool of yourself."

"The last thing I want to do is taint your image. Don't worry, little brother. I plan on leaving shortly."

Brodie felt a light tap on his shoulder. He turned around and was handed an envelope. He opened it and read the words he had been anxiously awaiting. He looked up at Buck, handed him his glass and, with excitement in his voice, said, "I have to go."

Several hours later, Brodie arrived at Grand Central Station holding tightly to the note. He had memorized the address, but wouldn't let go of the paper. Once he was out on the street, he walked toward Fifth Avenue. It had begun to snow and puddles formed on the ground beneath his feet. His toes began to stiffen from the cold, but he kept going.

The snow picked up and the cold wind made it difficult to move forward, but nothing was going to keep Brodie from finding Elizabeth. As he approached the address that had been printed on the paper, his heart began to pound. He was becoming extremely anxious, but was adamantabout finding the woman he loved with all of his heart.

Standing outside the building, Brodie hesitated, wondering if he would find yet another empty apartment. He took a deep breath and knocked on the door. After only a few moments, the door opened and Elizabeth stood in the doorway. She looked even more beautiful than Brodieremembered and he wanted to reach out and kiss her lips. But just as he started to step through the doorway, a man walked up beside Elizabeth and placed his hand around her slim waist. "Darling, who is this man?"

Initially, Elizabeth appeared shocked by Brodie's presence, but just as she had done so many times before, she acted her part perfectly. "Walter, this is Brodie Duke. He was someone who I met when I went to Illinois."

"Well, don't be rude. Ask him in."

"Brodie, please come in. It's been such a long time. How are you doing? Have you been able to stay sober?"

Brodie wasn't sure what to think. He knew Elizabeth was lying, but needed to know who this man was and, more importantly, what she had done with all his money. He stepped into the large foyer and looked around. The first thing he noticed was a painting he had purchased for her when they had been on a trip to Europe.

And then, he looked at her hand and saw a wedding band with a large diamond.

"Elizabeth, are you going to tell Walter, or do I need to?"

Without hesitating, Elizabeth responded, "Tell him what? That we knew each other in Illinois?"

"No. I meant about the affair we've been having."

Walter glared at Brodie and, with a booming voice, shouted out, "How dare you come into my home and accuse my wife of such an indecent act!"

"She's not the woman you think she is." Brodie pointed to the painting that he had purchased. "Elizabeth, tell him where you got that picture."

Walter walked up to Brodie and pushed him with his chest. "I believe you need to leave now. I've had enough of your accusations. And if you show up again, I'll call the police!"

Before Brodie realized it, he was back out on the street with the snow falling all around him. He didn't know where he would go. For months, his entire life had been centered on finding Elizabeth and finally making a life with her. He just couldn't believe she had lied to him and taken him for a fool.

Even though it was snowing and a sharp northern wind blew, Brodie only felt emotionally numb. He felt nothing as he walked the streets of New York City. Finally, as his fingers began to stiffen and he could no longer feel his feet, he walked into Park Avenue Hotel and reserved a room. Once inside his room, he laid down on the large bed and fell into a deep sleep. When he awoke, it was dark outside. He lit the bedside lamp, walked over to the water basin, and washed his face. He thought about going back to sleep, but decided to go down to the hotel bar where he could drink away the pain of rejection.

The hotel was beautifully decorated and it was clear that the clientele were wealthy individuals who could afford the best accommodations. Brodie walked through the lobby and entered a restaurant with a bar located against a back wall. Passing several tables, he noticed two women and a man who were sitting at one of them. He tipped his hat in their direction and then made his way to the bar where he ordered a whiskey neat. With thoughts of Elizabeth and her husband floating through his mind, he chugged the drink down and ordered another.

As he was swigging his second drink, one of the women from the table stood up and approached him. Brodie was beginning to feel the effects of the alcohol and decided that being with a woman might be what he needed. The woman was pleasant enough to look at, but at this point, looks didn't matter.

"Hello. I saw you come in a few minutes ago. Are you staying here at the hotel?"

Brodie was a little taken aback by the woman's forthrightness. "Yes."

"Oh, by the way, my name is Alice Webb. I've just arrived from Chicago. I'm here to do business. So, what's your name?"

At that moment, Brodie had an uneasy feeling well up inside him. He considered getting up to go back to his room, but given the effects of the alcohol, he decided to stay and continue to drink. "I'm Brodie Duke."

Alice's face took on a curious expression. "Duke. Are you the man who just shook up the tobacco industry?"

"No, that's my brother."

"Well, a nice-looking man like yourself must have his own claim to fame."

"People in Durham, North Carolina, refer to me as the Mayor of North Durham. Do you know that I've bought lots of real estate and stock in the railroads there?"

"Oh, have you?"

Brodie turned toward the bartender and pointed to his glass. Once the glass had been refilled, he turned back to Alice. "If it wasn't for me, my brothers wouldn't be as wealthy as they are." He pointed to himself. "I was the one who came to Durham first and started my own tobacco company."

"Well, isn't that interesting. You see, I own my own tobacco company in Texas. Have you ever heard of the Texas-Cuba Tobacco Company?"

Brodie thought it was interesting to meet a woman who ran her own business. "No, I don't think so."

"That's okay. It's doing extremely well. To be honest, I'm here to find some intelligent investors to assist in the company's growth."

Brodie took another swig of his drink. He wasn't sure what he thought of this woman. She definitely wasn't Elizabeth, but he did like the attention she was giving him.

Alice looked at him and asked, "Would it be okay if I join you?"

"Sure. It's a free country."

"It sure is."

Alice scooted a chair next to Brodie and intentionally sat so that her legs were touching his. He thought this was strange, but given how he was feeling, didn't think more of it. Over the next hour, Brodie continued drinking and was beginning to have a difficult time comprehending what was happening. At one point, Alice asked, "Brodie, how about I help you to your room?"

He slurred, "I don't need anybody to help me."

Brodie tried to stand but began to falter. Alice, with the help of the other people sitting at the table, assisted him to his room. Once inside the room, Brodie was placed on the bed and that was when everything went blank.

33

1905

Brodie awoke and the first thing he noticed were the bars on the window. He blinked a couple of times, trying to remember where he was, but he had no memories of how he had ended up in this room. He propped himself up on his elbow, looking around the small room with white walls and a particular smell that reminded him of the times he had been hospitalized.

The sheets were scratchy and, when he reached down to lift them off, he was shocked to find that he had been tied to the bedframe. Frightened by his situation, he began to yell. "Can anyone hear me? Please, there must be a mistake. Help me!"

After only a few moments, Brodie heard the sound of a key unlocking the door and a woman wearing a white uniform and nursing cap entered. "Mr. Duke, I'm glad to see that you are awake."

"Yes. But, where am I, and why am I tied to the bed like an animal?"

"I'm not at liberty to discuss this with you. I'll call the doctor and he'll determine if you can be untied."

"Please, you must help me. I've never hurt anyone and need to be released immediately!"

"Now, calm down. You don't want to appear uncooperative. If you do so, you may find yourself here for much longer than you'd like."

Brodie laid back in the bed and looked up at the ceiling. He could see where the paint was chipped and falling away. He tried to concentrate on how he had ended up in this place, but his mind was blank. As he waited for the doctor, he centered his attention on the few memories that formed in his head. He remembered seeing Elizabeth with her husband in the doorway of their New York brownstone. This memory was followed by a picture of being at the Park Avenue Hotel at the bar. As he pondered what took place next, a vision of a woman with her leg up against his took shape. But who was this woman and why was that the last thing he could remember?

His thoughts were interrupted by the sound of a key opening the door and a middle-aged man, dressed in a white coat, entering the room. The nurse stood behind the doctor, who was holding a pad of paper and looking at him with a peculiar expression on his face. "Mr. Duke, I'm Dr. Gregory. You're in Bellevue Hospital's psychiatric ward. Do you remember being admitted to the hospital?"

"No. I don't remember anything." Brodie paused, hoping to recall any detail, but he just couldn't.

"Several days ago, you were brought here by two detectives."

"But, why?"

"It appears you have been under the influence of some pretty powerful drugs."

"What?"

"Yes, you were close to death. It's likely that, if your son had not pursued a petition to the court to have you taken from the Park Avenue Hotel, you'd probably be dead."

"Now, I admit, I do drink too much, but I don't take drugs!"

"Well, drugs were in your system. Now, how they got there is what we need to find out."

"I'd like to know that myself."

"Nurse Carter, you can free Mr. Duke. I believe he'll be cooperative."

As the nurse untied Brodie, Dr. Gregory continued, "Your son would like to see you. Is it alright for him to come in?"

"Of course."

Nurse Carter left the room and returned moments later with Lawrence. She took a seat in the back of the room as the doctor excused himself. Brodie sat up in the bed and looked at his son. He couldn't believe how tall he was. It seemed like such a short period of time since Lawrence had been a small child. Lawrence pulled up a chair and sat next to his father. "Dad, how are you feeling?"

"Groggy, but I guess alright."

"Do you have any idea why you're here?"

"No."

"Are you sure you're telling me the truth?"

"Of course, I am. I want to know myself. All I can remember is leaving Buck's wedding in New Jersey and making my way to New York." Brodie thought it was best to leave out the part about visiting Elizabeth. Given that it was over between the two of them, he didn't think this detail was relevant to his present situation.

"Do you remember marrying a woman by the name of Alice Webb?"

"What are you talking about?" Brodie sat straight up and looked right at his son. "Why would I marry a woman I don't know? And anyway, I just divorced Minnie. Why would I marry someone so soon after going through that ordeal?"

"I don't know, Dad. After Buck's wedding, you went missing. No one could find you. And then, all of a sudden, Benjamin receives phone calls from a woman who identifies herself as Alice Webb. She tells Benjamin that the two of you are married."

"But I don't know an Alice Webb."

"Well, apparently you do. Rev. W.W. Coe of the Madison Square Presbyterian Church married the two of you on December 21st."

"December 21st? What day is it today?"

"January 11th."

"Are you telling me that I don't know what has happened to me since the beginning of December?"

"Yes. I was hoping you could tell us where you've been. All we know is that you checked into the Park Avenue Hotel on November 30th and rented a room with this Miss Webb."

Brodie thought for a moment before speaking. "Wait a minute. I do remember a woman sitting beside me in the hotel bar. I'd been drinking pretty heavily that night. The last thing I remember is this woman and two other people helping me to my room. And then everything else is a blur."

"Dad, you have to understand that it's hard to believe you. Given how you treated Minnie, as well as the amount of money that can't be accounted for, is an indication that you must know more about this than you're telling me."

Brodie stared right into his son's eyes. "Lawrence, you've got to believe me. This Miss Webb must have drugged me. I have no recollection of ever marrying her."

Lawrence shook his head in disbelief. "So, why should I believe you?"

Brodie didn't want to tell Lawrence the entire truth, but knew he had to. "Okay, there was another woman, but it wasn't some woman by the name of Alice Webb. Years ago, when I went to Illinois, to the Keeley Institute, I met a woman. Her name is Elizabeth. I fell in love with her, but didn't have any contact with her until about two years ago."

Lawrence sat back, folded his arms, and remained quiet.

"She lived in Washington, D.C., where I'd travel to see her. You can ask Minnie. She'll tell you that I received a call from her when I was in Brooklyn with her and Pearl. Minnie will vouch for how I left them to go to Washington. All I wanted was to be with Elizabeth. I truly loved her and wanted to spend the rest of my life with her. I'd have done anything for her. So, that was why I divorced Minnie."

"So, what happened to all the money you pulled out of your accounts?"

"I gave it to Elizabeth."

"So, you're telling me that all those accounts you emptied, and property you sold, was for the sole purpose of being with this woman?"

"Yes, exactly!"

"So, where is this woman named Elizabeth?"

"She went missing several months ago. I sent my private detective out to find her and I received a note at your uncle's wedding that she was living in New York. That's why I left the wedding so quickly. I went to find Elizabeth."

Brodie looked over at Lawrence, who didn't seem to believe him. This only made Brodie more adamant to explain. "Look, Son, I know I haven't been the best father, or husband to Minnie or your mother. I've drunk way too much over the years. I've done some very stupid things. But I didn't consent to marry anyone, particularly a woman I don't even know."

"Again, where is this woman who you proclaim to love so much that you were willing to publicly humiliate Minnie for?"

Brodie lowered his head. "When I received the note from my private detective, I went, that night, to her home in New York."

"And?"

"I found out that she was married."

"Okay, so let me get this straight. You left Buck's wedding and arrived here in New York that night, where you went to see this woman who you proclaim to love?"

"Yes. But when she opened the door, her husband was with her."

Lawrence began to chuckle and shake his head. "Dad, this doesn't look good at all. You didn't just get taken once, but twice."

Brodie had never felt as humiliated as he did at that moment. But, little did he know, that this was just the tip of the iceberg.

| 34 |

1905

Brodie woke from his slumber to the sound of a key opening the door to his room at Bellevue. It had been a week since he had discovered himself at the hospital, and he still couldn't remember the events that had transpired over the last month. Other than his son, he hadn't received any visitors and liked it that way. He felt like such a fool and preferred the isolation the hospital offered.

Little did Brodie know that, though he didn't want to face the world, people from all walks of life were talking about him. His story had made its way into every major newspaper in the country, causing a ripple effect that would forever change his life.

Once the door opened, the visitor walked toward the bed and leaned over. Due to the darkness of the room, Brodie had trouble identifying the intruder. When he finally recognized the man as his brother, Buck, he was consumed with fear. Buck appeared larger than life as he stood over him, causing Brodie to want to coil up in a ball. "What are you doing here, Buck?"

"What do you think?"

Brodie took a deep breath and raised his body into a seated position. "I don't know."

"Listen, I've been under a lot of stress in the last couple of months. There are a lot of people who have wanted to destroy my image since I have created the largest tobacco company in the world. And you, big brother, have destroyed it all on your own."

"What are you talking about?"

Buck flung the newspaper onto his bed and pointed to the picture of Brodie. The illustrator had drawn Brodie as an old, disheveled man who clearly looked intoxicated. There was a larger picture of a woman that Brodie recognized as the woman he had come to know as Alice Webb. The pictures made him sick to his stomach, but when he saw the headlines, his heart sank. **When Love is Blind: The experience of wealthy Brodie L. Duke with a "Woman with Schemes."**

"I would like for you to explain this."

"Buck, I really don't know what to say. I truly can't remember any of it."

"Brodie, all my life, I've had to tolerate you. You've been a thorn in this family's side for as long as I can remember. Why Pa doesn't disown you, I don't know. Do you have any idea how upset Pa is? Do you ever consider anyone else's feelings?"

Brodie sat staring at the newspaper. He wanted to defend himself, but didn't know what had actually happened.

"I just want you to know that, if something happens to Pa because of your reckless behavior, there will be consequences!"

And, with that, Buck turned and was gone.

For a long while, Brodie sat in a daze before he had the courage to read the article that apparently had made its way around the country.

New York-Somehow New York overlooked the announcement of the marriage of Brodie L. Duke and Miss Alice Webb on December 21, 1904. The fact that the ceremony was performed by Rev. W.W. Coe, chief assistant of Rev. Charles Parkhurst of Madison Square Presbyterian Church, who became famous some years ago because of his crusade against vice, ought to have attracted attention. Ordinarily, the mere name of Duke would have been enough to excite gossip. For Brodie L. Duke is the half-brother of James B. Duke, the head of the American Tobacco Trust.

It was James B. Duke who, starting in a small way at Durham, N.C., founded the tobacco trust and made it the great power that it is. Since that day, James B. Duke's progress to wealth has been phenomenal. The trust virtually controls the entire tobacco business of this country, and several years ago, invaded England and fought the big tobacco interests there to a standstill.

James B. Duke is the sturdy, square-jawed, silent type of man, who gives the impression of force, but carefully avoids notoriety. There are a dozen men connected with the tobacco trust who are more talked about than him and whose real achievements as moneymakers and business organizers are not half so great. Lately, he has built a palatial country place at Somerville, N.J., where he now makes his home. He, too, not long ago married a wife who was unknown to the society of millionaires, which men of his type usually aspire to enter in New York.

Brodie L. Duke is quite a different type of man. Through his family relationship, he has shared, to some extent, in the good fortune of James B. Duke, and has had the reputation of being wealthy. But most of his life has been spent in hard work in North Carolina, and the attractions of New York proved too much for him. He is said, in fact, to have dissipated a large part of his fortune before his marriage and to have been a frequent cause of anxiety to his family.

Two weeks after the quiet little ceremony at the home of Rev. W.W. Coe, a mysterious patient was taken one night to the psychiatric ward of Bellevue Hospital. Every care was taken to conceal the identity of the patient. It was not until the next day, when the detectives of District Attorney Jerome appeared at the hospital and demanded the delivery of some $40,000 in stocks and bonds, and a quantity of valuable jewelry, that it was revealed that Brodie L. Duke's family had taken steps to have him declared irresponsible. The next step was to secure his commitment to a private sanatorium at Flushing, L.I., where he was put under close guard.

Then the circumstances of Duke's marriage became public and, two days later, suit was brought for the annulment of the marriage. To one of his sons, Duke frankly expressed amazement when told that he was married. "I didn't know I married Miss Webb," he is reported to have said. "I don't remember having asked her to marry me, nor do I recollect appearing before the minister with her. It is all very strange."

At Bellevue Hospital, they said plainly that Duke was suffering from alcoholic dementia, and it was even intimated that his condition might have been brought about by the use of drugs. Naturally, Mrs. Alice Webb Duke had quite a different story to tell, and her friend, Mrs. Agnes Desplaines, bore her out in most of the details. But it happened that private detectives, employed by the Duke family, and the detectives from the District Attorney Jerome's office, had unearthed enough of the records of the two women to cast strong suspicion on them, and the grand jury was put to work investigating the matrimonial tangle.

For some time, the Dukes had not known where Brodie Duke was. He had been in the habit of spending a good deal of his time away from his North Carolina home. Last October, he dropped out of sight for an unusually long period. Then, one day, he turned up at Durham, N.C., with Miss Alice Webb. Then came another disappearance, and it was not until his son, Lawrence Duke, had arrived in New York to find out what had become of his father, that the truth was known. One day, late in November, Benjamin N. Duke, a half-brother of Brodie Duke, who lives at the Hoffman House, was called up at the hotel by a woman who said, "This is your new sister-in-law. I called you up to tell you that I have married your brother, Brodie. I want to tell you that we are very happy. Mr. Duke wants to talk to you himself."

Then Benjamin Duke heard some conversation and a voice, which he recognized as his brother's, come over the phone. It said, "This little Texas girl has got me and got me good."

Benjamin Duke asked his brother if he was satisfied, or something to that effect, and there was a conversation at the other end of the telephone in which he heard women's voices. Then his brother said, "Yes, it is alright. I am satisfied."

At the time the Dukes didn't know where Brodie Duke was. What really caused them to put private detectives to work was the knowledge which came to his family that Brodie Duke had come back to North Carolina and tried to wind up his affairs there, among other things asking that about $100,000 worth of securities being held there should be forwarded to him in New York. On top of that, they discovered that he had written a check for $4,200 on a bank where he had only $600 on deposit, and that the check had been returned. Next, they learned that an attempt had been made to borrow money on two of his notes for $16,500, which had finally come into the hands of a well-known money lender.

At once, one of his brothers and a son applied to the court for an order committing Brodie Duke to the hospital. Detectives were sent to the Park Avenue Hotel, a fashionable establishment where Brodie Duke and his wife were living. Duke himself made no resistance, but Mrs. Duke was not so passive. She abused the relatives, particularly the son, who was instrumental in getting his father away from her. The detectives pushed Duke out of the apartments, and the next day the bride was asked to leave the place. For a while, she went into hiding but, when at last she was located, she told a story in which sentiment and business were strongly mixed.

Mrs. Duke has all along claimed to have large property interests. She is about 50 years of age, perhaps five years the junior of her husband. For several years, she has figured as a promoter of a certain kind of industrial concern of more or less magnitude. Her business correspondence is written on nicely engraved stationery, under the heading of The Texas-Cuba Tobacco Company of which Alice M. Webb figures as the president. The offices of the concern are in the Continental Bank Building of Chicago and, according to Mrs. Duke, it owns a considerable area of tobacco land in Texas. She is also interested in the firm of Taylor, Webb & Co., which has its headquarters with the tobacco concern. Mrs. Duke is the Webb of the firm. It is engaged in promoting all sorts of projects and stock enterprises. According to Mrs. Duke, her first meeting with her husband came about in the way of business.

"I have large property interests in Texas," she explained, after her husband had been committed to the hospital. "It was in connection with these that I came to New York from Chicago in the latter part of November. I wanted to secure additional capital to develop the property and, naturally, I meant to seek wealthy investors. Of course, I'd heard of the Dukes as men of wealth. On arriving in New York, I sent a telegram to Brodie L. Duke, asking him for a business appointment. By mistake, my message fell into the hands of his brother, who came to see me at the Astor House."

"When I discovered that he was not the man I expected to meet, I told him my message had been intended for Brodie L. Duke. Then I explained what my mission was, and before leaving he made ma an offer of $15,000 a year for my services in his business affairs. I declined the offer after telling Mr. Duke that my services were not for sale."

"Then I sent a second telegram to Brodie L. Duke, at Durham, N.C, and we met for the first time at the Astor House. I explained my business proposition to him and he expressed great interest in it. I met Mr. Duke

by appointment a number of times, and he made inquiries about me and my business affairs. One day, to my great surprise, he said to me, "Little girl, I don't want your tobacco stock, and I don't want your lands, nor do I want to consider any of your business propositions. But I do want you."

"I was dumbfounded at what he said and explained to him that such a step would cause no end of comment on the part of his friends. I told him that his family would probably raise objections to this marriage, but he said he didn't care what the family thought and that he was old enough to know his own affairs."

"A few days later, I met Mr. Duke again and consented to marry him. I knew that, when our engagement was announced, there would be a great deal of publicity about it and I decided to go to some obscure hotel. Mr. Duke and I discussed our business projects every day, and he agreed to take charge of all my interest in Texas, and also got a financial interest in my lands in that state."

"He readily consented to put up the capital for the development of a large tract of land on which I had an option. In the meantime, to show good faith, Mr. Duke had a certified check made out and deposited it with his lawyer. He also entered into negotiations for $20,000 for the purchase of the land.

"When Mr. Duke and I were discussing our upcoming marriage one day, I asked him if his brothers and sons were likely to raise any objections to it. He said, "The family home is mine and my relatives will respect you or have to get out of it."

Mrs. Duke also had much to say about the plans she and her husband had formed for building a church in Durham and improving the condition of the poor people of the great tobacco city. "I want to deny emphatically," she said, "all the reports about Mr. Duke and me indulging to excess in drinking and that we were often in an intoxicated condition together. It is all a wicked falsehood, and intended by the members of the Duke family, who have been persecuting me ever since my marriage to Mr. Duke, to destroy my good name. I consented to an early marriage at the urgent plea of Mr. Duke. The following day we went on with our business arrangements, but Mr. Duke contracted a severe cold and his condition became so serious that I thought it safest to have the doctor give all his attention to him."

Mrs. Agnes Desplaines, who has figured as Mrs. Duke's closest friend, has called the Duke marriage a beautiful one. She declares that Miss Webb is a very capable businesswoman and that, when Mr. Duke came to see her, it was a case of love at first sight, for they soon stopped talking about tobacco. According to Mrs. Desplaines, the clever Miss Webb was all business, but the second time Mr. Duke called on her, he insisted upon marrying her.

"Finally," said Mrs. Desplaines, "he refused to talk business. Then Miss Webb saw it was no use to refuse and, as she really loved him, she at last consented to marry him, She was afraid his family would object, but Mr. Duke waived her objections aside and declared he would never be satisfied until he got her. It was a hasty courtship and a hasty marriage. If any woman could make a man happy, she is the one. Now they have torn him away from her in the very midst of their honeymoon. It was cruel to separate them, but it will not last."

These things, and many more, were told by Mrs. Desplaines to District Attorney Jerome, who has charge of all criminal cases in New York County. In the meantime, it was discovered that she has something of a record of her own, and that her acquaintance with Miss Alice Webb dated back many years. It seems that Mrs. Desplaines, in 1894, when the state legislature ordered a searching investigation of police corruption in New York City, appeared before the Lexow Committee and acknowledged that she was the owner of a Raines law hotel that had been raided by the police. The Raines law hotels are a peculiar institution in New York City, by which it is made possible to sell liquor on Sunday. There are some 7,000 of them licensed and, as a class, they are dens of vice and infamy.

There have been many interesting chapters in the life of Alice L. Webb-Powell-Hopkinson-Masterson-Duke since she left Erie County orphan asylum in Buffalo. The New York police say that Alice Webb first came to the city in 1878 to begin a life full of excitement. One of the first incidents in her career, that brought her notoriety, was her attempt to shoot a man named Murat Masterson, who represented himself to be a wealthy Arizona miner. The two had been associates for some time, and their quarrel was an ordinary case of jealousy, so common among people of a certain class. Masterson and Alice L. Webb were arrested but, as neither would make a complaint, both were discharged. This was in 1890.

Three years later, the woman brought a suit against George W. Hopkinson, a wealthy owner of perfumeries, for alimony. According to affidavits now on file, Hopkinson lived at a fashionable hotel in New York City in 1877. He had been introduced to a woman calling herself Alice Osborne, who told him that she had been married to a man called Osborne, and afterward been charged with endeavoring to blackmail Mr. Osborne's estate. Hopkinson induced Alice Osborne to leave the Desplaines boarding house. She set up an establishment of her own and lived in considerable luxury. Some years later, when Hopkinson tried to drop her acquaintance, he took the precaution to have papers duly drawn up and signed in the presence of his attorney. The woman acknowledged that she had never been his lawful wife, and for two or three years he heard nothing more of her. Then he began to receive gentle requests for money, and, in 1893, the woman, as Mrs. Hopkinson, began her action for alimony against him, saying that she had married Hopkinson on November 24, 1878, when she was 18 years old. Hopkinson denied ever having married her, said that she was at least 25 years old at the time he met her, and generally exposed the woman's character in court. The questionable authenticity of her marriage resulted in his attorney having the suit dismissed in 1895.

It has also been learned in the investigation of the woman's record, that Alice Webb married Edward H. Powell, a hotel clerk in Pittsburgh, PA, in 1895. Powell is now believed to be in Chicago or Allegheny City.

Further light was thrown on this remarkable case by a man named Dr. E. T. Osbaldeston, who was employed as a nurse in the Duke apartments during Mr. Duke's indisposition after his marriage. He told the criminal authorities that, when he first saw Duke, he was under the influence of liquor or drugs. "Mrs. Desplaines," he testified to the district attorney," mixed something, put what looked like whiskey in one glass and took from another what seemed to be milk. Soon after this was given to Mr. Duke, he fell back on his pillow, his jaw dropped and he was asleep and breathing hard." The nurse also declared that, on the day before the marriage, he found Duke so near death that he insisted that a doctor be called. The next day, Mrs. Desplaines told him Duke and Miss Webb had gone away to be married and the day after the marriage, so Osbaldeston told District Attorney Jerome, Mrs. Duke came to him and showed him her marriage certificate saying, "Now address me as Mrs. Duke with the $20,000. Oh my God, what I have gone through and suffered in the last few weeks to get this. I can't tell you. But, thank God, it is over."

It is a curious part of this extraordinary case that nearly everybody connected with it has a record. Osbaldeston admits that he was once arrested in Montreal with a woman named Louisa Weiss, who was accused of theft, and that he spent several years in an insane asylum there. In August 1892, he was shot while investigating a suspected dive in New York City. Later, he had a silver plate inserted in his skull to cover the hole made in it by a colored man who shot him while he was thus engaged in another raid.

In 1901, the Weiss woman went to Germany where Osbaldeston followed her. There, in the course of his life of adventure, he was assaulted by a man named Well, whom he shot dead. Osbaldeston was chased by a mob and fired at and killed their leader. Subsequently, he was set free on the grounds that he'd fired in self-defense. He was also once arrested in Washington, D.C., for extorting money from the owner of a massage establishment, but this case was dismissed.

While the examination of the persons principally involved in the Duke marriage tangle was underway, and evidence was being prepared for submission to the grand jury, District Attorney Jerome was informed that Mrs. Duke did not, in fact, own the valuable tobacco lands in Texas which had figured in her business relations with the impressionable Mr. Duke. She had once held title to some property, but it had previously been sold under sheriff's execution for $350 and, instead of being very valuable, it was probably worth only about that sum.

In any case, Mrs. Duke declared that she would stand on her rights as a lawful wife and began habeas corpus proceedings for the recovery of her husband from the hospital. The Duke family is equally determined that the separation shall be final, regardless of the mortification and scandal growing from the court proceedings.

One fact, which has come to light in the course of the inquiry made by the criminal authorities in this case, is that there are a number of disreputable women in the city of New York who live in good style, in pretentious quarters, and who make it their special business to keep informed about the habits of men of wealth, who are given to dissipation and loose living. They maintain elegantly furnished apartments, are women of good manners and pleasing address and, under the pretense of carrying on regular business operations, are really concerned with wheedling money out of their victims by both fair means and foul. Several of these cases, which have been uncovered, have been suppressed by the victims for fear of disgraceful publicity. The Duke Case has gone too far to be suppressed. Whether or not charges of conspiracy can be proved in court, exposure should help to check similar operations by women hanging on the fringes of society.

As Brodie finished reading the last words of the article, he knew he had become a victim and, thus, made to look like a fool.

But as bad as he looked to the world, as well as to his family, he wasn't insane and he would make sure everyone knew it.

| 35 |

1905

Not long after Buck left, Brodie was surprised to hear several loud voices from outside his door. He thought he recognized one of the voices and shouted out, "W.G., is that you?"

"Yes, Brodie. Can you please tell these people that it is imperative that I speak with you?"

"Let this man in to see me. If you don't, there will be consequences!"

Brodie heard the sound of the door opening and W.G. stepping through the open doorway. W.G. held a briefcase in his hand and appeared startled by Brodie's appearance. "Brodie, are you alright? I've been very concerned about you."

"Yes, I'm okay."

"I need to tell you some things that might upset you."

W.G. Bramham had been Brodie's personal secretary for years and had come up to New York to, not only find out how his boss was, but to inform him of what was happening. He had been a trusted friend and Brodie had always tried to keep him informed of his whereabouts.

Brodie noticed W.G. pick up the newspaper and read the headlines. "W.G., I didn't know this woman. I never met her in Durham. And you know that the only woman I've been seeing is Elizabeth. I don't remember ever asking this Alice woman to marry me and, to be honest, I can't remember ever going in front of a preacher to get married. I swear I was drugged."

"Right this very minute, your brother, Benjamin, and your son, Lawrence, are standing in front of a judge trying to declare you insane and have your financial holdings removed from your control."

Brodie sat straight up in bed. "What are you talking about?"

"They want to make sure that your marriage with Alice Webb is annulled."

"Well, I certainly want this marriage annulled, but I am not insane. I know she, or this Agnes Desplaines woman, drugged me and were trying to get their hands on my money."

W.G. shook his head. "Given the amount of time we haven't communicated, I needed to make sure of your mental state before I file a motion with the judge.

"W.G., you've got to believe I was drugged. Now that the drugs are out of my system, I'm fine."

W.G. stared a moment at Brodie and then stated, "I can clearly see you're sane."

"Thank you for believing me. Now, W.G., what can I do?"

"I'm going to file a motion that the judge speak to you in person before he makes a judgment pertaining to your sanity."

Brodie sat back and shook his head. He couldn't believe his own son would try to declare him insane. And Benjamin had always been sympathetic toward him. Feelings of anger toward them rose up and he wanted to hit something but, instead of acting out, he balled up his fist and hit the bed.

"W.G., you have to do everything you can to get me out of here. I am the victim here. Yes, I admit, I drink too much and can be tempted by a nice-looking woman, but I did nothing wrong. I was drugged and taken advantage of."

"Brodie, I'll see what I can do. But, please don't act out, and please demonstrate to everyone you come in contact with that you are sane."

"I will. Thank you, W.G. You have no idea how much I appreciate all you're doing."

"Brodie, this isn't likely to go away anytime soon. But I believe you have been taken advantage of, and I don't want to see your rights taken from you."

"Buck came by earlier. He was furious. He told me that Pa is very upset. Please tell Pa that I'm okay. I don't want anything to happen to him. I know Buck doesn't want to have anything to do with me, but I do care about my father."

"I'll send him a telegram, informing him of our meeting." W.G. hesitated a moment before speaking. "Oh, and one last thing. Did you know that the authorities recovered over $40,000 worth of stocks and jewelry in your hotel room?"

Brodie looked down and covered his face with his hands. "I swear I have no idea how those women were able to get their hands on my money."

"I guess it's best to tell you everything."

Brodie looked up at W.G., trying to prepare himself for what might come next. "How can there be more? I was drugged, married off to a woman I don't know, and have been institutionalized."

W.G. looked down at a bill from the Park Avenue Hotel. "Well, apparently, your new wife and her friends charged your room for over four thousand dollars."

"What?"

"Before I came here, I spoke to the hotel manager, who told me that people were constantly complaining about the noise that came from your room."

Brodie tried to process everything that W.G. was telling him. He knew he had messed up, but as bad as it was, Brodie knew he wasn't insane. "W.G., I need your help."

"I'm here for you."

Brodie stood up and looked straight into W.G.'s eyes. "I need for you to promise me that you will do everything you can to make sure I'm not declared insane. And if that means fighting my son and brother, then do it!"

For the next couple of weeks, while Brodie waited in Bellevue, W.G. Bramham worked alongside a team of lawyers to prove that his client was sane. It was a difficult fight given all of the national attention the case was receiving. To make matters worse, Benjamin and Lawrence hired their own lawyers to prove that Brodie was insane and should have his finances taken over by a commission. But, the worst part of the ordeal came from Alice Webb, who wouldn't give up her position that Brodie willingly married her.

36

1905

Days after Brodie was released from Bellevue, he received a telegram from W.G. Bramham that his father had fallen and had broken his hip bone. At first, he thought he should rush home to Durham, but realized he probably wouldn't be welcome. So, he decided to stay in New York where he could stay on top of the legal mess he had apparently created.

In late April, Brodie took the train south to Durham. It had been close to six months since he had been home, and he knew he needed to see his father. As he was jostled by the movement of the train, Brodie tried to remember better days and it was then that he pulled out the wooden fox that he had always kept inside his coat pocket. As he rubbed the smooth wood, his thoughts returned to his simple life as a boy. He took the fox and brought it up to his nose, smelling the wood and trying to remember the days when it was just him, his father, and Sidney.

Before he realized it, tears started falling down his cheeks. *"Sidney, if only you had lived. If only you could be with me now. I hate how Benjamin and Buck are so close. That should be us. Why, God? Why did you take him away?"*

Brodie turned his head so that no one could see his tears. He stared out the window at the trees and fields as the train moved down the track. As each mile passed by, Brodie became increasingly fearful of seeing his father. He knew he had caused him a great deal of pain and felt a strong sense of guilt.

Once the train came to a halt, he picked up his bag and walked down the steps onto the platform. At first, he wondered if he was in the right place. There were throngs of people everywhere, many he didn't recognize. He knew the American Tobacco Company, along with the different mills, had been hiring, but he was shocked by the sheer number of people.

Brodie looked over at the Hotel Carrolina, a hotel that Julian Shakespeare Carr had built in 1893. The beauty of the structure on the corner of Corcoran and Peabody Streets seemed out of place alongside the plain buildings that surrounded it. He decided to walk to his house on Duke Street and unpack before making his way to see his father. But, as he was walking away from the crowds of people, he felt the stares of many of the pedestrians. Several were pointing in his direction, speaking in hushed voices, while others were more blatant in their comments. "Brodie Duke, we were wondering when you were going to show your face back here in Durham."

Brodie looked around to see who had made this comment, but was taken aback by the number of people glaring at him. Instead of commenting, he decided to keep his head down and walk in the direction of his home. Once he reached the front steps, he looked up at his house and noted the poor condition it was in. The outside paint had become discolored from the smoke of the tobacco factories. The wood had chipped and the porch needed to have boards replaced. He took a mental note of the things that needed to be done, wondering if anyone had been here since he left.

When he opened the door and stepped in, he was saddened by what he saw. Spider webs hung in almost every corner of the room and a coat of dust covered every surface. Dead flies and bugs were scattered all over the floor and a stale scent filled his nostrils.

Brodie grabbed his bag and walked back to his bedroom. When he entered, a feeling of loneliness swept over him. What had he done to arrive at this point in time? He was a laughingstock to everyone and his own family wanted nothing to do with him. Memories of when the children and Minnie occupied this space came rushing through his mind. And, in that moment, all he wanted to do was get out, go anywhere, be somewhere other than here.

Without thinking, he ran out of the house and headed the few blocks to his father's home. As he approached the front steps, he noticed that there were several carriages lined up on the street. He wondered why so many people would be here but, as much as he didn't want to see any other family members, he needed to see his father.

Brodie knocked on the large door several times. After a few minutes of waiting, he decided to see if it was open. He turned the knob and slowly opened the door. He could hear voices from the back of the house and decided to make his way closer in. Once he filled the space of his father's bedroom doorway, he could see Benjamin and Sarah, along with Lawrence. His first instinct was to leave, but he knew he had to face them at some point, and what better time than in the presence of his father.

Washington was lying in his bed, propped up by pillows. Brodie was initially taken aback by the changes in his father's appearance. He had drastically aged and the color of his skin was an ashy gray. Once Washington spotted his son in the doorway, he extended his hand outward. "Son, you're home." He took a deep breath before speaking again. "Please, come closer."

No one spoke as they exited the bedroom, allowing Brodie the opportunity to draw close to his father's bed. Benjamin gave him a stern look and, under his breath, stated in a firm voice, "Don't make him upset any more than you already have."

Brodie glanced at his family members as they left the room and then sat down on the edge of the bed. "Pa, I'm so sorry for everything."

"I missed you, Son."

"I missed you as well."

"Brodie, do you remember when it was just the three of us, living off of the land and never knowing if we were going to have enough to eat?" Tears started streaming down Washington's face. He took a deep breath and, with a cracked voice, stated, "I really had everything I ever needed or wanted with you and Sidney."

Brodie began to weep and placed his head down next to his father's. Washington placed his hand on Brodie's shoulder and began to pat it. "I love you, Son. I hope you know that."

"Pa, I do. I'm so sorry for the hardship I've brought on you."

"Brodie, the good Lord is calling me home."

"Don't say that. You can get better."

Washington took in a deep breath. "No. I know it's my time to leave this world."

For a few minutes, silence filled the room and then, in a soft voice, Washington whispered, "I'm going to miss you."

Brodie began to sob. He wiped the tears from his face. "I'm going to miss you as well."

On May 8th, surrounded by his family, Washington Duke passed away. On May 10th, all the businesses in Durham closed and a funeral procession left Trinity College and made its way to Main Street Methodist Church on the corner of Chapel Hill and Duke Streets. Thousands lined the street to pay their respects. The student body of Trinity College walked in the procession behind the casket. After the service, Washington was laid to rest in Maplewood Cemetery.

"Prior to the funeral, a reporter walking through the crowded flower-filled rooms of Fairview, Washington's home, noted Brodie Duke sitting on the staircase, away from the crush, and watching the people file into the room where the casket lay. The newsman added, "He looked small and frail and pitiful, this son that the old man had loved."

| 37 |

1905

Brodie observed as distant family members walked through the doors of Fairview and made their way to Washington's library. Many of them he didn't recognize, causing him to wonder how they were all somehow connected to the man who was now resting in the mausoleum located in Maplewood Cemetery. Some, who had very little in the way of fine clothing, appeared nervously excited at the prospect of an inheritance that would somehow change their lives.

Brodie took his place on the far-left side of the room where Pearl and Mabel were seated. He sat next to his youngest daughter, squeezing her hand and presenting an awkward smile. It was clear that she was hesitant to speak and Brodie could totally understand why. The last year had been a whirlwind of events that were humiliating for everyone associated with Brodie. Pearl, who had the ability to somehow look beyond all of Brodie's blunders, asked, "How are you, Daddy?"

Brodie shook his head before responding, "I knew my father would die one day, but I never thought it would be so difficult."

Mabel responded with a coldness in her voice. "If you would've spent more time with him, you probably wouldn't be feeling so much guilt. He was a kind man who only wanted the best for you. But you wouldn't know that, given you were so busy ruining your life and that of everyone associated with you."

Brodie wasn't sure what to say, so he remained silent. Pearl looked at her sister. "Mabel, that's an awful thing to say to our father."

"No, Pearl, Mabel is right. I have been neglectful as a son, and also as a father."

"And let's not forget how horrible a husband you were to Minnie. She only wanted what was best for you and all you did was treat her like the dirt off the bottom of your shoes."

Mabel crossed her arms and looked straight ahead. Pearl glanced at her sister and then turned her attention to her father. "Daddy, I'll never understand why you married that woman in New York. You couldn't wait until you were divorced from Minnie, and then you jumped right into a marriage with that crooked woman who is clearly a gold digger."

"I know nobody believes me, but I swear I was drugged. I don't remember anything after having drinks with her in the hotel bar."

Mabel leaned over her sister and pointed at her father. "Can't you see how your drinking has led you down into the pits of hell? And, now look, no one wants to have anything to do with you!"

Brodie was overcome with a gut-wrenching pain that radiated from his chest down. He had a hard time breathing, but didn't want his daughters to see how much pain he was in. All he wanted to do was leave, but knew that the scene of him leaving would cause even further ridicule.

In that moment, Buck and Benjamin walked out of a side door and toward the front row. Neither looked in his direction, which Brodie was thankful for. J.E. Stagg, the attorney presiding over the reading of the will, arrived and strode to the table that faced the crowd. He took several papers out of his briefcase and placed them in a neat pile in front of him. "Ladies and gentlemen, I have been asked to read the will of Mr. Washington Duke."

Several people in the back of the room began to whisper. Mr. Stagg looked in the direction of the noise and spoke. "I'd appreciate it if no one interrupts until I've finished."

Brodie glanced around the room and noted the many familiar faces, along with some he had never seen before. He knew his father had always been generous to his sibling's families and wasn't surprised to see them here. He also noted a black man leaning against the wall in the back of the room.

John Merrick was dressed in a coat and tie and didn't appear any different from the upper-class citizens of Durham, except for the color of his skin. Anyone close to Washington knew why John was present. It had nothing to do with receiving any finances for himself. No, it went deeper than that.

As Brodie looked in his direction, John nodded his head as a show of respect. This made Brodie feel uncomfortable. There was nothing about the way he had been acting in the past year that should encourage anyone to respect him. Brodie believed, on the other hand, that John deserved respect from everyone in this room, and also in the city of Durham.

Brodie knew that John had been born and raised before the Civil War by his mother, who had been a slave. Once slavery was abolished, they moved to Chapel Hill, where she was hired to clean houses. Over time, John found a job as a brick mason and was one of the men who had built Shaw University in Raleigh. Times had been difficult for John, but he always could envision a life where he would do more than just manual labor.

John had become friends with a barber in Raleigh during the time that Durham's population was increasing, so he moved to Durham to open up his own barbershop. He settled in Hayti and built a house on Fayetteville Street. Over time, he opened several shops, in and around Durham, all segregated. It was in one of these shops that Washington Duke became a regular customer.

The men had a lot in common, but the main thread that tied their relationship together was their love for their churches. Both men were Methodist and both had a strong faith in Jesus Christ. So, when Washington would come in to get a haircut and shave, their conversations would ultimately lead back to their faith and love for their churches.

Brodie would never forget one particular day that he had stopped in to get a haircut. Washington was sitting in the chair and was so engrossed in a conversation with John, that he didn't notice his presence. John was telling Washington about an insurance company that he had begun. "Yes, Mr. Duke, I have to do something. I have witnessed too many of my friends and family members suffering because they didn't have the money to bury their loved ones."

Washington asked, in a gentle voice, "How do you plan to resolve this issue?"

"I know many of my kind are poor and can't afford an insurance policy. And, even if they could, no insurance companies, owned by white folk, are going to supply them a policy. So, I'm going to ask each person who will purchase a policy from me, to give ten cents per month. And, if they are current with their payments at the time of their loved one's death, I'm going to write them a check for one hundred dollars. That should be enough for the burial and a headstone."

Brodie could see the expression on Washington's face in the mirror. He looked up at John with a grin covering his face. "John, I think that is a wonderful idea. You are a very intelligent man. But I believe it is your compassion for others that makes you standout. I believe you will create a business that will be, not only successful here in Durham, but one that people will recognize all over the country."

Brodie was brought back to the present by the sound of J.E. Stagg calling the room to attention. He felt a strong impulse to look back at John, standing against the back wall, surrounded by a sea of white folk. He smiled in his direction and tipped his head. In that moment, he had a deep respect for this man who had been such a good friend to his father.

J.E. Stagg began to read the will. *"I, Washington Duke, of sound mind and body, would like to appoint my sons, James Buchanan and Benjamin Newton, as executors of my estate. I would like for each of them to receive thirty percent of the overall value of my estate. I leave to my son, Brodie Leonidas, and his four children, twenty-eight percent of the overall value of my estate. The remaining twelve percent will go to Mary Stagg, George Lyon, and Buchanan Lyon. The estate will remain in a trust. I would like Fairview, my house, and all personal property to go to James Buchanan."*

People begun to murmur as the words began to sink in. Brodie remained silent and tried to understand why his father had given him less than his brothers. Initially, a strong feeling of jealousy swept over him. He didn't want to feel this way and tried to focus his thoughts on his last interaction with his father. He knew that Washington had cared deeply for him and was somehow protecting him from the horrendous handling of his own finances.

Brodie looked over at Mabel and Pearl and noticed the smiles on their faces. He watched as the two women clutched each other's hands with excitement. It was evident that they were thankful for how Washington had divided his portion, so that Brodie's children could immediately reap the benefit of being a Duke. Brodie couldn't fault them for anticipating the opportunities the money would provide to them and their families. Anyway, he still had plenty of money flowing in from his properties and stock dividends.

J.E. Stagg's loud voice interrupted his thoughts. "Ladies and gentlemen, I would like to continue. As we all know, Washington, knowing he was nearing the end of his life, made several large contributions, the largest to Trinity College. It is difficult to know the exact amount Washington contributed to this college, but it sizable, to say the least. There are several other organizations he has named in his will that are listed below: to the North Carolina Methodist Church, he left five thousand dollars; to the Western North Carolina Conference, he left five thousand dollars; to Watts Hospital, he left three thousand dollars; to the Oxford Orphanage, he left three thousand dollars; and to the Raleigh Methodist Orphanage, he left three thousand dollars."

J.E. Stagg paused a moment before continuing. His eyes looked toward the back of the room as he spoke. "Mr. Merrick, Washington left a note at the bottom of his will to personally thank you for your service and friendship over the many years you served as his barber. Out of respect for your faith and love for the Methodist Church, he has left five thousand dollars for the Kittrell Institute, as well as twenty-five hundred dollars each, for the Western North Carolina and North Carolina Conference of the African Methodist Church."

Several people began to express their dismay at the generosity Washington displayed toward the black community. At this point,

Buck rose and addressed the crowd. "I want to thank all of you for coming today. My father was a very generous and compassionate man. He never saw the color of a man's skin and he would appreciate it if you would remember him by respecting his wishes."

People began to get up and the sound of chair legs scratching against the wooden floor could be heard around the room. Some of Washington's distant relatives began to huddle together in small groups, discussing their feelings about Washington's will. Brodie looked over at where John Merrick had stood and noticed he was gone. As Brodie stood up to leave, he heard Pearl and Mabel discussing their newfound wealth. No one approached him as he slipped out the door.

Before heading home, Brodie made his way to Maplewood Cemetery and to the neoclassical designed mausoleum, where Washington now rested. As he approached the structure, he couldn't help but notice the large columns, along with the intricately designed building. His father's name loomed above the door declaring it as the place where his father and family members would be buried.

He took out his key and opened the large doors leading inside. The stained-glass window at the far end allowed beams of afternoon sunlight to project across the space, giving the room an eerie feel. Brodie walked in, closed the door, and walked over to the marble vault where Washington was buried. He placed his hand on the cold stone, and then, as if to draw closer to his father, pressed his entire body against the wall.

Brodie stood still, absorbing the enormity of losing his father. The reality of who his father had been, and the barrier of love he had created to protect Brodie, was becoming clear. It was only now, with his father gone, that he realized how different life would be. After pulling back from the stone, he touched his sister, Mary Elizabeth's, vault. He remembered how happy his father had been when the mausoleum was completed in 1894, so that his daughter would have a proper place of burial. At the time, Brodie didn't understand why his father visited the mausoleum so often. But now, he did.

Before leaving, he placed his hand on Martha's vault. It seemed so long ago that she had passed from this world. Once the structure was finished, Washington had asked Brodie if he would like Martha's remains placed in the mausoleum. At first, he declined, but over time, he had changed his mind. And now, as he walked among the deceased, he was grateful for having them all together.

38

1906

The torrential rain let up long enough for Brodie to make his way from his office on Main Street to his home. As he walked, the mud from the road splattered onto his pants causing him to cuss under his breath. Just as he was turning onto Duke Street, a Rolls Royce, with a chauffeur driving his brother, Ben, veered around the corner, spewing muddy water everywhere.

Brodie knew that his brother and his nephew, Angier, had recently purchased automobiles, but this was the first time he had encountered either of them. Only a few Durham citizens had bought an automobile, due to the high cost and unreliable nature of the machine. Most people were still dependent on their horse and buggy to get around town. So, when the brown liquid seeped into his coat and pants, he instantly swore out loud.

Brodie heard his brother, Ben, telling his chauffeur to pull over and, once the car stopped, Ben called out, "Brodie, come in and take a seat."

"I'm covered with mud."

"That's okay. I'll have it cleaned later today."

Brodie lowered his head, crammed inside the small space, and sat down, trying to keep an arm's length between him and his brother. He rubbed his fingers against the paneling and the cushioned seat. He was definitely impressed with the interior and the smell of the leather backing. "So, this is what all the fuss is about?"

"I thought you'd like it. It definitely can't replace the horse and buggy, but it sure is nice to be out of the elements." Ben signaled for the driver to ride down Duke Street, passing the warehouses on the right and Brodie's house on the left.

Brodie sat back and didn't say anything to his brother. Even though it had been almost a year since his institutionalization, neither brother had made an effort to communicate. After a few minutes of becoming acclimated to his first ride in an automobile, Brodie spoke. "How have you been feeling lately? I received word that your health hasn't been good."

"I have my good and bad days. I happen to be feeling pretty well at this point in time." Ben paused a moment before continuing. "I don't know if you heard about Buck's breakup with Lillian?"

"Yes. It seems the only one of us who has been successful in marriage is you."

"I give Sarah all the credit for that. When we moved to New York, she was not happy. But I'm excited to say that she has made the most of it."

"Speaking of your family, how is Angier? I heard about his accident with the gun. I'm sorry that he had to have his right hand amputated."

"Thanks. It was a freaky accident, but I'm glad it wasn't any worse. I love my son, but he takes a little after his uncle in the way he enjoys life a little too much."

Brodie smiled at the thought of his nephew living a carefree life. He then changed the subject. "I was hoping that Pa would leave Fairview to you."

"I think Pa thought if he left it to Buck, he would have a reason to come back to Durham. But I don't see that happening. Buck has too much going on in New York. And, now that the federal government is filing a suit against the American Tobacco Company, Buck will be too preoccupied to move home."

"So, what kind of defense is Buck giving the federal government?"

"He's told them that he never bought a company in order to eliminate it, but as a form ofinvestment."

"That sounds like Buck. What do you think is going to happen?"

"It doesn't look good but, as you know, you can't ever discount our brother's innovative ways. He's already looking into using hydroelectric power to operate the textile mills. I believe we are just in the beginning stages of finding ways to use electricity. I personally wouldn't be surprised if he ends up making a fortune off developing power companies all over the south."

Brodie leaned his back into the firm cushion and closed his eyes. "That sounds just like him. Never satisfied with just getting by, but always looking forward."

"Big Brother, I need to ask you something?"

Brodie tensed up, unsure of what Ben wanted to talk about. "What do you need to know?"

"Are you Daniel Quiggs?"

Brodie shivered in response to the question. He wasn't sure if he wanted to tell his brother the truth. It was only a year ago that Ben wanted to proclaim him insane and have his property placed in trust for life. "Why do you want to know?"

"Maybe, I hoped you would feel comfortable telling me the truth."

Brodie paused a moment, keeping his eyes shut. "Yes, I was arrested in New York for being intoxicated. When I was booked, I felt it would be best to keep our names out of the papers, so I told the arresting officer that my name was Daniel Quiggs."

"Brodie, I do appreciate how you tried to keep our names out of the papers, but didn't you think people would naturally assume it was you? Given the fact that you had your wallet on you with over five thousand dollars inside?"

Brodie began to feel uncomfortable. He didn't want to be questioned by his brother for his behavior. "You can get your chauffeur to drop me off at my house."

"Brodie, look, I'm sorry. Believe it or not, I do care about you."

"Yeah, right."

Ben waited a moment and then said, "I just hate how you and Buck aren't speaking. No matter what you've done in the past, the one thing Pa taught us was to value family. And no matter what you've done, you are my brother."

"You mean half-brother."

"Look, I wish I could remember Sidney, but I was just too young. I think about how horrible it was for you to lose him and Artelia. Even though she wasn't your biological mother, I believe her death hurt you the most."

Brodie didn't know what to think. He always believed Ben had a good heart and wanted the best for him. Ben was the one who had paid off his debts and purchased the mills from him when he had no other way to pay his outstanding obligations. He thought it best to change the subject. "Everyone is talking about the Durham and Southern Railway line you financed and how it now connects Durham to Dunn as well as to your textile plants in Erwin. I especially think it's wonderful how it has a couple of passenger cars for people to get to parts of North Carolina that haven't been previously accessible."

Ben smiled before responding. "That railroad cost me over a million dollars, but I believe I'll quickly recoup my money. I feel very blessed to have been given the opportunity to help others. And, by the way, I've purchased four acres right across from Main Street Methodist Church, where I'm going to build a house for Sarah and me to enjoy when we are in Durham."

Brodie sat up. For some reason, he was happy to know that Ben would be moving back to Durham. "I'm glad to hear that."

"Between the textile mills and my position as president of the Citizens National Bank, I need to be here. Anyway, traveling back and forth to New York is exhausting."

"What do you mean by that? I've heard that you and Buck have purchased private railroad cars to get you back and forth."

"Even with a private car, I'm tired of all the travel. Speaking of travel, have you heard anything from Richard Wright?"

"I see him occasionally. He's been working on the trolley system here in Durham, as well as building his cigarette packaging machine company. Every time I speak to Nannie, she tells me that he's in some foreign country, selling either the Bonsack machine or his packaging machine."

"You know it was a real blessing when he wanted out of the company. At first, I thought it would be a real blow for us, given what an excellent salesman he was. But, over time, I've realized that he wanted to captain the ship and we both know that couldn't happen with Buck."

As the Rolls Royce pulled in front of Brodie's house, Ben leaned in toward his brother. "Look, Brodie, I truly hope the best for you. I know you've had some tough blows in life, but I really hope that, one day, you'll find someone to love."

"Thanks."

"Have you ever thought about asking Nannie Wright out?"

"No. We're just friends and both of us want to keep it that way."

"Well, maybe someone will show up."

"Thanks, Ben, for stopping. It was really nice catching up with you."

"You take care, Big Brother."

"You, too."

Once Brodie climbed out of the car and walked toward his house, he turned to watch the Rolls Royce pull away. At that moment, a feeling of loneliness swept over him like a cold chill. He shivered as he walked inside the empty house and poured himself a drink.

| 39 |

1906-1908

Brodie couldn't believe he was right back in the same situation he had been in with Minnie. Soon after arriving home to Durham, he had served Alice Webb papers for an absolute divorce. But it wasn't until the following March that Justice Blanchard, in a New York court, granted him the judgment he had requested. Even following the divorce, Alice Webb took advantage of her last name and started a business called the Alice Webb Duke Tobacco Company. Months later, the owner of the building, where she held a lease, took her to court to have the company dissolved due to her unwillingness to pay her bills.

Brodie was dumbfounded by the actions of Alice Webb. He still had little memory of what exactly had happened in New York. One thing was clear; he wanted nothing more to do with this woman who had caused such havoc in his life. So, it wasn't surprising when Brodie heard that Alice Webb had been arrested for writing bad checks. She pleaded that she was under the influence of stimulants and narcotics she had taken to alleviate the pain of a pleurisy attack. Later that month, an article in the Durham Sun stated, "*What a tangled Webb she can constantly weave, when she undertakes the public to deceive; and then, to add to her infamous fame, she keeps right on using Brodie's name.*"

At the time, Brodie also had some legal issues he needed to clean up. He had lost money in the trade of cotton commodities and the brokers wanted their money. Twice he had been to court and won the judgment. But on November 25, 1907, a jury before Supreme Court Justice Newberger, awarded A.L. Norden and Company $5,623 to be paid in full. Unlike his earlier divorce proceedings, when Brodie had managed to sway the court, this time he was unable to use his power or influence to alter the judgment.

As much as he considered changing, Brodie continued to pursue a lifestyle without boundaries. Maybe he thought he would find some form of satisfaction or fulfillment in his outlandish pursuits of fun. An Atlanta newspaper posted an article sharing that Brodie had been spotted with a group of six friends heading to Birmingham. Another article, in Pittsburgh, commented on a night that Brodie spent over ten thousand dollars for a dinner, handing out large tips to the wait staff, and even giving the leader of the orchestra money for changing the songs in the program.

But, no matter where he went, Brodie always considered Durham to be his home. In June 1908, he stood alongside hundreds of people on the campus of Trinity College to, once again, pay homage to his father.

Brodie had heard about the bronze statue that had been created by Edward Valentine, a well-known southern sculptor, and was as excited to see it as anyone. A.T. Ragland and T.J. Walker of Richmond, Virginia, had led the campaign to raise the money for the monument that was now being placed at the entrance to Trinity College. Brodie had gladly contributed to the statue's creation, along with over two hundred other donors.

Students, Durham citizens, and Trinity College alumni, stood shoulder to shoulder, waiting for the unveiling. Buck and Benjamin were seated on the stage, along with several other Durham dignitaries. Brodie hadn't been asked to be one of the select few to be seated on stage, which suited him just fine. He preferred to stand among the ordinary citizens of Durham, a place where he felt more comfortable. Brodie was also aware of Buck's continued hostility toward him, never having given up the notion that he had had something to do with their father's death. So, Brodie gladly stood at a distance, where he could enjoy the moment without his brother glaring down at him.

John C. Kilgo, Trinity College's president, stood up to speak. "We are here today to pay homage to a man who loved this city, as well as this college. His generosity and devotion to education have enabled us to become an institution that we can all be proud of. Before unveiling the statue, I would like to read the inscription that has been etched onto its base: WASHINGTON DUKE / 1820-1905 / ANIMATED BY LOFTY PRINCIPLES HE EVER CHERISHED THE / WELFARE OF HIS COUNTRY WITH THE ARDOR OF A TRUE / PATRIOT; DILIGENT IN BUSINESS HE ACQUIRED RICHES, BUT / IN THE ENJOYMENT OF THEM DID NOT FORGET TO SHARE / WITH THE LESS FORTUNATE; A PATRON OF LEARNING HE / FOSTERED AN INSTITUTION WHICH PLACED WITHIN THE REACH / OF ASPIRING YOUTH THE IMMORTAL GIFT OF KNOWLEDGE; AND / WHEN THE ACTIVITIES OF HIS EARLY LIFE AND THE STERNER / STRUGGLES OF HIS MATURER

YEARS HAD PASSED HE ENTERED / UPON A SERENE OLD AGE CHEERED BY A LOWLY PIETY AND / SUSTAINED BY AN UNFAILING TRUST IN GOD, WHO IN ALL THE / VICISSITUDES OF LIFE HAD KEPT HIM SINGLE IN HIS AIMS, / SINCERE IN HIS FRIENDSHIPS AND TRUE TO HIMSELF. The north face reads:FRIEND TO TRUTH! OF SOUL SINCERE, / IN ACTION FAITHFUL, AND IN HONOR CLEAR. The east face reads: PHILANTHROPIST. The west face reads: PATRIOT.

Once he finished reading the inscription, John Kilgo spoke with a deep sincerity in his voice. "Washington Duke was a man of integrity, of great character, and his life's work will never be forgotten. But, most of all, Washington Duke was my friend."

There was an eruption of applause which gave Brodie goosebumps. He had never felt more honored to be Washington's son than at this moment in time. He smiled at the fact that this man everyone was celebrating had been, not only a great man, but also an incredible father.

John Kilgo motioned for everyone to be quiet. "At this time, Mary Washington Stagg, Washington's great-granddaughter, will pull the cord to unveil the statue."

Everyone was standing on their tiptoes, trying to get a first glimpse of the larger-than-life statue. As the little girl pulled the cord, and the cover slipped down to the ground, loud applause erupted. Brodie looked at the statue of his father and was immediately struck by the likeness. He was taken aback by the facial expression, one of repose and meditation; an attitude he had seen many times when visiting the older man in the quietness of his study.

Brodie was close to tears as he stared at his father's likeness etched in stone. He knew his father would have felt both honored, and a little embarrassed, by all the attention. Just as he started moving closer to the bronzed statue, someone tapped him on the shoulder. He turned around and was face-to-face with a dark-skinned woman. For a moment, not recognizing her, he was about to tell her that she had made a mistake. But then she spoke. "Brodie, do you remember me?"

The sound of her voice was familiar but unrecognizable. "I'm Caroline."

Brodie looked at the older woman, who had been such an important part of his life, and smiled. "Oh, Caroline." He stopped speaking, finding it hard to believe she was actually standing in front of him. "I can't tell you how much I've missed you. What happened? Did you locate your family?"

"The night your father told me to leave, I traveled north in pursuit of freedom, as well as a reunion with my family. But, when I got up to Maryland, I had nothing. I was hired to work for a wealthy family as their nannie. I stayed there until the war was over." Caroline paused, as if she was reflecting back on those days so long ago. "I desperately wanted to find my family but realized I had no way of knowing where they were."

Brodie pointed to a bench at the far corner of the grounds. "Come over here, so we can talk." He led her over and sat down. He could see people pointing at the odd-looking couple, but didn't care. He only wanted to hear the story of how Caroline had survived and how she had made it back to Durham. "Caroline, please tell me more. I missed you so much when you left. I must admit I was angry with my father for letting you leave."

Caroline smiled. "Brodie, you have no idea how much I missed all of you. I want you to know I kept one of the books you gave me. Every night, for years, I pulled it out and read it, remembering the time I was with your family. So many times I wanted to return to Durham but just didn't know how."

"Did you get married and have children?"

"No. I was so busy raising the children of the people who I worked for, that I never met anyone. But, over time, I was able to put away a little money. A couple of years ago, I made the decision to come back to Durham to try and find you."

"Did you see Pa before he died?"

"No. I made it to Durham a few months after his death."

"Oh, Caroline, I wish I'd known you were here."

"That's okay. I found a nice family to work for. They treat me well and even give me books to read."

Brodie sat up straight and, with eagerness in his voice, asked, "Would you like to work for me? I have a large house and could use the help."

"No. I'm happy with the family I'm with. But, thank you."

Caroline looked at Brodie with a strange expression. "Brodie, are you okay?"

"Not really. I miss Pa more than I ever thought I would, and I've made a mess out of my marriages, as well as my kids don't really want to have anything to do with me."

It was clear that Caroline wanted to reach over and touch Brodie, but both knew it wouldn't be perceived well. So, they sat in silence for a few moments. Then, in a confident voice, the older woman spoke. "I believe in you Brodie Duke. I believe you're going to take these last years the Good Lord has given you, and you're going to be just fine."

Caroline then stood and, with tears in her eyes, walked away, never to be seen again.

| 40 |

1908-1909

Brodie couldn't shake off the effect of Caroline's words and, for the first time in decades, he experienced a diminished desire to drink. Instead of spending time at Carrington or Mangum Tavern, Brodie began walking from his home to downtown, conversing with the people he met along the way.

There was one local man who Brodie found himself bantering with on a daily basis. Leander Rochelle was typically sitting on his porch, watching the world go by, when Brodie passed by during his daily walk. He knew that Leander was a conservative and Brodie loved to flaunt the fact that Theodore Roosevelt, a Republican, had been such a successful president, and that it looked like William Howard Taft, also a Republican, was going to win in November. It was late September and everyone was beginning to discuss the presidential race with the conservative, William Jennings Bryan, as the Democratic nominee.

When Brodie saw Leander sitting on his porch, he yelled out so the local could definitely hear him. "William Bryan doesn't have a chance in hell to win in November."

"What are you talking about Brodie Duke? This nation needs a more conservative president. And anyway, why are you favoring the liberal Republicans? You know they are determined to bring down the American Tobacco Company with their pursuit of breaking up monopolies?"

Brodie yelled out, "That's true, but that's not my concern. Buck is having to deal with that, not me."

"Come over here and let me tell you why a conservative like Bryan will make a good president."

Leander's daughter, Wylanta, yelled out, "Brodie, I wouldn't come over here if I were you."

"And, Wylanta, why shouldn't I?"

"You know my father will talk your ear off."

Intrigued by Wylanta's words, and with the lack of anything better to do, Brodie walked up the sidewalk and onto the porch. Leander was sitting in a chair, while Wylanta was leaning on the rail that bordered the porch. The young woman shook her head. "Don't tell me that I didn't warn you, Mr. Duke."

Leander motioned for Brodie to sit down in one of the empty chairs that lined the porch. "So, tell me what you believe Taft is going to do for you going forward?"

Brodie sat down and turned the chair facing Leander "These last eight years with Roosevelt have been good for the country. Now, unlike my brother, I'm more concerned about the common man and his rights."

Leander looked intently at Brodie. "Well, I'm one of those common men and I personally believe everything is moving way too fast."

"Now, Daddy, let's not bore Mr. Duke with all your philosophical beliefs about the desire to keep things the way they've been since the Civil War."

Brodie looked at Wylanta and noticed, for the first time, how she had grown into an attractive young lady. "Wylanta, what about you? Do you want to be able to vote one day?"

"Of course, I do. I differ from my father in his views about women's rights. I believe it's deplorable that women don't have the ability to vote at this point in time."

Leander began to interrupt his daughter, but Brodie cut him off. "Now, Leander, let's let your daughter speak her mind."

Leander folded his arms over his chest and grunted.

Brodie then looked at Wylanta and, for the first time, felt a desire to get to know this young woman. "Wylanta, how old are you?"

"I'm twenty-six."

"Tell me about your plans for the future."

"I'd like to attend college, but that's probably not likely."

Leander abruptly interjected, "Now, Wylanta, you know we would send you to college if we could afford it, but we don't have the money to send you to school. Anyway, you don't need a college education. You need a husband to take care of you."

"Daddy, I don't just want to be someone's wife. I want to do something good for this world. Maybe I could help with the women's suffrage movement."

Leander shook his head, but remained silent. Brodie looked at Wylanta and noticed how excited she was about the possibility of bettering herself. "Wylanta, if you were to go anywhere to college, where would it be?"

Wylanta looked at Brodie with a quizzical look. "If I could go anywhere, it would be Trinity Washington University."

Brodie asked, "And why there?"

"The school is located in Washington, D.C., our nation's capital. I could be among all the politicians where I could learn more about our government and how it works. I want to learn everything I can about this nation and what is good for women." Wylanta looked toward her dad and then continued. "Daddy, I know you would love for me to stay here and get married, but I believe there is more to life than just being a wife and a mother."

Leander looked at Brodie. "Do you see what I'm having to deal with? I'm sure your daughters did what you wanted them to do?"

Brodie laughed to himself. He thought about Mabel and how she had eloped, and then how Pearl moved to California before marrying a man from Chattanooga. "I wish I could say that was true, but it isn't. Both of my daughters have minds of their own."

The next day, when Brodie walked by the Rochelle house, Wylanta was sitting alone on her family's porch. He wasn't sure if he wanted to approach her without her father being present, but when she saw him, she yelled out, "Mr. Duke, how are you today?"

"I'm doing well. I hope you are."

"I am. Please come and sit a spell. Daddy is taking a nap and should be out in a few minutes."

Brodie came up and sat down in the rocking chair next to Wylanta. She turned and smiled at him. "Mr. Duke, can I ask you a question?"

"Sure."

"If you could change anything in your life, what would it be?"

"Oh my. Wylanta, I don't think we have enough time to answer that question."

"I don't believe that. You have done so much good for this town. You've traveled the world and made a lot of money. And, from what Daddy says, you've been very generous with giving your land away for so many different needs. He told me that you were even considered the Mayor of North Durham. That sounds like a lot to me."

Brodie smiled as he listened to this young woman speak so highly of him. His impulse was to stop her and tell her the truth, but he didn't want to put a damper on the conversation. "I have done some good for this town. But I also know I've hurt some people along the way."

"That's hard for me to believe."

"Well, enough about me. I want to know more about your aspirations."

Wylanta leaned in as she spoke. "I wish I could define exactly what it is that I want to do, but there are so many directions I could go in. If only I had the ability to go to college. Daddy doesn't understand this. He thinks I'm smart enough, almost too smart for my own well-being."

Brodie stood up before speaking. "Wylanta, I have to go now, but I'd like to talk to you more about your dreams."

Wylanta stood and looked Brodie in the eye. "I'd like that very much."

Over the next few months, Brodie intentionally walked past the Rochelle house, always hoping to spend a few minutes talking to Wylanta. After having numerous conversations about her desire to go to college, he made a decision and was ready to share it with both Wylanta and her parents.

41

1909

Brodie knew his idea was outlandish and he wasn't sure if Leander and his wife, Jeanette, would agree to it. He also knew that it made perfect sense and he was willing to do what it took to see it through. So, on one of the hottest August days, Brodie headed out to the Rochelle house where he hoped he could speak with Leander and Jeanette, without Wylanta being present.

When Brodie turned the corner onto Main Street, Leander was out on the porch fanning the flies away. Brodie made his way up the sidewalk and up the steps onto the porch. "It sure is a hot one."

Leander continued to use his fan, trying to swat at each fly as they circled around him. "It sure is. One day, I hope someone invents a machine that can keep the flies away. I guess if your brothers can figure out a way to give us electricity here in Durham, surely someone could create a fan to move around the air."

"I believe it will be sooner than later. Buck has been working on hydroelectricity for a while. If he could just figure out a way to move the electricity away from the rivers and into Durham, you might just have your fan become reality."

"I hope so. What have you been up to?"

"Not much. I'm building more store space in the center of town. I've also decided to donate some land for a park. I think I'll call it Duke Park. It'll be nice to see more common spaces in and around Durham for people to enjoy."

"Well, we have Lakewood Amusement Park just a trolley ride away."

"Richard Wright sure knew what he was doing when he created that park at the end of the trolley line. I'm hoping the trolley line will head toward the north, but it doesn't seem likely. Now that more people are driving automobiles, I guess there isn't as much of a need for the trolley."

Leander kept fanning. "Not everyone can afford an automobile. I know the workers at the mills and the tobacco factories aren't making enough money for an automobile."

Brodie sat still for a moment. "Is Jeanette around?"

"Yes. She's in the kitchen."

"Can you get her to come out here so we can talk?"

Leander gave Brodie a quizzical look and then got up, opened the screen door, and yelled, "Jeanette, Brodie Duke is here and he wants to talk with us."

A voice could be heard from the back of the house. "I'm coming."

Jeanette, a thin woman with gray hair, walked out of the house with a dishrag in her hand. "Well hello, Brodie. Can I get you a glass of tea or lemonade?"

"No. This won't take long."

Jeanette sat down and Brodie scooted his chair so that he was facing the couple. He cleared his throat and began. "I've been giving this a lot of thought and I've decided that I'd like to pay for Wylanta to go to college."

Leander immediately responded. "Brodie, that's a nice gesture, but we can't accept."

Jeanette gave her husband a stern look and then spoke. "Leander, let's not rush into a decision. We both know how much Wylanta wants to go to college. Now, Brodie, we couldn't just take your money. If there was a way that we could pay you back, we would consider it."

"Now, you two know that I have a lot of money that's just sitting in the bank collecting dust. In the last year, with my mind clear from abstaining from alcohol, I've been trying to find ways to use it in a productive manner. I can tell you, I've thrown more money away than I care to admit. But, I believe, Wylanta would take full advantage of an education and, then, if she gets a good job, she can pay me back."

Just about this time, Wylanta walked up the steps and observed the scene in front of her. "So, what are the three of you talking about?"

For a moment, no one spoke. Once Wylanta was up on the porch, leaning on the rail, Jeanette said, "Mr. Duke would like to pay for you to go to college."

Brodie looked at Leander to see his expression. It was clear that he wasn't totally sold on the idea. Wylanta, on the other hand, was beaming. She looked at Brodie and, with an endearing voice, asked, "You would do that for me?"

Brodie felt awkward looking up at Wylanta, so he stood. "I was just telling your parents that I believe you would do well in college. I think it would be wonderful for you to experience living in Washington and, hopefully, find what will make you happy."

Wylanta seemed dazed. "You would do that for me?"

Brodie smiled. "Yes, I would do that for you."

As much as Leander didn't want to accept Brodie's offer, he eventually conceded, and Wylanta left for Trinity Washington University in early September. After she had been gone for a few weeks, Brodie received a letter from her. As he inspected the envelope, with the elegant cursive writing, he smiled. Once he opened the letter, he raised the paper up to his nose and smelled the scent of Wylanta's perfume.

Brodie was struck with feelings that, he believed, were inappropriate, but then he had to question why she would lace the letter with perfume. And, as he read the words that were meant only for his eyes, he became even more confused.

Dear Brodie, (I hope it's okay to call you by your first name)

I wanted to let you know how truly grateful I am for this opportunity to attend college. I never thought I would be able to go off to school and actually study subjects that I'm interested in. And you made it all possible! I wish you could come visit me and see the campus. It's so beautiful here.

There are so many things I want to share. I'm taking a literature class and reading several interesting books. I believe my favorite is the The Gift of the Magi. I know you have lots of money, but I believe you can relate to the importance of sacrificing for someone you love. When I read the story, I started crying. Just thinking about this gift you have given me, means more than you will ever know.

I need to close for now, but would love to hear from you.

With Deep Gratitude,

Wylanta

Brodie sat back in the leather-bound chair situated in his library, surrounded by books he had never even opened. He heard the ticking of the grandfather clock in the hallway and smelled the bread that the cook was baking in the kitchen. He brought the letter up to his nose, enjoying the scent that reminded him of the young woman who was capturing his heart. He pulled out his ink and pen and began to write.

Dear Wylanta,

I received your letter today. It made me smile to know how much you are enjoying being at school in Washington. I've spent a lot of time there in my past and know what a beautiful place it is. I would love to come there and spend some time with you.

I feel a little awkward telling you this, given our age difference, but I honestly feel a connection with you that I've never felt before. I know you are fully aware of my failed marriages and how foolish I've been in the past. But I can tell you that, in the last year, I've truly tried to change.

I'd love to share with you so many things and take you places that I truly believe you would appreciate. When I think of you, I feel like I can be the best version of myself.

You are ever in my thoughts,

Brodie

Over the next several months, Wylanta and Brodie wrote to each other often, neither sure if this relationship could actually evolve into anything more than a benefactor taking care of a beneficiary. But as much as they told themselves that the age difference was too large to overcome, their feelings spoke something entirely different.

| 42 |

1909

For the first time in decades, Brodie was excited about the holiday season. He took great care when picking out a Christmas tree and had ornaments shipped to Durham from all over the country. He, along with his house staff, spent hours decorating the tree, ensuring it was just right. His staff, who were used to a house void of the holiday season cheer, were ecstatic to see the changes in their boss.

Brodie decided to have an elaborate holiday party on Christmas Eve. He invited the Rochelle's, along with many other Durham residents. Given Brodie's reputation for being overly generous, the party was sure to be an event that everyone would talk about for weeks. Brodie had hired an orchestra as well as commissioned one of the best chefs from New York City.

Wylanta was to arrive home two days before Christmas. As much as Brodie wanted to spend time with her, Wylanta had asked him to be discreet and keep his distance for the time being. It was difficult for Brodie, but he honored her wishes.

Before anyone arrived for the party, the house staff, along with several other hired hands, worked tirelessly to create a magical environment for the guests. Candles flickered from every windowsill and the tree was lit up, showcasing the beautiful ornaments. But it was what was under the tree that brought Brodie the most joy. It was full of gifts for the children attending the party as well as one wrapped package that he intended to give to Wylanta.

Once the party began, Brodie stood in the foyer welcoming his guests. The orchestra played Christmas songs and the smell of the fir tree filled the air with the scent of the holiday season. The candles twinkled, along with the diamonds the women wore around their necks, creating a perfect setting for a memorable evening.

Brodie was extremely nervous as he waited to see Wylanta enter. He knew he shouldn't feel this way, but his heart was ruling his mind and emotions. He had loved Martha and lusted after Elizabeth, but never had Brodie desired to be with a woman who he appreciated for her intellect physical appearance, as well as for her heart.

Brodie knew there would be resistance, but he didn't care. People would talk and many would try to persuade him that he was once again being foolish. But, as he watched Wylanta walk through the door, with the candles flickering and the music playing, all he cared about was being with this woman.

The wait staff, dressed in formal wear, walked among the guests, offering appetizers and champagne. The children who attended were offered punch and cookies in a back room where toys had been set up to entertain them. Once it was clear that everyone had arrived, the guests were escorted to a large dining room that had been prepared with the finest silver, crystal glasses, and linens.

Brodie had placed engraved name cards at each place, making sure that Wylanta would be seated next to him. To make it less obvious, he had placed her mother, Jeanette, and father, Leander, on her other side. Once everyone was seated, Brodie rose from his seat at the head of the table and clinked his knife against the fine crystal glass to catch the attention of all his guests. "Ladies and gentlemen, I want to thank you for coming tonight. As many of you know, this is the first time, in a long time, that I have hosted such a festive event. I want to raise a toast to this evening and hope that we will have many future occasions like this one."

As Brodie raised his glass, he looked around the room and finally his eyes settled on Wylanta, who was looking at him with a gleam in her eye and a smile that almost brought him to his knees. He sat back down and, as the food was being served, Wylanta leaned in and whispered, "Brodie this is the most magical night of my life. I never thought I'd experience anything like this."

Brodie reached under the table and grasped Wylanta's hand. "I would love to share many more nights just like this one with you."

Brodie understood the importance of discretion and quickly removed his hand so he wouldn't draw attention. He spent much of the evening conversing with all of his guests, expressing his gratitude for their attendance at his holiday party. After a wonderful dinner of roast beef, turkey, and cranberry sauce, Brodie escorted his guests to the parlor where he distributed gifts to the children.

It had been a long time since he had been around small children and he found them entertaining. He beamed while observing the reactions of the children, as they pulled off the ribbons and tore the wrapping paper from their gifts. Many were pleasantly surprised at the extravagance of the toys, showering him with hugs, while others jumped up and down with joy.

As the party began to wane and his guests were leaving, Brodie decided to pull Wylanta aside to give her the one gift he was most excited about. Leander and Jeanette appeared preoccupied, which Brodie was thankful for. At this point, he didn't know, for sure, where their relationship was headed and didn't want to arouse unwarranted suspicions.

"Wylanta, I have something for you."

"Brodie, you didn't have to get me anything. You have given me the gift of education, which I can never repay."

Brodie handed Wylanta a wrapped present and stood next to her, anxious to see her response. "I hope you like it."

The young woman seemed giddy as she unfolded the paper and found a silk bag. She reached inside and pulled out a gold comb with a flower decoration made out of diamonds and rubies. At first, she didn't react, which caused Brodie to become extremely anxious, wondering if he'd made a mistake. But, then Wylanta smiled at him and, for that moment, it was as if they were alone in the room. The magic spell was suddenly broken by the sound of Leander's voice. "Brodie, I'd like to speak to you in private."

Jeanette stood next to Wylanta as Brodie and Leander went back to Brodie's library. Once they were in the room with the door closed, Leander got right to the point. "What are you thinking?"

"Leander, what are you saying?"

"I can see that there is something going on between you and my daughter. Hell, you're old enough to be Wylanta's father!"

Brodie wasn't sure what to say, but knew he had to be cautious. "Leander, I only gave your daughter a comb for her hair."

"That isn't just an ordinary comb."

Brodie kept his composure as he responded, "Look, Wylanta told me about a story she was reading in college, where a woman receives a comb as a gift. So, I thought I would give her a comb, just to let her know that I am proud of how well she is doing in school."

Leander looked right at Brodie before continuing. "Listen, as a father, I'm concerned for my daughter. I know how your relationships have turned out and I don't want my daughter to be hurt."

"I can understand your concerns. I think you have a very intelligent daughter, who has a mind of her own. I believe she can take care of herself and make good decisions."

"Brodie, I'm not going to allow you to influence my daughter with extravagant gifts, only for her to become one of your women who you get tired of and then throw away."

The words hurt more than Brodie wanted to admit. He knew he had made some serious mistakes regarding his past romantic relationships. He also knew that his reputation for drinking and gambling didn't help, but he had changed in the last year. "Leander, I hear you. I promise I'll only see her in your company or with a chaperone. You're probably right about being concerned about me. I would be concerned if one of my daughters came home with an older man. Now, how about let's go back to my guests, so I can properly send them off."

The two men walked back into the parlor where the last of the guests remained. Wylanta was standing in front of a mirror admiring her new comb. She looked so beautiful, standing there, that Brodie was tempted to walk up to her but thought better of it. Leander glared at Brodie. "Jeanette and Wylanta, it is time to go. I'm sure Mr. Duke has much to do to prepare for Christmas."

But that was the furthest thing from the truth. Brodie wanted to tell Leander that he had no plans and his children were all celebrating with their spouses' families. He wanted to tell him that the only person he wanted to spend Christmas with was his daughter,

Wylanta. But mostly, Brodie wanted to tell Leander that he loved Wylanta and planned to someday make her his wife.

43

1909-1910

The next morning, Brodie woke to a cold chill that caused him to pull the blankets up tight around his neck. At first, he thought he might be ill but, as he lay in the bed with no one else in the house, a deep-seated loneliness swept over him. He had allowed all of the staff to take the day off to be with their families, leaving him alone for the first time in months. He reached out for the wooden fox that he kept on his night table and placed it in the palm of his hand. He rotated the object around and around, hoping to find some solace from it, but none came.

After an hour of trying to avoid getting up, he finally rose and reached for his robe. He then walked over to the fireplace located on the other side of the room, balled up some paper, and lit it with a match. He placed the burning paper under some wood that had been prepared for a fire and waited for the wood to begin burning.

Once the fire was going and the room began to warm, Brodie dressed and made his way downstairs. The staff had cleared away the dishes and brought order to each of the rooms before leaving. He retrieved the newspaper from the front porch and made a cup of coffee. The coffee wasn't very good, but it did bring some warmth to his chilled body. He opened up the newspaper and read it from cover to cover.

Brodie was overtaken by feelings of loneliness and he knew that, if he didn't get out of the house, he might reach for a drink. So, he walked out the back to the stables, saddled a horse, and began to ride. Without a destination in mind, he allowed the horse to dictate the direction. He rode past First Presbyterian Church on Main Street and headed east. As he was approaching Dillard Street, he spotted Nannie walking toward the house that Richard had purchased from E.J. Parrish in 1899.

He slowed the horse down to keep pace with this woman who he considered to be a true friend. "Nannie, what are you doing walking outside on this cold Christmas day?"

"Brodie, I could ask you the same question." She paused a moment. "Anyway, I needed to borrow some sugar for a cake I'm baking for Christmas dinner."

"Is Richard home?"

"He is, in body, but it's clear he's preoccupied with some business deal. Why don't you stop by and come in for a visit. It'll be awhile before we eat. I'm sure he'd like to spend some time with a man his age, instead of all these children and women."

Brodie laughed. "I don't know. I don't want to intrude."

"Oh, you'd be doing all of us a favor if you could entertain him for a while. He just doesn't do well if he isn't working, even if it is Christmas."

Brodie thought the visit might be a good distraction from his desire to be with Wylanta and decided to see Richard. After he made sure his horse was secured, he walked up the steps and knocked. A girl with curly hair opened the door and looked up. "Can I help you?"

"Yes, I just spoke to your Aunt Nannie and she invited me to come visit with your Uncle Richard."

The little girl pulled the door back and pointed toward the back room. "He's back there."

Brodie walked toward the back of the house and looked inside a room where Richard was sitting behind a large desk. He knocked on the door frame, before entering. Richard looked up and stood. "Well, well, Brodie Duke. What are you doing out and about on Christmas Day?"

"My children are all with their spouses and I've sent the house staff home. I was out riding my horse and spotted Nannie walking back from an errand."

Richard leaned back in his chair. "So, I haven't seen your name in the newspaper lately. Does this suggest that you may have quit all your foolishness?"

Brodie had always felt a little uneasy around Richard. He, like his brother, Buck, was always focused first on his work, above all else. "I guess it does. I've been busy with building more rental properties and trying to sell all those lots that I purchased from you and Julian Carr."

"I wish we'd been able to hold on to all those lots in Trinity Park but, with all my travels and Julian's investment in the textile mills, it just made more sense for you to handle the sale of the property."

Brodie looked around the room and noticed all the imported furniture and expensive paintings. "So, I've heard that you've been selling a lot of your packaging machines."

"I have. I'm still selling some of the Bonsack machines, but I like the fact that I don't have to travel so far to sell my packaging machines. I'm also trying to teach my nephews, Richard Jr. and Tom Jr., how to run the business."

About that time, Nannie stepped inside the room. "It is about time to serve dinner. Brodie, why don't you stay and eat with us?"

"I don't want to intrude."

"You won't be intruding. We have a lot of food and it would be nice to have a guest for Christmas."

Brodie hesitated a moment but, after thinking about the empty house he would be going home to, he thought it would be nice to be surrounded by friends. "Sure, if it isn't too much trouble."

After dinner, and spending time listening to Richard speak of his trips to Asia and Europe, Brodie made his way back home. Once he was inside, he built a fire and was just sitting down to read a book, when he heard a knock on the front door. He wasn't expecting visitors and called out, "Who is it?"

"It's me, Wylanta."

Brodie opened the door and asked, "Wylanta, what are you doing here?"

"Can I come in? I can't stay but a minute. I came after Mom and Dad went to sleep, but I had to see you."

"Come in."

Brodie was trying to figure out why Wylanta had come. Thinking of the words Leander had spoken last night, he was sure she was going to say she couldn't see him again. "Can I take your coat?"

"No, I have only a moment before my absence may be noticed."

"What's wrong? Are you okay?"

Wylanta looked down and it was clear she was crying. "Brodie, I don't understand what is happening here?"

"What do you mean?"

This young woman, who could have anyone she desired, was clearly upset. She lifted her head and looked right at Brodie. "Between you and me."

All Brodie wanted to do was take Wylanta into his arms and kiss her but, as difficult as it was, he held back. He knew that, for this relationship to ever work, he had to respect her and give her an opportunity to make sense of her own feelings. "Wylanta, you know that I've been married several times and none of them worked out well. I can understand your father's concerns. I'd have my own concerns if my daughter brought home an older man."

"But I don't care about the age difference. All I know is that I've never felt this way about anyone before."

"Look, if we have any chance of being together, we need to be smart about this. First of all, I think both of us need to have some space to consider if this is truly what we want. I suggest you go back to school and see how you feel. We can write to each other and see what happens."

"But I want to be with you now."

Brodie could no longer restrain his feelings for Wylanta. He reached over, pulled her into his body and stroked her hair. "I'm not going anywhere." He kissed her gently on the forehead and then released her. "Please, go home. Once you get back to school, write me. I promise to write back. Then we can decide over the next few months if we are meant to be together."

Brodie took his finger and wiped the tears from her cheek. And before dashing out of the door, Wylanta leaned into Brodie, brushed her lips up against his, and left.

| 44 |

1910

Brodie placed his key inside the lock, turned it, and opened the P.O. Box. For weeks, since Wylanta left, he had walked to the post office, hoping to hear from her. He had opened this particular P.O. Box to avoid letters arriving at his office or home. In the past, there had been letters intercepted by both the office and house staff, leaving him no other option.

Ever since Wylanta left in January, there had been no letters. It was now the middle of February and his hopes to be with this woman were beginning to diminish. He took a deep breath and said a little prayer before pulling open the small door. Once the door was open, he instantly smelled the scent of Wylanta's perfume, causing him to jump with anticipation.

Hardly able to keep his composure, he pulled the letter out, tucked the envelope into his coat pocket, and quickly locked the box without being noticed. As he walked in the direction of his house, Brodie's heart began beating at a rapid pace and he was unable to take another step. He began to play out the worst-case scenarios and knew he needed to open the letter in order to ease his mind. So, with shaking hands, he pulled the flap back and read:

Dear Brodie,

I tried to pretend that our relationship didn't exist and that I could find a young man who would provoke the same feelings I have for you. But, in reality, I can't stop thinking about you. I actually went out on a few dates to test my feelings, which brought me to the conclusion that I'm in love with you.

Brodie, I know we are far apart in age, but I believe we were meant to be together, even if it is only for a little while. Your generosity, as well as your willingness to send me to school, have truly touched my heart. Every time I open a book or write an essay, I can't help but think about you and why I'm here.

Darling, please write back soon. I miss you so much and can't go another day without hearing from you.

Love,

Wylanta

Brodie read the letter several times before the truth sank in. It was like a dream. He had been betrayed and taken for a fool so many times that it was hard to believe that this honest and intelligent woman actually wanted to be with him.

As soon as he arrived home, he went into his study, and made sure the door was securely closed. He walked over to his desk, took a piece of stationery from the top drawer, and dipped his pen into the inkwell.

Dear Wylanta,

Your letter arrived safely on Saturday. I was so glad to hear from you. I must admit I was concerned that you may have changed your mind during your absence. You have come to mean so much to me and I must admit that I haven't thought of anyone but you since you left in January.

I would love to plan a trip to Washington to see you. Please write back soon.

Love,

Brodie

The following months were filled with train rides to Washington to see Wylanta. In early April, as the cherry blossoms covered the trees, Wylanta and Brodie sat out on the lawn in front of the United States Capitol Building, enjoying the warm temperatures. Wylanta had fixed a picnic and the two sat on a blanket among perfect strangers.

Brodie had realized, over the course of time, that he loved Wylanta and wanted her to be his wife. He knew there would be obstacles to overcome, but he was willing to do anything to make her happy, and that included purchasing a beautiful engagement ring. So, after his previous visit with her in Washington, he'd taken a trip into New York City and picked out a ring that he believed would suit her perfectly.

After they finished their picnic lunch and were gazing out over the crowds of people, Brodie reached over and took her hand in his. "Wylanta, I have something to ask you."

"Yes, Brodie. What would you like to ask?

"I love you so much. You're the first person that I've ever known who truly understands me. When I'm with you, I feel a peace I've never known before. Oh, I wish we were closer in age, but there is nothing we can do about that. All I know is that I want you to be my wife."

Brodie pulled out the ring, looked Wylanta in the eyes, and asked, "Will you marry me?"

Wylanta looked down at the diamond ring and then up into Brodie's eyes. "Yes. Oh, yes. I would love to marry you."

Several people within earshot of the couple began to snicker at the sight of this older man asking this young woman to marry him. But even the snickering didn't take away from the joy the couple felt at the thought of being together.

Brodie sat back and smiled. "Darling, I'd like for you to finish this school year. I'll come up in early June and we can get married at the Presbyterian Church here in Washington."

"Oh, Brodie, I can't wait to be your wife. I know my parents will probably not agree to this, so I would prefer we not say anything until we're married. Once we are man and wife, they'll have to accept it."

"You're probably right. I believe my children will give me a hard time as well. Let's keep it a secret as long as possible. We may not have a large wedding, but I promise you a wonderful honeymoon to anywhere you'd like to go. I know you would love Europe in the summer. We could go to London and Paris. I've also heard Barcelona is magnificent."

"I don't care about a honeymoon. All I want is to be with you. Just the other day, I walked by a shop that sells exquisite satin." Wylanta beamed as she thought about the dress she intended to make. "I'll go back and purchase the material. Oh, Brodie, I can't wait to get started on it."

Brodie couldn't take his eyes off of Wylanta as she shared her ideas about the dress and their upcoming wedding. "I know you'll be a beautiful bride."

"And you, my old man, are going to be a handsome groom."

For the next two months, Brodie tried to keep the news of his upcoming wedding a secret. He spent very little time out and tried to avoid conversations that might hint at his upcoming marriage. The last thing he wanted was for the press to get hold of the news and distort the truth, as they had done so many times before.

In early June, days before Brodie's departure, he went to purchase his train ticket. While waiting in line, he noticed a reporter from the Herald-Sun standing close by, appearing to be engrossed in reading a newspaper. Once the ticket was in hand, Brodie began walking toward home. After walking several blocks, he looked back and saw the young man following him. Brodie abruptly stopped and turned around. "Can I help you?"

The young man seemed unperturbed by the question. "Yes, you can."

"And what can I help you with?"

"I've been watching you for the last couple of months. I even took a train to Washington, D.C., where I saw you with a young woman by the name of Wylanta Rochelle."

Brodie had never grown comfortable with the press and how they were always snooping around, trying to create a story out of nothing. He knew his blunder with Alice Webb had created a ripple effect, but he didn't want his marriage to Wylanta to be seen as anything other than what it was, a union between two people who loved each other. "Look, young man, I'd appreciate it if you would keep your nose out of my business."

"Mr. Duke, I can't do that. Like it or not, you and your family are news. And, if you're planning on marrying Miss Rochelle, I plan to be the first to report it to the world."

Brodie knew that there was nothing he could do to stop this man from writing his story, but he was surely not going to give him any information about his plans. "If you'll excuse me, I have some matters that need my attention."

"I'll see you around, Mr. Duke. And, good luck with your upcoming marriage."

Brodie practically ran home. Once he got inside, he slammed the door so loud that Mary, one of his house staff, came running over to him. "Mr. Duke, are you okay?"

"No, I'm not."

Brodie thought Mary might have her own suspicions about what was happening. He knew it was best to calm down and pretend like everything was status quo. He took a couple of deep breaths before speaking, "Mary, I'm sorry. I just had a bad day at the office. I'll be okay. Oh, and if you want to leave after serving dinner, please feel free to go."

"Thank you, Mr. Duke. It would be nice to get home before dark."

On June 9th, Brodie packed a small bag and made his way to the train station. At first, when he arrived at the station, he thought he had been able to keep the news away from the press, but then, out of the corner of his eye, he spotted the young reporter speaking to several other members of the press. Brodie pushed his way past them and entered the private train car that he had reserved. He locked the door behind him, sat down, and breathed a sigh of relief.

But little did he know of the chaotic turn of events that he was about to encounter.

| 45 |

1910

Once the train came to an abrupt stop, Brodie knew he had to get off and face the crowd of reporters and photographers, who were hungering for a story; one that they believed would be as outlandish as his debacle with Alice Webb. He had contacted Wylanta, warning her of the potential harassment by the press, but nothing prepared him for the number of reporters who were now approaching him. It was clear that their wedding was spiraling away from being a quiet affair and, once again, Brodie's life was becoming a public spectacle.

His plan was to meet Wylanta at city hall to obtain a marriage license and, then, the two were to make their way to the First Presbyterian Church, where the ceremony would be held. Brodie was several minutes late to the city hall, due to the men who stood in his way, trying to ask questions and shout out accusations. Once inside the office, he spotted Wylanta sitting in the corner, trying to stay as inconspicuous as possible.

Brodie, followed by a dozen reporters, walked into the office, closing the door behind him. He rushed over to Wylanta, concerned for her welfare. "Darling, I'm so sorry. I never thought our marriage would be so newsworthy. Please, forgive me for being late. I love you so much. If you don't want to marry me, I totally understand."

Wylanta looked up at Brodie. "I love you, and there is nothing I want more than to be your wife."

Brodie gently took Wylanta's hand in his. They walked up to the counter together, where they filled out all of the information needed to receive the license. As they were getting ready to leave, the clerk said, "Please understand that the minister has to sign the license in order for it to be valid."

Brodie responded, "Thank you. I don't believe that will be an issue."

Before opening the door, Brodie looked at Wylanta, "It would be better for you to take a separate cab to the church. I'll meet you there. We've been told to enter at the back entrance of the church." Brodie reached for Wylanta's hand and said quietly, "I love you and can't wait for you to be Mrs. Brodie Duke."

Brodie left first, followed by the majority of the reporters. He looked back and spotted Wylanta slipping away and hoped that she would be able to arrive at the church without incident. Once the cab pulled up in front of the church, Brodie hurried to the back entrance and opened the door that led to large hallway. He knew it wouldn't be long before the reporters arrived and needed to find the reverend to get the license signed as quickly as possible.

Donald MacLeod, the reverend for First Presbyterian, was sitting in his office when Brodie came through the door. "Reverend MacLeod, it's nice to meet you. I'm Brodie Duke and my fiancée, Wylanta Rochelle, will be joining us in a few minutes."

Brodie looked at the reverend and noticed the reserved expression on his face. He didn't speak, which made Brodie anxious. "Reverend MacLeod, I sent you a letter a week ago, asking if you would conduct my marriage ceremony. I was assuming there wouldn't be a problem."

The reverend cleared his throat and finally spoke. "Mr. Duke, I don't know who you think I am, but I take marriage very seriously."

Brodie was confused by his statement. "Reverend, I do as well. I love Wylanta and believe we will be together until death."

"Mr. Duke, I've been doing some research on your past."

"What does my past have to do with this?"

The reverend stood and looked right at Brodie. "It has everything to do with this. I have to sign my name to the license, representing the church and state, and given that you have been married three previous times and divorced twice, I cannot give my consent for this marriage."

"Do you mean to tell me that you will not sign the license?"

"That is exactly what I'm saying."

"But you don't understand. Wylanta and I love each other very much. I know it might look suspicious to you, that I would choose to marry someone so young, but she is the love of my life. Of all the women I've been with, Wylanta is the one woman I truly believe God has chosen to be my wife until death."

"Mr. Duke, I have made my decision. So, I'd appreciate it if you would kindly leave my office."

Brodie was stunned and didn't move.

"Mr. Duke, I want you to leave now or I'll be forced to call the authorities."

Brodie wasn't expecting this. He never thought that this Presbyterian minister would turn him away. As he turned to leave, he saw Wylanta standing in the doorway wearing her wedding dress. "Wylanta, how long have you been standing there?"

Wylanta looked close to tears. "Long enough."

"Darling, I'm not giving up. Let's find a place for you to sit, while I figure this out."

The two went into the sanctuary and found a pew in the back, tucked away from where anyone would notice them. Wylanta sat down, looking defeated, in her wrinkled satin dress and white veil. Brodie sat down next to her and lifted her face, staring right at her. "I promise, I'll be back as soon as I can. Try and stay quiet and out of sight,"

"Brodie, where are you going?"

"Wylanta, you need to trust me. I have an idea, but I need to go alone. Hopefully, the press will leave you alone. But, if they come in and ask you where I am, try to ignore them."

Wylanta shook her head and looked down toward the floor. Brodie went over and lifted her head in his hands. "Darling, I promise you that we'll be married once I can find a solution. I'll be back as soon as I can. I love you so much."

And, with that, Brodie ran out the back door and slipped past the reporters. He knew they were likely to search for Wylanta in the sanctuary and assume the worst, but he couldn't focus on that now. He needed to figure this out and do it without the press finding him.

He walked toward the city hall, remembering a judge he had once worked with while coming up to visit Elizabeth. When he entered the building, he hoped that W.S. Robinson would be in his office but, when he walked by Robinson's office, he noticed an unfamiliar name on the door. He walked in and went up to a woman sitting behind a desk.

The woman looked up at Brodie. “Can I help you?”

“Yes, I’m looking for W.S. Robinson.”

“I’m sorry, but he is no longer an acting judge.”

Brodie’s body slumped over. If he didn’t love Wylanta so much, he would’ve given up. The woman appeared to see his disappointment. “He usually can be found in the café next door.”

“Thank you so much.”

Brodie ran out of the building and walked into the café, spotting W.S. in a corner booth, and walked over to where the older man was sitting. “W.S., I’m not sure if you remember me.”

“Brodie Duke. How can anyone ever forget you? You’ve been in the newspapers more than anyone I know. What can I do to help you?”

“I’m in need of a clerk of court who is willing to sign my marriage license and conduct a marriage ceremony.”

“Why should I be surprised that you want to marry again?”

“Look, W.S., the press has been chasing me around this town and I had to leave my fiancée at First Presbyterian Church.” He paused a moment, allowing W.S. time to process what he was saying. “I’m concerned they are going to harass her. She’s only twenty-eight years old. My children are trying to get me to give up this notion of marriage. I just heard that they have sent my personal secretary to stop me.”

“Well, maybe you should consider all these obstacles as a sign that it isn’t a good idea to marry this young woman.”

“W.S., please. I’ve never felt like this before. Wylanta is a very special woman who I truly love with my whole heart.”

“Well, I do know one clerk who might be willing to marry you, but you’re going to have to travel to Camden, New Jersey.”

“I don’t care how far we have to go.”

W.S. took a piece of paper and pen and wrote down an address. "Tell him that I sent you."

"Thank you so much. I promise you won't regret this."

And, with note in hand, Brodie left to return to the church, praying that Wylanta was still waiting for him.

46

1910

Traveling back to the church, all Brodie could think about was being in Wylanta's arms and declaring to the world that she was his wife. But he knew that his troubles weren't over yet. As he approached the church, he saw several dozen reporters circling around Reverend MacLeod. Brodie called out to the driver, "Can you please circle the block so I can get out in back of the church?"

"Sure, but it will cost you."

"I don't care how much it costs. I need to enter the church without being noticed."

Once the car had stopped, Brodie called to the driver as he was climbing out of the car. "Please stay here and keep the motor running. I'll be right back." Brodie raced in and found Wylanta asleep on a back pew. He went over and gently shook her. "Darling, we need to leave now."

"Oh, Brodie, you won't believe what happened while you were gone."

"Come on. Once we get out of the city, I want to hear all about it."

Brodie took Wylanta's hand and they ran out the back entrance of the church and sprinted to the cab. A reporter spotted them and called out, "Mr. Duke, stop!" Several other reporters ran toward them. Brodie and Wylanta, who were a couple steps ahead, slipped into the cab, quickly closing the door, as a reporter pressed up to the car window. Brodie yelled at the driver. "Please go as fast you can! There will be a large tip for you if you can get us away from the reporters."

The driver looked over his shoulder. "Yes, sir! I don't know why they're so interested in you, but I can say that I've never had reporters pursuing my cab before."

"Please take a left up here." Brodie sat back and took a deep breath. He couldn't remember ever running so fast in his life.

"So, where can I take you?"

"Camden, New Jersey."

"What!"

"You heard me. We need to get to Camden tonight."

Brodie looked over at Wylanta, who burst out laughing. "Brodie, I knew marrying you would be an adventure, but I never imagined that we would be chased by reporters and have to leave Washington to get married."

Brodie smiled at Wylanta. She looked beautiful in her white dress, stained with splattered mud. Her hair had fallen from its hairpins but she didn't seem to care, which made her look even more desirable. "Oh, Wylanta, I love you so much."

"And I, you."

"You were going to tell me something that happened in the church."

"Oh, it's nothing. The reporters found me and tried to make it out that you were intoxicated and had left me at the altar." Then Wylanta smiled at Brodie. "But I knew better than that."

Brodie kissed Wylanta. "Thank you for believing in me."

Wylanta tried to smooth out the wrinkles in her dress. "So why are we headed to Camden, New Jersey?"

"I found someone to marry us there tonight."

"That's wonderful."

Wylanta moved close to Brodie, snuggling up to him, as they made the long drive. It was close to midnight when they arrived at 444 Stevens Street. There was a light on in the front room and Brodie could hear voices. He left Wylanta in the cab while he went up to the door and knocked. A middle-aged man opened the door and looked at Brodie. "You must be Brodie Duke. W.S. Robinson told me to expect you."

"Yes. Can we come in?"

"Of course."

Brodie waved at Wylanta, who left the cab and walked up toward the door. He took her hand and squeezed it. "We're actually going to get married."

Once inside, Brodie noticed some flowers and a plate of cookies. A woman looked in their direction. "You can't have a wedding without a bouquet and a reception."

The woman reached over and took Wylanta's hand. "Come with me, and let's get you sorted out."

The two women went upstairs, leaving Brodie in the room with the man and two other people. The man who'd answered the door reached out his hand. "My name is Frank Garrison and I'm a justice of the peace. I'll be conducting the ceremony." He turned toward a couple standing beside him. "This is Frank Hill. He and his wife will be the witnesses."

"It's nice meeting all of you. I really appreciate this."

Frank Garrison showed Brodie some papers. "Now, one thing that we need to document is that you own property in New Jersey."

"But I don't."

"Well, after you sign these papers, you'll own a residence at 112 North New Jersey Avenue."

"How much will it cost me?"

"Don't worry about that. I can assure you that you can definitely afford this property. This way, you won't have to wait until Monday. And we don't want those annoying reporters to get in the way of your holy matrimony."

"You're right about that."

Brodie signed the papers and, just as he placed the pen on the table, Wylanta stepped into the room. Her hair had been fixed and the light from the candles enhanced her features. He felt like the luckiest man that ever walked the earth.

Frank Garrison cleared his throat as he looked at Wylanta. "Are you ready to take this man as your husband?"

"I surely am."

"Okay, then let's make this union official."

The ceremony was short but intimate. Once it was over, Brodie took Wylanta in his arms and the two embraced as he kissed her on the lips. Mrs. Hill went into the kitchen and came out with coffee and cookies. Once everyone was served, Frank Garrison raised his coffee cup to toast the couple. "I hope that you live a long and happy life together."

Brodie became a little choked up and his voice cracked. "Thank you so much for being willing to conduct this ceremony. I'll never forget any of you." He looked at Wylanta. "You have made me the luckiest man alive."

| 47 |

1910

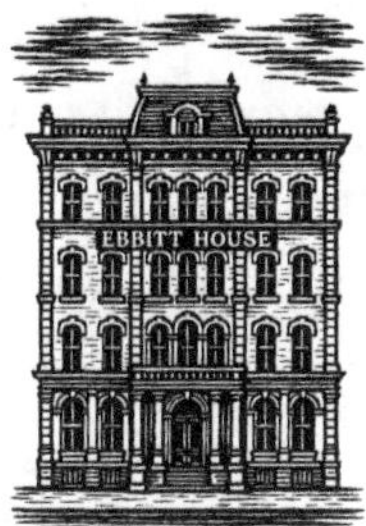

Brodie smiled as he listened to Wylanta read the newspaper article published by Camden, New Jersey's Courier-Post. "*June 13- Love, and love alone is the bond which holds the youthful Mrs. Brodie L. Duke to her 63-year-old husband whom she married at Camden, New Jersey, Saturday. She loves him to distraction, according to her own admission, does not care for his gold and would rather stay here in Washington than live on the Duke estate at Durham, North Carolina. Mrs. Duke talked freely about her future plans this morning.*

"I'm very happy," she said, as she gazed out of the window at the Ebbitt House drawing room. I've loved Brodie for five years, so why shouldn't I be happy?"

Mrs. Duke wore a close-fitting black dress, unrelieved by trimmings. Large diamonds flashed in her earrings and she wore several expensive rings, which were gifts from her husband.

"Yes, we are very happy, aren't we, Baby?" She said, turning toward her husband.

"I don't think we shall go to Durham yet. Mr. Duke has some business matters to arrange, and some of his family evidently didn't want him to marry me. So, it must all be arranged."

"We shall stay here for a few days anyway. I like Washington and social life here is so much nicer than down in Carolina. I shouldn't wonder if we decided to live her for quite a while."

"Oh, yes. There is something else I want you to deny for me," and the latest Mrs. Duke's eyes flashed. "I want you to say I was not waiting at the church for Mr. Duke. The idea! Why, he had to come after me two or three times. Didn't you, Brodie?"

Mr. Duke admitted he did.

"It must be kind of nice to be married to a millionaire," was ventured. Mr. Duke's money had nothing whatever to do with it," retorted Mrs. Duke, emphatically. "I should have married him if he hadn't a penny, and if it was necessary, I'd work for him, He has always been very kind to me, and I think the reason he didn't get along well with the others was that they didn't really care for him. It is different this time."

Mrs. Duke said, among other things, that her husband had given her seventeen hats.

Both seemed to realize that they were going to have a little trouble with his family. Several telegrams from Durham arrived for Mr. Duke yesterday and he hinted that they were on their way to Washington, presumably to talk matters over."

And, sure enough, several days after the wedding, Mabel, Pearl, and Lawrence, showed up at the Ebbitt House. Brodie was in the hotel lobby enjoying a cup of coffee when he saw his children arrive at the entrance. He preferred to speak with them alone to save Wylanta from the backlash that was primarily meant for him. Given that Wylanta hadn't come down from the room yet, he thought this would be a good time to speak with his children. He stood up and waved in their direction. "Pearl, I'm over here."

All three of them marched over and stood over him as he sat back down with his coffee cup in hand. Mabel was the first to speak. "Daddy, we have had it!"

"Well, Mabel, it is nice seeing you, too."

Lawrence was the next one to interject his thoughts. "Father, I can't believe you would do this to us!"

"Do what? I married a woman who I love very much. How does that have anything to do with you?"

Mabel placed her hands on her hips. "It has everything to do with us. Whenever you go off and do something crazy, we become the target of every newspaper reporter within a hundred miles."

"Well, I'm sorry for that, but I'm not sorry at all for marrying Wylanta. Unlike Alice or Minnie, I love her with my whole heart. My only regret is that we couldn't have known each other earlier."

Pearl asked, in a calm voice, "Daddy, do you really love her? She's so much younger than you. Most women who marry older men are gold diggers."

Brodie looked up at his three adult children. "I know all of you have always found me a little peculiar. And after the Alice Webb debacle, I can understand your concern. But I can tell you that I've never been so sure of anything in my life. I love Wylanta and she loves me."

Mabel shook her head in disbelief. "We came here to bring you home and, hopefully talk some sense into you."

Brodie stood up and looked straight at Mabel. "My darling daughter, you have never been happy with me as your father. I know it upsets you that my brothers have done so well and I have chosen a different path. And, now, you're probably concerned that

Wylanta will be spending my money. Money that you probably believe is yours."

It was clear from Mabel's expression that Brodie had spoken what his daughter was thinking. "Well, yes. If I'm to be completely honest, I am concerned about the money you have spent on this woman."

Lawrence spoke up. "Look, Father, we are concerned about the money, but we are also concerned that you are being taken advantage of."

Brodie smiled. "I can promise you that Wylanta has never taken advantage of me. To be honest, I pursued her. I love Wylanta, and I feel so blessed to be able to spend the rest of my life with the one person who seems to know me and love me, despite my imperfections."

Just about that time, Wylanta walked over and stood next to Brodie. "Darling, I'd like for you to meet my three children." Brodie placed his arm around Wylanta's slim waist, emphasizing to his children, and others who might be watching, that he loved this woman. Brodie pointed to each child as he introduced them. "This is Mabel Goodall, my oldest, and this is Lawrence, and Pearl Bachman is my youngest. They've come to Washington to check on my welfare."

Wylanta looked first at Mabel, then Lawrence, and lastly, Pearl. She directed her attention onto the younger woman. "Pearl, I've always wanted to meet the girl who has a textile mill named after her. Your father has spoken highly about each one of you." She paused a moment before continuing. "I feel so blessed to be a part of your family."

Pearl smiled at Wylanta. "Wylanta, you need to understand that we've gone through some rough spots along the way regarding our father. We love him and only want what is best for him."

"I can understand your concerns. I just want you to know that I love your father very much and want to spend as many years together as the Good Lord gives us. I made a vow to love him through the good days, and bad ones, and I promise you that I intend on keeping my vow."

Pearl smiled in acceptance while Mabel and Lawrence didn't appear to believe Wylanta's words. Wylanta said, "I'm sure all of you are tired from your trip. Why don't you get checked in and settled? Once you have, we'd love to take you to one of our favorite restaurants."

Brodie knew it would take a while for Mabel and Lawrence to soften up to the idea that Wylanta truly loved him and wanted the best for him. He had witnessed his children's disapproval on so many occasions that their behavior didn't surprise him one bit. On the other hand, Pearl seemed to accept this young woman as her father's new wife, making him feel elated that the two women could possibly become friends.

48

1910

The thunderous applause caught Brodie off guard. For some reason, he never thought that his contribution of land would create such a reaction from Durham's black community. He felt honored to give what he could for the sole purpose of bettering the educational opportunities of individuals who had been enslaved less than fifty years ago.

On this particular night, St. Joseph's A.M.E. church, located on Fayetteville Street, was full to the rafters. The women were dressed in their Sunday best and the men wore their coats and ties with pride. Glancing around the room, it was hard not to notice the few white men and women sprinkled among the crowd.

The program began with Judge Jeter C. Pritchard announcing the agenda for the evening. Once his introduction was complete, a choir, made up of over a dozen men and women, began to sing so loudly and with such enthusiasm, that the building shook. The scene was mesmerizing as the entire audience rose and rocked back and forth to the pulsating vibration of the music.

Brodie had recently returned to attending church alongside Wylanta, but what he was experiencing at this moment was in no way similar to what he typically heard at Memorial Methodist Church. There, each Sunday service began at 11:00am and ended promptly at noon. The parishioners were always subdued and the routine of the worship service could be predicted down to the minute. The choir, usually made up of people in the latter stages of their life, would sing with little to no enthusiasm. The parishioners were no better, as they sifted through their hymnals and muttered the words, cautious not to be heard by the people surrounding them.

Brodie had been placed at the front of the church alongside Dr. James Shepherd, the newly nominated president of the National Religious Training School. John Merrick and Dr. Aaron Moore were also seated nearby with their families. Julian Shakespeare Carr was present due to his generous donation to the school. Brodie thought about the complex nature of this man whom he respected deeply. Julian had hired black men to work in the William T. Blackwell Company long before other tobacco factories or cotton mills in and around Durham had made the move to employee them.

Brodie had never forgotten the days when he would pass the William T. Blackwell Company and hear men's voices singing gospel songs in such unison that it would cause him to stop and listen. If he was ever to become a believer in a good God, it would be due to the peace he felt when listening to these men sing as they worked.

He turned his attention to Judge Pritchard as he spoke his last words. "I am glad in my heart to see colored people following in the footsteps of white people with their advantages received only through centuries of work."

Another eruption of applause shook the building causing Brodie to feel a sense of pride in his donation, as well as with this city that had come together to advance the educational opportunities of their fellow citizens. Brodie knew that there remained a deep-seated resentment among much of the white community, but this religious training school was a true indication of how Durham was advancing in the pursuit of equality among all of its citizens.

Brodie's thoughts were interrupted by the sound of John Merrick's daughter as she sang an unfamiliar hymn. He had never heard such a radiant voice in all the years he had attended church or other theatrical productions. He closed his eyes and was transported back to the days of his youth. A peace came over him and he reached for the wooden fox that he kept in his coat pocket. He thought of Sidney and his father as they worked in the fields together, just the three of them. Life had been hard back then but, even so, he treasured every memory of the days of his youth.

His thoughts were again interrupted when he heard Judge Pritchard call out his name, followed by a round of applause. "I want to personally thank Brodie Duke for his kind donation of land, worth over three thousand dollars."

Dr. Shepherd turned toward Brodie, encouraging him to stand. He hesitated a moment, feeling awkward at all the praise, but then rose and looked back at the large crowd. He had never felt such admiration from others in the way that he did that night. For once, he believed he had done more than just donate land; he had contributed to a cause much greater than himself.

Once the program was over, he walked over to Dr. Moore. "I want to thank you, once again, for coming to my aid that night so many years ago."

"You are quite welcome. I believed back then, and more so now, that the Lord has a special purpose for you. You will never know how much your donation means to our community."

Brodie thought for a moment before responding. "It's strange. When I began buying up land in and around Durham, I never thought anything of it. But now, with Durham growing so rapidly, I believe I can actually make a difference."

"The Lord works in mysterious ways. He is definitely working through you. I was glad to hear that you have been attending church. I hope you'll find the peace that, I believe, you've been hungering for all your life."

Brodie nodded as Dr. Moore excused himself and turned around to find Julian Carr standing alone. "So, Julian, it's good to see you here. I wanted to congratulate you on your recent election to the State House of Representatives. I know we have some differences of opinion regarding politics, but I'm glad you'll be there to advocate for more roads in and around Durham."

"I appreciate that. I've been blessed with a successful business career and believe that I have something to offer the people."

"You do, at that."

"Brodie, on another note, I have said some things I shouldn't have said in a public forum about our colored friends, but I do believe that education and religion are the two institutions that will make us all better, no matter what color we are."

"My father would totally agree with you. Washington believed that all men were created equal and would've loved to have been here celebrating this new religious school."

"Washington was a good man. You know, whenever I go past his statue at the Trinity College entrance, I stop and pay my respects."

"That means a lot to me."

"So how is your young wife doing?"

"Julian, she is truly the love of my life. I no longer feel the need to go out like I did before. All I want to do is spend time with her. My only regret is that we didn't meet in my youth. But, even so, I feel blessed to have her as my wife."

"I'm happy for you, Brodie."

"Thank you, Julian."

49

1911

Brodie had just arrived home from a meeting in North Durham and found no one stirring downstairs. The help had left, leaving Wylanta alone. Once Brodie entered the front door, a stirring set in and all he desired was to be upstairs to join his wife in bed. Just the thought of her cotton lingerie pressed against her bare skin made him quicken his steps. But, as he approached the closed door to their bedroom, he was overtaken by the sound of weeping.

Unsure if he should enter, he called out, "Wylanta, are you okay? Is it alright if I come in?"

Brodie could hear the sound of sniffles. "Yes, my love. Please."

Once he opened the door, Brodie could see Wylanta lying on the bed in a fetal position. Concerned for her, he ran over and sat down on the edge of the bed. She wore no makeup and her hair created a halo, highlighting her youth. He wasn't sure how to respond to her, given that he had never seen her so distressed. "Darling, what's wrong?"

Wylanta placed her hands over her face as she let out a loud sob. Not sure what to do, Brodie placed his hand on her shoulder, moving the auburn curls from her face. "Darling, no matter what's wrong, I'm here for you."

"Oh, Brodie, I don't know what to do."

"What do you mean?"

"It's Daddy. He's been arrested."

Brodie stiffened with concern. "Why?"

"The police raided his store and found him selling alcohol. They're threatening to sentence him to roadwork."

"Are you sure?"

"Yes. My mother just left a few minutes ago. She's frantic with worry. The police have threatened to close the store all together."

Brodie sat for a minute, unable to think of what to say. He had his suspicions but couldn't believe that Leander would run a blind tiger operation. "Darling, I'll look into it first thing in the morning. I knew the police were cracking down on this sort of thing, but didn't realize it would become so serious."

Wylanta looked up at Brodie with a pitiful look. "Oh, Baby, would you do that for me?"

"Of course, I will. I can't promise you anything, but I'll do my best."

Wylanta took Brodie's hands in hers. "You've been so kind to me and my family."

Brodie leaned in and softly kissed the tears off of her cheek. "I love you so much."

The next day, Brodie inquired and discovered that it was, indeed, a serious situation. Given the strict prohibition laws that Durham conservatives had put into place, he wasn't able to influence anyone to drop the charges. That afternoon, Leander stood in front of Judge Allen, who sentenced him to six months in jail plus court costs. Wylanta, her mother, and her sisters, stood in the back of the courtroom holding on to each other as the sentence was read. Thankfully, Judge Allen sentenced the older man to only jail time, without hard labor but, even so, it was difficult for Wylanta and her family to believe that Leander had to spend time in jail for six long months.

Over the next few months, Wylanta spent most of her time helping her mother and sisters run the store. At night, she returned home exhausted, which greatly concerned Brodie. He hated seeing Wylanta so sad and had an idea he believed would cheer her up. "Wylanta, why don't we take a trip to Charlotte? I can have our chauffeur drive us and we can enjoy a few days in a nice hotel."

Wylanta looked at Brodie with a concerned expression. "I'm not sure."

"Please. If you need help with the store, I can hire someone."

"It would be nice to get away."

Brodie leaned in and kissed Wylanta on the forehead. "Good, it's settled."

The next morning, Brodie's chauffer, Jim, pulled the car up in front of their house. Wylanta took a seat in the back with Brodie, while Jim drove the couple toward Charlotte. The September warm temperatures and clear skies made it a perfect day for a drive. Brodie held Wylanta's hand and watched her as she took in the scenes of the fields and pine trees that bordered the road.

As they approached Lexington, North Carolina, Jim drove around a sharp curve and slammed right into a horse. The animal fell to the ground, clearly injured. A farmer, who had witnessed the incident, appeared from across a field, running in the direction of the car. Jim had turned the car off and stepped out to determine the extent of the horse's injuries. The farmer came around the car and leaned down, also checking on the condition of the horse. He rose and stared right at Jim. "What were you thinking, going so fast?"

Jim was clearly upset over the animal's injuries. "I'm sorry. I didn't see it as I came around the curve."

Brodie spoke up. "Mister, it was clearly an accident. I'll be glad to pay for the damages."

"I knew there would be no good to come from these contraptions," the farmer stated as he pointed at the car.

"Again, I'll be glad to pay you what you believe the horse is worth."

It was clear that the farmer was irate as he turned toward Brodie and yelled, "You're not going to get away with this so easily! I'm going to press charges."

Brodie couldn't believe the words he was hearing. "Mister, what's your name?"

"My name is June Leonard."

"Mr. Leonard, I have the money to pay you for the horse."

"There needs to be consequences for people like you, with your fancy cars speeding down the road."

Just about this time, a sheriff came down the road on horseback. He leaned down and asked, "June, what's going on here?"

"This man and his fancy car were speeding around the corner and hit my horse."

By this time, Brodie was becoming annoyed by the circumstances. "Sheriff, I'll be glad to pay Mr. Leonard what, he believes, he should get for the damages to the horse."

The sheriff looked right at Brodie. "What's your name and where did you come from?"

"My name is Brodie Duke and we were driving to Charlotte from Durham."

The sheriff paused a moment before speaking. "Brodie Duke. Are you one of those Dukes who own the American Tobacco Company?"

"Well, yes and no."

"Are you giving me a hard time?"

"No, sir. My brother, Buck, is the man behind the American Tobacco Company."

"Well, anyone who can afford a car like yours has to be doing alright."

"Look, can I just pay Mr. Leonard and be on my way?"

"It doesn't work like that in these parts. I'm going to have to arrest you. Tomorrow, you can present your case in front of the judge. He'll be the one to determine how much Mr. Leonard should receive for his horse."

Brodie looked over at Wylanta and could see how upset she was. Both of them were leery of the judicial system after Leander's recent incarceration. Wylanta took hold of Brodie's arm and, with tears in her eyes, pleaded to Brodie, "Look, just do what they tell you to do. I can't stand the thought of you spending time in jail."

The sheriff looked at Brodie. "I think it's best to listen to your daughter."

"She isn't my daughter. She's my wife."

Both Mr. Leonard and the sheriff looked at Brodie and Wylanta. "Now I know you must have a lot of money. No woman would be attracted to a man your age, unless you have a lot of money."

Instantly, Brodie was filled with a strong feeling of agitation. He had seen the newspaper articles highlighting the differences in their ages, but this came across as a personal vendetta. If he didn't care so much about taking care of Wylanta, he would've leaned in and punched the sheriff. But, before he could react, the sheriff stated, in a firm voice, "I want you to get back in the car and I'm going to follow you to the local courthouse. I don't want you to get any ideas about running off. I know who you are and I know some people in Durham who would be glad to help me out."

Once they arrived in Lexington, Brodie was ordered to pay fifty dollars and return to the courthouse the next morning. The closest city that had a vacant hotel room was High Point. So, instead of the nice getaway that Brodie had planned for Wylanta, they stayed in a worn down room with very few amenities. The next day, Brodie appeared before the judge and paid the fine. After they left the courthouse, neither felt like going on to Charlotte, so they headed back to Durham, with hopes that their troubles were behind them.

50

1911

It had been years since Brodie had been in the same room with his brother, Buck. When he'd heard that Buck was going to be present for the fundraiser, he almost declined the invitation, but thought better of it. Given that he was being honored for his donation of land for the Sheltering Home Circle of the King's Daughters, he knew he had to attend, no matter the awkwardness between the two men.

The intent of the house would be to shelter older women who were widowed and lacked the means for a home. When Brodie had been approached for a donation, he thought of women like Nannie, who without her brother, Richard, would surely be homeless. In the past month, he had been introduced to several recently widowed women who attended Memorial Methodist Church; women who had no place to live.

Benjamin had graciously offered to host the fundraiser at his new home, Four Acres, located across Chapel Hill Street from Memorial Methodist Church. When Brodie and Wylanta arrived, several cars were parked along the street, indicating that the fundraiser would be a success. He knew that everyone who received an invitation would attend if, for no other reason, than to see the house that had been called one of the most impressive homes in Durham.

Brodie tried to stay calm and not think about his upcoming interaction with Buck, but he found it difficult to keep his mind off of the dialogue that might transpire between the two of them. Upon entering the doorway, an impeccably dressed butler took their coats and escorted them to where the party was being held.

As they walked through the foyer, he looked around the room, unable to take his eyes off of the incredible woodwork and modern fixtures. The expensive artwork, along with the beautiful chandeliers, made it a very welcoming space. Once they entered the room where the party was being held, he took hold of Wylanta's hand. She, in return, squeezed his hand and quietly said, "It's going to be fine. Remember, I'm proud of you and the man you've become."

Brodie responded, "You'll never know how much I love you."

Brodie spotted Benjamin and Sarah and walked up to them. "Benjamin, I don't believe you have had the honor of meeting my wife, Wylanta."

"Wylanta, it's a privilege to finally meet you. I've heard that you've been such a positive influence in my brother's life and, for that, I'm truly grateful."

Wylanta smiled at both Benjamin and Sarah. "I love your brother very much and am also grateful to have him as my husband."

Sarah took Wylanta by the hand. "Come with me. I'd like to introduce you to several of my dear friends."

As the women walked away, Brodie looked over at Benjamin. "Brother, I want to thank you for your kindness toward Wylanta. I know everyone speaks of our age difference, but I do love her very much."

"I can see that. And I'm very happy to hear that. On another note, have you recently spoken to Buck?"

"No. To be honest, I'm not sure if he'll even speak to me. I can understand how, in the past, I was a thorn in his side, but I'm different now."

"Let's go over and speak with him together," Benjamin said, as they walked across the room to where Buck and his wife, Nanaline, were standing. As they drew closer, Brodie couldn't help but notice the grim expression on his brother's face, an indication that his brother's feelings hadn't changed over the course of time. In a very stale voice, Buck said, "Brodie, I heard you'd be here."

"Yes. As you probably know, I donated the land for the shelter on the corner of Buchanan and a new street that I'm calling Gloria, because I feel glory over aiding such a wonderful cause."

"Now that's interesting. You sure didn't feel glory over your actions in New York with that woman, Alice Webb."

Brodie felt anger simmer up inside him. He couldn't understand why his brother couldn't see that he had changed. "I do regret my actions in New York and am truly sorry for the impact it had on your reputation."

Buck didn't respond.

Benjamin quickly intervened. "Thankfully, we can all agree on the need for this shelter. I, for one, appreciate that we can come together as a family and support these women."

Instead of agreeing, Buck turned and walked away. Benjamin looked directly at Brodie. "You know he has a lot going on with the Supreme Court ruling against the American Tobacco Company."

Brodie, out of frustration with Buck, responded, "He never could be satisfied with just the initial company we built. That's one reason I pulled back from being an active business partner. Over the years, I've seen how many small tobacco companies couldn't compete with him. I personally think it's a good thing for the tobacco farmers, as well as other manufacturers, to be able to have a piece of the tobacco business."

Benjamin remained silent, clearly not wanting to choose sides on this issue. Brodie couldn't help but point out the obvious. "Shoot, he had a monopoly on almost every facet of the industry."

Benjamin shook his head. "I can't argue that point with you. All I know is that, every time he saw a smaller company that might be a good investment, he took advantage by obtaining it. In his mind, it was just business."

Brodie shook his head. "It's always been about business."

Benjamin remarked, "I can see why you think that way. I'm sorry that you two haven't been able to resolve your differences. I wish I could tell you what to do, but I don't have the words. One thing is sure, for the first time ever, Buck seems happy about being a husband to his wife, Nanaline, and the upcoming birth of their baby."

Brodie didn't know how he felt about his brother and felt it was best to change the subject. "By the way, how are your children?"

"Angier is enjoying life. He doesn't have our drive but, I guess since he was born into wealth, he doesn't see the reason to work hard. It's Mary that I'm more concerned about. She's started seeing Prince Pignatelli, a distant cousin of the king of Spain. He seems infatuated with her and wants her to spend time with him in Europe. Both Sarah and I are concerned about his domineering nature, but hesitant to interfere. We just don't want to push her away."

"I can relate to that. I hardly see my children any more. Mabel and Lawrence are furious with me about Wylanta, even though it's clear that we love each other. I hardly see Pearl and Woodward lives in California with his mother, Minnie." Brodie paused a moment before speaking. "I wish I'd spent more time with them, particularly Woodward, as they were growing up."

"Well, we can't go back but, hopefully, you can make an effort to see more of him in the future." Benjamin looked him in the eye. "I have to go and check on things before the auction. I see Richard Wright over in the corner. I'm sure he'd be glad to talk with you."

Brodie made his way over to where Richard was sitting and sat down in a chair facing him. "Well, I'm surprised to see you here. I thought you'd be on one of your trips to Egypt or South Africa selling one of your machines."

"I leave in a week to go to China and Japan. I hope to obtain several contracts for the Bonsack machine, along with my packaging machines. I made it a special point to be in Durham when I heard your brother was going to be in town. Julian and I heard he's interested in purchasing the Durham Traction Company from us."

"I thought I heard that might be happening. Why would you sell him your company?"

"I believe Julian and I have come to a standstill in providing the electricity that people are asking for. Your brother has spent more money than we can afford in developing alternating current to the mills here and around Durham. I've found, over time, that I just can't compete with him regarding anything to do with business. Anyway, I'm getting older and have decided to focus on my machine factory and creating a telephone and telegraph company."

By this time, Wylanta had made her way over to Brodie and sat down in a chair next to him. "Richard, I'm not sure if you've met my lovely bride, Wylanta."

"No, I don't think I have." Richard looked directly at Wylanta. "I'm glad that you and Brodie have found each other."

"Well, thank you, Richard."

Richard stared off into the distance, clearly distracted by a past memory. "I've only known love once. Mamie and I were together for only a short period of time, but she was all the love I needed in this lifetime."

Wylanta leaned in and smiled at Brodie. "I know people don't understand why I would want to marry a man so much older than me. But I love Brodie and I believe we're good for each other."

Richard smiled. "It definitely appears that way." Richard reached for his cane and stood up. "Now, if you two would excuse me, I need to see if I can speak with Buck."

Wylanta looked at Brodie for a moment. "So how did it go with Buck?"

"Not good. I still think he believes I had something to do with Pa's death."

Wylanta reached for his hand. "I'm sorry. But I know what will make you feel better once this evening is over and we get back home."

Brodie smiled at his wife. "Now, Mrs. Duke, are you propositioning me?"

"I think I am, Mr. Duke. I think I am."

| 51 |

1914-1915

The next few years were marked by Brodie and Wylanta's extreme generosity. People from all walks of life were blessed by the couple's willingness to give in small and large ways. Lottie Riley Lawrence sent a thank you note for the spoons she received as a wedding gift. Mrs. Smith sent a thank you note for the doll the couple gave to her daughter. Wylanta received a letter from her sister, thanking her for a check for $25. Her sister emphasized that she didn't want to send the letter to Brodie's office because Mr. Carver would open it and Brodie wouldn't see it. She ended the letter by stating how the world is a better place because Brodie is in it.

The couple enjoyed each other's company and life was good. But, just as the two were beginning to believe that no bad could happen, several events occurred that changed everything. The first event occurred in the form of a fire that destroyed the entire 100 block of Main Street where Brodie's office was located. Due to the lack of a water supply, the fire continued until all the buildings on this block were burned to the ground.

Brodie also became informed that Benjamin was experiencing debilitating dizzy spells that the doctor had no cure for. Benjamin would feel normal for weeks and then, without warning, he would be taken to the ground with such horrendous episodes that he couldn't leave his bedroom. Brodie visited him when he could but, ultimately, Benjamin moved to St. Petersburg, Florida, where his doctor believed the climate would assist in his recovery. Once Benjamin moved, Brodie realized how much he missed his half-brother and the relationship that they had fostered over time.

But it was the news Brodie received in June 1914 that caused him extreme heartache. The Herald Sun reported, *Brodie Duke's Son met tragic Death. Woodward Duke killed in Automobile Accident in Utah—Driving in Mountain—Woodward Duke, son of Brodie L. Duke, millionaire tobacco king, was instantly killed this afternoon at a point eighteen miles southwest of Park City, which is thirty miles from Salt Lake City. Duke was one of a party of five Los Angeles men on a trans-continental automobile tour from the west coast to New York. In Chalk Creek Canyon, the three-ton car skidded off a bank and went into Chalk Creek, the water of which is six feet deep. Young Duke was pinned under the front end and steering gear and was almost instantly killed. The party flagged a train and were taken to Park City with the body. The party had left Pasadena about a week ago for New York.*

Heavy rain and thunderstorms lit up the sky as the mourners stood outside of the stoic marble mausoleum that loomed over all the other headstones in Maplewood Cemetery. Brodie clung onto

Wylanta on one side of the walk that led to the stairs leading up to the open door of the building. Pearl, Mabel, and Lawrence, circled around Minnie on the other side of the walkway. Everyone was wet and, even though it was warm, Brodie felt a chill as the pastor spoke about Woodward and how his life had been shortened for a purpose that no one would understand in this life on earth.

Brodie reached out and covered Wylanta with his umbrella, causing the rain to gush over his head. It didn't matter that the rain had seeped under his coat and was drenching his clothes. Being soaked didn't matter. Nothing mattered now. He felt grief and regret all tied up into a ball of emotion that was suffocating.

Brodie glanced across the space that separated him from his children and the woman who he had hurt so many years ago. Tears came to his eyes as he replayed in his mind his horrendous treatment of this woman, who had only wanted the best for him and his children. He lifted his head and looked over at them, only to have Mabel return his stare with a scornful look. He quickly turned his head and focused on the marble interior where his son's body now resided.

After hearing about his son's death, he had shared with Wylanta all of the details of his relationship with Minnie and how badly he had treated her. He knew his wife might possibly find his actions unforgivable, but thought it was better for her to hear the truth directly from him.

The night the telegram arrived, Brodie had stepped outside and sat on the back porch. Wylanta had followed and sat next to him under the bright moon that litup the night sky. Shock had taken over and Brodie sat stunned from the news. He pulled out the wooden fox from his pocket and rubbed the smooth surface between his fingers. And then, in a quiet voice, he said, "I didn't fight for him."

Wylanta quietly rocked in the chair, staring in his direction. That was one thing Brodie loved about this woman. She understood him like no one else ever had. "I should've fought harder for him, but I didn't. He was so young when the divorce was finalized and I rarely made an effort to be with him."

It was then that the tears began to flow. "Wylanta, how can you love me when I have hurt so many people in my life?"

At that moment, Wylanta rose from her chair, leaned over, and ran her fingers through his hair. "I was so consumed with Elizabeth at the time, I couldn't see the people who loved me."

Wylanta leaned in and kissed Brodie on his forehead. Her love was too much for him to bear at that moment. He sat erect and looked her in the eyes. "How can you love me? You deserve someone better than me! Can't you see that?"

"Shhh."

"I mean it. I've been foolish and hurtful to everyone. Minnie never deserved my abuse and my other children don't want to have anything to do with me. I'm too old to become a father again, so you'll never know what it's like to have a child. I'm depriving you of having a family of your own. Don't you see it would be best for you to be with someone younger? Someone who can give you a family of your own."

Wylanta looked right into Brodie's eyes. "I don't want to be with anyone but you. I love you and that's all I need. I know about your past and that's all it is to me, your past. When we were married, I promised you that I'll be with you until death and, Brodie Duke that is exactly what I plan on doing."

Brodie felt Wylanta squeeze his hand and a sense of calm came over him. The rain became lighter as the small group of mourners sang a stanza of "Amazing Grace". Once the pastor finished speaking, Minnie walked up and entered the small room where Woodward's body had been placed. He knew his presence wouldn't be well-received, but believed he needed to somehow convey his deep regret to Minnie.

Brodie broke away from Wylanta's grasp and followed Minnie up the stairs and into the mausoleum. Minnie was softly crying as she touched the marble vault. "Brodie, I wish you would've gotten to know our son."

Brodie remained silent as he stood beside this woman who he'd hurt so deeply. Minnie took her finger and traced Woodward's name etched in the marble. "He only wanted to be a part of your life. And, even though I married again, and Woodward had a father who loved him, he only wanted to be with you."

"I'm so sorry for the hurt that I caused you and Woodward. I have no excuse."

Minnie stared into Brodie's eyes. "Wylanta appears to be a very kind woman who loves you very much. Treasure your relationship with her and never take her for granted."

And, with that, Brodie watched as Minnie left the mausoleum and was immediately surrounded by his children. Wylanta came to his side and placed her arm through his. But, even with her loving support, he couldn't help but stare at his estranged family as they walked down the sloping path, entered a car, and drove away, leaving him filled with a tangled mess of regrets.

52

1917-1919

The stomach pains had started as a mild inconvenience and could easily be attributed to certain foods. Brodie had lessened his alcohol intake and believed that whatever was causing the pain would run its course. But on this particular cold day in January, he was overcome with an agonizing pain in his gut.

Brodie had been in the parlor when the pain gripped him and caused him to lean over. Wylanta had left earlier for a dress fitting and wouldn't be home for hours. Irma, one of his house staff, was in the next room humming a spiritual song as she wiped down the furniture. As much as he wanted to believe the pain would subside, he now knew he had to call for help. "Irma, can you come here?"

Irma, who was in the middle of her song, didn't hear Brodie's cry. After waiting a moment, and seeing no response, Brodie called out again. "Irma, I need you to come here!"

Irma came in with some polish in one hand and a rag in the other. "Yes, sir. What's wrong, Mr. Duke?"

"Irma, I need you to call for the doctor."

"Yes, sir." Irma placed the rag and polish on the table, then scuttled out of the room in the direction of the back hall where the phone was located. Brodie could hear her speaking to someone in a loud voice. Once she had hung up the phone, she rushed back into the room. "Mr. Duke, can I get you anything? Would you like a cup of tea or some hot soup?"

The pain had only intensified and Brodie was beginning to feel light-headed. "Help me to the sofa so I can lie down."

Irma reached over and allowed Brodie to place his weight on her shoulder. The two slowly walked across the room where Brodie almost fell to the floor. Once his head hit the cushion, he passed out. When he awakened, he looked up to see Wylanta towering over him. His vision was blurred and he grabbed for his stomach. "Wylanta, I've never felt such pain."

"Darling, I'm here."

Moments later, a man holding a black satchel was peering down at him. "Brodie, we need to transport you to the hospital."

"To the hospital? Can't you just give me some medicine to stop the pain in my stomach?"

"I wish I could but, at this point, I'm not totally sure what's triggering your symptoms."

The pain was causing Brodie to black out and, when he woke again, he was lying in the back of a large car. He looked around and was face to face with a man in a white coat. "We'll give you something for the pain after you've been examined. We should be arriving at the hospital in a little while. If you need to grip my hand through the pain, please do." Brodie had never felt this way before and fear crept in. He tried to calm down, but every time the wheels hit a rock, his stomach cramped with a sharp pain.

Finally, the car pulled up in front of a large building. Once the car was stopped, two men pulled him out of the vehicle and carried him through the doors and into an examining room. A doctor approached and pulled a chair up beside him. "Mr. Duke, my name is Dr. Johnson and I'll be examining you."

Brodie could hardly speak. "Please, doctor, can you give me something for the pain?"

"I need to examine you first. Once I do, I'll determine what to prescribe for the pain."

All Brodie could do was to lie there, helpless and alone. He had never experienced pain like this in his life and was beginning to think he'd rather die. After what seemed like hours, the doctor prescribed some medicine and he was transported to a private room. He slept for over twenty-four hours and, when he finally awakened, Wylanta was sitting by his bed.

Brodie was too weak to speak, but tried to smile at this young woman who had given up her life for him. In a slurred voice, he spoke. "Wylanta, my beautiful Wylanta."

Wylanta reached over and placed her finger on his lips. "Darling, don't speak."

He gazed around the room and realized he wasn't home. "Where am I?"

"You're at Tucker Sanitarium in Richmond, Virginia."

The pain had dulled, but he was groggy from the medicine. "I love you, Wylanta. Will you be my wife?"

"Honey, I am your wife."

Brodie kept his eyes closed as he murmured, "Wylanta, you're so beautiful. Why do you want to be with an old man like me?"

"Darling, you are my old man and I love you so much. I promised you when we were married that I'd be here for you till death. And I believe that isn't going to be anytime soon."

"I don't want to die. I want to spend more time with you. I want to buy you nice clothes and take you to the seashore. You're the only woman who has ever gotten me."

"Darling, I feel the same way about you. Now get some sleep and, hopefully, you'll feel better in the morning."

Brodie never fully recovered from the stomach problems. He was confined to Tucker Sanitarium for several months before he was finally released. But, even after returning home, he continued to be plagued with stomach pain.

Over the next two years, Brodie rarely left the house. He conducted most of his business from his home and entertained very little. His house staff, some of whom had been with him for years, became like family as they did their daily chores and tried to take his mind off of the unrelenting pain. Irma, particularly, would keep him company when Wylanta would leave. She would often sit and have him tell her stories about his childhood and the days when life had seemed so simple.

One day, when the pain seemed unbearable, Wylanta, along with the house staff, gathered in his room. Irma came to his bedside and began to sing a hymn. He liked it when she sang spiritual songs. It reminded him of the nights, so long ago, when Washington would get out his Bible and read to him and Sidney. He lay there and clutched the wooden fox in his hand. "Irma, did I tell you that Sidney made this fox just for me?"

"Yes, Mr. Duke."

"We had such good times running in the woods and going down to the river to catch fish." Brodie took a deep breath before continuing. "And then, there was the day that he saved me." Tears started to well up and trickle down his cheeks. "He was such a good brother."

The woman used her apron to wipe her eyes. "I'm sure he was, Mr. Duke. I'm sure he was."

Brodie's breathing became labored and he looked up at the ceiling. As he gazed upward, he saw a vision of Sidney beckoning him to follow him across the rocks to the other side of the river. "Sidney," Brodie called out. "Sidney, I'm coming."

| 53 |

1919

On February 2, 1919, Brodie Duke passed away. His wife, Wylanta, along with his house staff, were by his side. One visitor who observed the last moments of Brodie's life noted their grief in a newspaper article that was published days later. "*One of the most touching incidents in connection with Brodie's death was the genuine grief of his family servants, many of them having lived at his home place since their childhood.*"

Brodie's funeral was held at his home on Duke Street, where Dr. T.A. Smoot, the pastor of a leading Methodist church located in Richmond, Virginia, presided over the service. William Few, the president of Trinity College, attended. After leaving the service, William Few wrote Buck a letter sharing his thoughts. He stated that Brodie had paid for Dr. Smoot's education at Trinity College, which provided the reverend plenty of stories to share with the mourners. In the letter, he states that he had not informed Benjamin of his brother's death and would leave that to Buck's discretion.

Newspapers from all over the country used the occasion of Brodie's death to, once again, bring to light his scandalous past. But, one article published in the Morning Herald on February 5th, provided a different perspective.

The death of Brodie Duke removed from the activities of life a man, in many respects, above the average and certainly one with an extraordinary number of remarkable traits. Had he confined his efforts, initiative, and business acumen, strictly to the business end of life, he would doubtless have died known as one of the world's greatest financial giants. But he was human and not just a money-making machine. He loved life and its pleasures, and sacrificed business in order to get his share of the world's joys.

Brodie Duke lived more varied stories than even a dozen speculative romance novels could ever invent. His life was tempestuous - a continuous picture of events, and in all his ups and downs, he ever remained optimistic.

It was Brodie Duke who first commenced the manufacturing of tobacco in Durham in the days when the Bull was in its infancy—he saw the possibilities of the manufactured article and, with his father, Washington Duke, started the business that finally made the Dukes the biggest in the tobacco world. When the American Tobacco Company was formed, through the genius of J.B. Duke, his half-brother, Brodie sold out, taking in a million and more dollars and went into real estate and other enterprises.

While his life was a busy one, a peculiar one, he made many strong friends and was always loyal to them. His passing will be regretted.

Just here, it may not be amiss to say that the first time we ever saw Brodie Duke was at a meeting of the Commonwealth Club of Durham—a commercial organization that had for its purpose, the up-

building of the Bull City. It was in October, back in 1890—and at that meeting, we recall distinctly those present were: Mr. James Southgate, one of Durham's best citizens; Mr. Robert Rogers, a real estate dealer; Mr. A.E. Lloyd, a hardware merchant; Colonel W.A. Albright, a postmaster; Mr. Albert Kramer, a tobacconist; R.E. Carr, a newspaper reporter; Captain J.E. Freeland, a merchant; and H.J. Bass, a tobacconist. And, strange as it may appear, all of those men assembled there have died.

Some of them lived to see Durham get her own, but all of them have now passed to their reward. Of the entire gathering this writer alone remains. This was a regular meeting, but the members didn't turn out. It was the first week in Durham—and we listened to Brodie Duke with peculiar interest. He was an original talker—he thought and he got up and, finally, said, "I tell you fellers that we can't stick like bark on a tree—so d—d tight it won't come off. We've got to be like the branches of the tree—we must expand—we must make Durham bigger and we must put up the coin if we expect to get men to come here."

This general proposition was agreed upon by those present—and the three big additions, which were then just mapped off for Durham, were discussed. There was the East End Company, the Consolidated Land Company, and a few others—and enough town lots laid out to take care of thirty thousand people. The blueprints looked good. And we all felt like Brodie Duke felt, that we mustn't remain like the bark on a tree—so d—d tight it wouldn't come off—but the land boom failed and Durham continued to grow, naturally pushed along by the same spirit as expressed by the man who died Saturday.

In late February, Fidelity Bank was named as the administrator of Brodie's estate. Given that Brodie left no will, it was necessary for the estate to be divided by the heirs, according to the law. Wylanta hired the firm of Bryant and Brogden to represent her, while Mabel, Pearl, and Lawrence, hired the firm of Fuller and Reade. At this point in time, the estate was estimated to be worth close to four hundred thousand dollars.

Soon after Brodie's death, Wylanta left the house that Brodie had built in 1882, and moved to 607 Watts Street, which she would make her primary residence until her death in 1980. Soon after her departure, the house, along with the sixteen acres located on the corner of Morgan, Duke, and Main Streets, went up for sale. William Erwin, along with John Sprunt Hill, pushed for the city to buy the property and build a city park on the grounds. But instead, the city purchased Brodie's homestead and, in 1922, construction was completed on a new high school building. Brodie's house remained on the property until 1930, at which time the house was demolished and a home economics building replaced it.

Ironically, Wylanta would also have her share of husbands. Two years after Brodie's death, Wylanta married Isaac Richardson Strayhorn, a prosecuting attorney. But, after only two years, Isaac was killed in a car accident while the couple was visiting Guillaumes, France. Wylanta was injured but, over time, was able to fully recover from her injuries.

Seven years after Isaac's death, Wylanta married Connor Woodard Aycock. Dr. David Scanlon presided over the ceremony in her home on Watts Street. The couple was married for eleven years before Connor passed away at home from a heart attack.

Then, Wylanta, at the age of 60, married Perry Clayton Eldridge, 39, of Buffalo, New York. After only a year of marriage, the couple divorced in Dade County, Florida.

Wylanta's last attempt at love was with Thomas Michael Holt. The couple was married on October 22, 1949. Thomas was also involved in a car accident in June 1953, but survived. The couple divorced in Orange County, Florida, in 1954.

Wylanta lived her final years in the house at 607 Watts Street and attended First Presbyterian Church on Main Street. She was buried in Maplewood Cemetery in Durham.

Minnie, Brodie's second wife, married Frank May, and lived in Pasadena, California, until her death on December 26, 1920.

Mabel, Brodie's oldest daughter, died in 1957 and was buried at Maplewood Cemetery. Lawrence died in 1956, and is also buried at Maplewood, while Pearl, who died in 1938, is buried in Chattanooga, Tennessee.

Epilogue

After much research, it is clear that Brodie and Buck never reconciled their differences. Buck did find love with his second wife, Nanaline Holt Inman, and, at the age of fifty-five, became a father to his only child, Doris Duke. He loved his wife and daughter deeply. There are records to indicate that, as a small child, Doris would sit with her father as he conducted business. It is clear that he hoped to prepare his daughter for what life would bring after his death.

After the breakup of the American Tobacco Company, Buck spent little time dabbling in the tobacco business, instead turning his focus and time on expanding the power company that he had founded for the purpose of providing electricity to the mills in and around the Carolinas. At the time of his death, he had been working on the transition between hydroelectricity and steam.

It wasn't until the final years of his life that Buck began to understand the importance of giving back to the community where he had been raised. In 1924, with the assistance of several influential men, Buck created the Duke Endowment Fund. This fund would provide resources for the expansion of Trinity College and, ultimately, change the name of this institution to Duke University. In addition to providing money for Duke University, money was also allocated to several other smaller universities as well as to the Methodist Church. Like his father, Buck also donated to the religious, medical, and educational needs of the black community.

It is unclear, due to Benjamin's debilitating illness, whether he and his half-brother, Brodie, ever completely reconciled their differences. Given Benjamin's demeanor and desire to meet the needs of the people around him, I do believe the brothers held no grudges. Benjamin and Sarah were married for fifty-four years and it is clear that they loved each other deeply. They had three children. Their first child, George Washington Duke, died at the age of two. The couple was blessed with two more children, Angier Buchanan and Mary Lillian.

Mary became romantically involved with a prince from Spain, Prince Ludovic Pignatelli D'Aragon, a distant cousin to the king. When she broke off the relationship, newspaper articles from all corners of the world reported that the prince was despondent and tried to kill himself by shooting a bullet into his chest. Several years later, when Mary was twenty-seven, she married Anthony Drexel Biddle, Jr., of Philadelphia, who was seventeen at the time. To keep it all in the family, Angier, at the age of thirty, married Anthony's sister, Cordelia, who was only sixteen when they spoke their wedding vows.

Benjamin would experience heartache in 1923 from the death of his son, Angier. Angier had been in Greenwich, Connecticut, with several friends. The group had spent time at a country club and were making their way back to Angier's yacht on his dinghy, when the boat capsized, tossing Angier into the water. Even though he had lost one of his arms in a previous accident, he was known to be a strong swimmer. His friends believe he hit his head when he fell out of the boat and was unable to come to the surface.

Benjamin died in 1929, one of the last of the founding fathers of Durham. Sarah, his loving wife, was ever by his side until the end. William Few, President of Trinity College, believed Benjamin deserved to have a memorial built to honor his devotion to Trinity

College but, because of the great depression, the funds were never raised.

Before his own death in 1925, Buck chose a piece of land, on top of a hill, specifically for Duke Chapel to be built. This magnificent structure towers over the university and can be seen from downtown Durham. Given that there would be no memorial for Benjamin, a crypt was built inside the chapel where the bodies of Washington, Buck, and Benjamin now reside. The land in front of the chapel slopes downward into a valley that Buck specified for a lake. But in 1930, the university ran short of the needed funds and the lake had to be removed from the plans.

In 1934, Dr. Frederick M. Hanes, head of the Department of Medicine, encouraged Sarah Duke to create an iris garden where the lake was to be. The garden brought Sarah a great deal of pleasure until her death in 1936. In 1938, Mary Biddle, Sarah's daughter, honored her mother by donating the money to finish the garden her mother had loved. And today, the Sarah P. Duke Gardens, brings joy to the thousands of visitors who walk through its gates.

Acknowledgments

First and foremost, I want to thank God, the ultimate creator, who in His infinite wisdom provided me a gift for telling stories. Second, I want to thank my husband Jay, who has been willing to listen to my countless accounts of the men and women who made Durham the city it is today. I want to thank my brothers, Bill, Richard, and Rob Hawkins for their encouragement to keep writing about the city we all have called home. A special thanks goes out to my editor, Debbie Zaccardelli, for her willingness to do the tedious work of transforming my rough drafts to works of art. I am grateful for my granddaughter, Ellie Kate Thomas, who, with the help of AI, created the illustrations for each chapter. Lastly, I want to thank my daughter, Hannah Darrah, for being willing to apply her visual artistry to creating the cover as well as checking behind me on all the minute details involved with publishing this book.

www.ingramcontent.com/pod-product-compliance
Lightning Source LLC
Chambersburg PA
CBHW060540310726
48982CB00009B/1319/J

* 9 7 8 0 9 9 8 6 5 1 4 8 4 *